STILL LIFE

by

Jon M. Skillman

COPYRIGHT © 2004

STILL IN PLAY
Not Quite Par for the Course

By

Jon M. Skillman

ALL RIGHT RESERVED. NO PART OF THIS BOOK MAY BE REPRODUCED IN ANY FORM OR BY ANY ELECTRONIC OR MECHANICAL MEANS INCLUDING INFORMATION STORAGE AND RETRIEVAL SYSTEMS WITHOUT THE PERMISSION IN WRITING FROM THE PUBLISHER OR AUTHOR EXCEPT FOR A REVIEWER WHO MAY QUOTE BRIEF PASSAGES IN A REVIEW.

ISBN 1-930002-54-8

I & L PUBLISHING
174 OAK DR. PKWY
OROVILLE, CA. 95966
PH: (530) 589-5048
FX: (530) 589-3551
E-MAIL: INLPUBLISHER@OROVILLECITY.COM

FIRST EDITION
FOR ORDERING AND DISTRIBUTING CONTACT
I&L PUBLISHING

Printed in the United States by Morris Publishing
3212 East Highway 30
Kearney, NE 68847
1-800-650-7888

To
My Mommy

You always gave me the freedom to dream and the encouragement to try.

To
Mrs. Weber
My seventh grade
teacher. You saw something in
me to suggest I pursue a career in
writing. You also knew what a horrific
speller I am. I have used that as an excuse for
fifty-three years but now, spell-checker has
set me free. I only wish I had heeded your words
sooner so I could tell you how much I appreciate your
time and effort in planting a seed in such hard
and
barren
soil.

CONTENTS

PLAYERS..1-24

BEFORE THE GAME...25-34

THE FRONT NINE...35-141

AT THE TURN...142-151

THE BACK NINE...152-278

THE AFTERMATH...279-296

GLOSSARY OF GOLF TERMS............................297-308

ACKNOWLEDGMENTS

Writing is a solitary and at times all consuming endeavor and it cannot be accomplished without the patience, sacrifice and support of an understanding spouse. Thank you Trish for possessing all of these traits and most of all for being my wife.

A crust of praise and a few crumbs of recognition are the sustenance upon which writers feed. The positive feedback from Joyce Maltby, Durant Brown, Ada Lee, Chippie Bohn, Bobbie Haken, and others has continually nourished me back from the depths of self doubt. Thank you all for your kind words and support.

Golf may be an individual game but when it is played in the company of special people it becomes a true joy.

To the Kiln Creek Golf Club Senior Men

You have given me the selfless gift of friendship. Friendship which will endure well beyond our final round.

You have also given me a rich pool of character traits from which these composite, fictitious, characters evolved.

PROLOGUE

When exceptionally slow play hobbles their weekly round of golf, a foursome of senior men suddenly find themselves engaged in meaningful dialogue. Well there is some meaningful and some not so. Anyway, they discuss weighty issues such as "The Golden Years", aging gracefully understanding women and other oxymora that muddle the minds of aging American males.

Hole by hole the men, in typical male pattern banter, try to validate their existence in a new millennium, an age in which their values are now deemed worthless. They are frustrated by the changing world around them yet thankful to still be a part of it, or in golf terms, *still in play.*

In between shots they complain about, the impatience and irresponsibility of youth, the lack of loyalty and sportsmanship, the apparent relocation of morality from Dubuque to La-La land, and, ...understanding women.

The babble and bickering is somewhat tempered when a romance begins to bloom between the widower in the group and a widow playing in the group ahead. A flurry of unsolicited, overzealous, albeit well intentioned wooing advise does little to sharpen Cupid's aim and the romance flounders in an on again, off again manner.

As the four men play and talk their way around the golf course, they begin to realize just how close they themselves have become. This creates a crisis in masculine verbal expression. Being emotionally illiterate, they resort to the language of jabs, jokes and innuendo to convey their true feelings. A language they are aptly fluent in.

In the end, the game of golf is tallied on the scorecard and the wagers are settled. There are, however, no scorecards for the games of life and love.

IN MEMORY OF GEORGE LEE

My swing doctor
My confidant
My buddy

DALE

Dale Iverson, as usual, was the first of his foursome to arrive at the course. In fact, he was usually the very first golfer to enter the clubhouse. Dale had always been an early riser. Time was important to him. Was he a prudent user of time? No. He was more of a time conservator, a collector. He enjoyed having time to stop and talk or spin a yarn or two and Dale Iverson was an excellent spinner of yarns and weaver of words.

Dale's rugged looks and free movement belied his actual age, which now stood one year shy of Medicare. At six foot three and one hundred and seventy pounds, he could be described as lanky but preferred to refer to himself as a tower of power, a pillar of love.

Heredity had blessed him with a metabolism that converted fats and sugars into a non-stick substance that slid through him with the ease of spam.

Gray had invaded his temples and was quickly infiltrating his full head of dark brown hair. Chiseled facial features draped with thick tanned skin produced the outdoor look of a waterman or construction worker of which he was neither. A pair of coal dark eyes, one slightly larger than the other, appeared sunken in relation to a very prominent nose.

Growing up in the Tidewater Region of Virginia, as the only child of a prominent attorney, afforded Dale a very carefree childhood. He was a happy child prone to mischief; mischief that at times smudged the letter of the law. He always wore a smile, which helped conceal his rascality. He was an easy kid to like.

The day after his graduation from high school, Dale surprised his friends and shocked his parents by enlisting in the Marine Corps. It was just something guys D.I. back then and in Dale's case it also satisfied a court ordered ultimatum.

His perpetual smile D.I. not set well with the ever-somber Corps. In fact, Dale's drill instructor took exceptional exception to it.

"Marine!"

"YES SIR!"

"Do you find something funny here?"

"NO SIR!"

"Then wipe that smile off your face or I'll knock it off!"

"YES SIR!"

It took three knocks and a couple of slaps to realign Dale's face into a half smile, half sneer that satisfied both he and the Corps. This half smile, half sneer, which his friends refer to as a smear, still resides under his nose to this very day.

The disipline and absolute authority had arrived in his life at just the right time and Dale credits the Corps for molding him into the man he had become.

Although he spent just four years in the Marine Corps, Dale would forever be a Marine. His drill instructor had left a definite impression on him and Dale held D.I.'s in the highest regard. For this reason, all Dale's friends addressed him as, "The D.I." or simply D.I. Not because fate had actually blessed him with those very initials, but because they knew, in his heart, Dale Iverson was a D.I. He wore his pseudo moniker with pride and honor.

Dale's golfing buddies realized that he had more tales and war stories than a four-year hitch could possibly provide. They did concede, however, that the stories were probably true but questioned Dales actual involvement in any of them. The general consensus was that Dale simply edited the point of view into the first person to make the story more

enlisting in the Marine Corps. It was just something guys did back then and in Dale's case it also satisfied a court ordered ultimatum.

His perpetual smile did not set well with the ever-somber Corps. In fact, Dale's drill instructor took exceptional exception to it.

"Marine!"

"YES SIR!"

"Do you find something funny here?"

"NO SIR!"

"Then wipe that smile off your face or I'll knock it off!"

"YES SIR!"

It took three knocks and a couple of slaps to realign Dale's face into a half smile, half sneer that satisfied both he and the Corps. This half smile, half sneer, which his friends refer to as a smear, still resides under his nose to this very day.

The disipline and absolute authority had arrived in his life at just the right time and Dale credits the Corps for molding him into the man he had become.

Although he spent just four years in the Marine Corps, Dale would forever be a Marine. His drill instructor had left a definite impression on him and Dale held D.I.'s in the highest regard. For this reason, all Dale's friends addressed him as, "The D.I." or simply D.I. Not because fate had actually blessed him with those very initials, but because they knew, in his heart, Dale Iverson was a D.I. He wore his pseudo moniker with pride and honor.

Dale's golfing buddies realized that he had more tales and war stories than a four-year hitch could possibly provide. They did concede, however, that the stories were probably true but questioned Dales actual involvement in any of them. The general consensus was that Dale simply edited the point of view into the first person to make the story more interesting. Whether Dale actually believed he lived them was not really important. His friends looked beyond any indiscretions or acts of plagiarism and focused on the honorable man they knew him to be. He had proven himself a true friend and one who could be counted upon when the chips were down.

Besides they liked his style. They marveled at his uncanny knack of modifying and embellishing his stories then artfully inserting them into any conversation. They never tired of hearing the same story because they never heard the same story. Dale was a BS artist and when he told a story it was a masterpiece.

D.I. had a cutting wit, a sarcastic wit that was rarely unleashed in anger. Those who knew him understood but others might misconstrue his humor as rudeness. When he spoke, he was heard. It wasn't that he was obnoxiously loud; it was just that he was hard to ignore. His deep resonant voice tempered by a thick southern drawl fell slowly and quite lightly on the ear.

After his hitch in the Corps, Dale showcased his vocal talents and gifts of gab by working in sales. His father, not willing to give up on his own plans for Dale, tried to coerce him into returning to school and obtaining a law degree. He had always envisioned Dale as a junior partner and eventually taking over the firm, but Dale lacked both desire and motivation.

Dale married Donna, a girl he had dated in high school and they settled down and raised two sons and a daughter. It wasn't a Harlequin romance. It wasn't the Hollywood style of love. It was simply what folks did in those days; they got married and raised a family. Although the marriage may have lacked a wildfire passion, it was solidly rooted in deep respect and genuine affection

D.I.'s mid-life crisis, produced an affair that would shake the marriage to its foundation and test the solidity of its footing. The union endured but Dale never forgave himself for betraying Donna's trust and breaching the security of their marriage. The deep wounds healed, with time, but the scars would forever recall the pain.

Dale changed jobs several times but they were all sales related and with local companies. He had developed a vast network of contacts and acquaintances, which made him a valuable asset to any company as well as the community.

When Dale's father died suddenly, the shock hit his mother so hard she couldn't cope. Seven months later, a minor case of the flu advanced into full-blown pneumonia and she succumbed to her lack of will.

Grief hesitated while Dale tended to all the moral and legal tasks that death entails, but when he finally drew a restful breath, grief enveloped him like the gloom of night.

Dale, being the only heir, found himself financially secure at the relatively young age of forty-two. With work no longer a necessity, Dale started cutting back on his work schedule. He eventually cut deep enough to sever all ties with the working world and became a man of leisure.

He was ill-prepared for a Life of Riley. He had no hobbies to speak of, no plans of any sort.........He was vulnerable. Then it happened. Dale's father-in-law introduced him to the game of golf. For this, Dale never knew whether to thank him or kill him.

He wasn't exactly athletic, but he considered himself coordinated enough to hit a stationary ball with a big stick. After all, how hard could it be? He took to the game like a duck to L'orange and it roasted him well done.

Not being one easily dissuaded, Dl persevered and worked hard enough to play to an eighteen handicap, bogey shooter, or as he often referred to himself, not quite up to par. Dale's mood swings were directly proportional to his golf swing and Donna need not ask how his game went. It was understood.

Dale grew to love the game and particularly the three men who would soon join him for their standing Friday morning round of camaraderie, levity and of course.........golf.

BARNEY

Barney Melton was right on schedule but Barney's schedule normally ran fifteen to twenty minutes later than everyone else's. He tried to be punctual but circumstance simply would not allow it. At sixty-three years of age, Barney's main circumstance was short term memory, or more precisely, the lack there of. His brain was no longer the multi-task organ it once was. The old adage "can't walk and chew gum at the same time", pretty much described Barney's thought process. His train of thought could be easily derailed by an outside stimulus or transient neurological spark. His flights of fancy had no ETA or destination. His mental meandering lacked direction and purpose. His mind was a free wheeling vagabond. These were not necessarily bad things but they did make him prone to forgetfulness.

Today, Barney had forgotten his golf shoes. He was half way to the course when the realization struck him. The neurological spark that zapped the shoes into Barney's consciousness also derailed Barney's driving function and instigated an involuntary, nearly catastrophic u-turn. This was not an isolated incident and for this reason, most of Barney's friends preferred not to be a passenger in Barney's car. And, because of his habitual tardiness, they preferred not to have Barney Melton as a passenger in their cars. Barney logged a lot of solo driving time.

Barney was granted the nickname "Deputy" in honor of his slight resemblance to and fondness for the lovable yet over reactive deputy, Barney Fife, on the Andy Griffith Show. He, like "The D.I.", took satisfaction in his nickname considering it a gesture of genuine affection from his friends.

When a certain purple Dinosaur hit the scene, someone suggested changing "The Deputy", to "Barneysaurus". When Barney flew into a Barney Fife like rage, no one could possibly draw a comparison between "The Deputy" and a honey dripping, extinct, purple reptile. "The Deputy" was the only handle that fit Barney Melton.

A native Virginian, Barney grew up one year behind D.I. Although they were not friends in their youth, they had become very close friends over the last few years. They met on the golf course and now lived in the same neighborhood but for obvious reasons seldom carpooled to the golf course.

Barney, despite his small stature, was very athletic and had lettered in baseball and track in high school. He picked up the game of golf rather late in life as a favor to his doctor. With his quick hands and perfect timing he generated enough club head speed to out drive his larger cohorts, a reality that at least one of his playmates had trouble dealing with. The others, while not awestruck, did respect his abilities. Barney possessed the potential to out score his partners on any given day but a pessimistic view of the world as a whole and life in particular, inhibited his game and limited his potential.

This pessimism stemmed from a life long series of bad experiences, some of which Barney had little or no control over and others he failed to take control of or responsibility for. An abusive, alcoholic father dimmed Barney's outlook early in his childhood. Barney's parents divorced when he was seven, an event that tore at his being. He dearly loved the sober, caring, gentle man his father could be, but he despised the drunken beast that filled him with fear and hate. Barney could not understand why or what caused his father's transformation, he only knew it hurt to love him.

Barney was a bright boy, a boy who let his intelligence impede his learning. He became bored with school and dropped out in his junior year. He joined the Air Force. It was just something guys did back then. It took little time for him to become disenchanted with military life. His promotion to Airman 2nd class came quickly, just before he developed a propensity for insubordination. He felt the chain of command began with him, and those of higher rank represented the missing links in human evolution. He managed to keep his stripes but there would be no additions. An understanding sergeant, who appreciated Barney's hard work and shared in his assessment of higher echelon, saved Barney's butt more than once. Barney was fortunate to be discharged honorably and the false pride of forty-six months of time in grade was all he carried through the main gate. A duffel bag containing all of his government issue, lay at the bottom of a dumpster behind the chow hall.

Several jobs in the private sector didn't improve Barney's cynical opinion on life. He found little difference between civilian management and that which he had experienced in the military. He worked hard but his attitude kept him from moving up.

At twenty-five he met, fell in love with and married Barbara, a woman of independent means. Her financial standing was not what attracted him to her. He fell in love with her tenderness, her complete acceptance of him and her ability to make him feel truly and unconditionally loved, a feeling he had not known before. A feeling that lifted the aura of gloom and doom from around him.

Barney's pride would not allow him to consider using Barbara's money for anything that may prove beneficial to him. But she knew of his frustrations and begged him to let her help. He had obtained his high school diploma by attending night school and now she wanted him to quit work and go to college full time. Barney knew in his heart that she was probably right but it went against his masculine need of self-reliance. She finally convinced him that they were a team. No! More than a team, a unit and what was good for one, benefited the whole. It would strengthen their marriage. It would make her happy. And, it would enrich both their lives.

Two years at a community college produced a AA degree. Barney then transferred to a four-year school and received his BA degree in business. He had kept a close eye on the business community, looking for a niche or a need that had not as yet been filled. He was very skilled in market research and had a knack for finding opportunities where others did not. He had learned it wasn't necessary to be knowledgeable in any particular product or service. What was important was identifying the areas that held the highest potential for growth then putting together a team of competent professionals to handle the nuts and bolts of forming and running the company. This he discovered, was his forte. Before he realized it, he owned a string of successful unrelated businesses that were making him very comfortable financially.

Life was good for Barney. He managed to be successful without being obsessive. He allowed those he hired to run his enterprises, to do so. He had complete faith in them. He was also aware of every move they made.

He was devoted to his wife and gave his rapidly expanding family top priority in time and attention. It was his family that paid him the highest dividends.

Barney was forty-six when his last child spread her wings and flew the coup. This event sent Barbara into a mild depression. Barney was able to lift her spirit by taking her on a series of trips to places they had often talked about. They sold their large, memory laden home and moved into an upscale condo community. Barney managed to get her interested in community activities and their social life began to blossom. They settled into a life of mutual satisfaction and shared experiences. It pleased Barney to see her grow as a person, to grow in his heart. It was impossible to love her more, but he did.

Then in a split second, she was gone. In the time it takes a traffic light to switch from red to green, she was gone. She didn't see the signal runner, he was hidden by the van beside her. Barney had warned her of such a circumstance but her mind was elsewhere. When the light turned green, she drove forward. She was gone.

In the months following the accident, Barney mired himself in grief and self-pity. He lost his will. Friends and family feared for his sanity and grew concerned about him becoming self-destructive. His children tried their best but they were scattered far and wide, all with full and busy lives of their own. Some offered to have Barney move in with them but he would not hear of it.

In the end, it was Dale, "The D.I", Iverson who took Barney under his wing. He sympathized and consoled Barney in his grief. As time passed, he encouraged and nagged Barney to get out and do things. But, Barney's loss was debilitating. All the negativism and skepticism that Barbara had swept away returned with a vengeance. Barney truly didn't care whether he lived or died, Dale Iverson did. They didn't call him "The D.I" for nothing. Barney Melton was going to shape up or ship out.

It wasn't easy for either one of them. There were times they nearly went to blows and things were said that would have caused a lesser man to throw in the towel. But, D.I. persisted and slowly Barney began to rebuild his life. But without its foundation, its focal point, Barney's life would never be the same.

Dale Iverson got him through the day but night fell heavily on Barney Melton.

VINCE

Vince Denevi looked up from his morning cup of coffee. Out the kitchen window of his condo he could see the parking lot. He felt apprehensive, even though he knew Wally would be there soon. Vince Denevi was not hyper by nature but waiting really put his nerves in a snit. Patience was a virtue that had somehow eluded him, when he was ready to go, he was ready to go.

"What time is Wally picking you up?" his wife asked. She knew the answer was eight o'clock, it had been eight o'clock for the past eight years. Every Friday morning eight o'clock sharp, Wally's car would pull up in front of their condo and put an end to her husband's anxiety. Every Friday morning at 7:45 she would ask the same question hoping to ease his restlessness.

Vince appreciated Wally's willingness to drive him to the course and took pride in always being ready. He made it a point to be out the door before Wally's car came to a complete stop.

Vince was a big man, a once powerful man with a massive upper body. In his youth, he wore a belt strictly as a fashion accessory. Now at sixty-five, his belt served more as a flesh dam which strained to counteract gravity and hold back years of the good life.

His facial features had not changed significantly over the years. It was easy to imagine him as the handsome Italian boy he had been. He still had a full head of jet black hair, dashing dark eyes and smooth olive skin. He had a prominent chin punctuated with a deep cleft that drove the young ladies wild and young men mad. As a young man, Vince was seldom wanting for female companionship. He took full advantage of his advantages.

Vince was born in New Jersey, which tagged him a "Yankee" to those of southern breeding. He grew up in a blue collar neighborhood with his sister and four brothers.

All six Denevi children were handsome but his sister was drop dead gorgeous. She was closest to him in age and Vince took it upon himself to be her protector and confidant. She would be his only ally in an on-going conflict with his male siblings.

His closeness to her gave Vince a keen insight into the mysterious female psyche. They told each other everything. They talked about dating, desires, and needs. They respected each other's opinion and heeded each other's advice. They formed their own mutual admiration society, slash, support system.

There was a constant competition between the Denevi boys for their father's favor and their father did little to discourage. In fact he played it to his benefit. Vince realized this early on and fell from grace by refusing to play the game. When he graduated from high school, he further lowered his standing by enlisting in the navy instead of driving for his father's small trucking firm. It was just something guys did back then, but his father never forgave him.

Vince met Tiffany while he was stationed in San Diego. He knew the moment he saw her that she was the one for him. The feeling lacked mutuality. He soon discovered, not all women and especially California women, fell for his Jersey style of charm. She was from a different culture, a culture of elegance and grace, a culture that perceived him as being a tad slow and a bit crude. His Jersey accent and cocky manner shown dimly on their elitist attitude casting him in an unfavorable light. Vince was out of his league.

Anybody who really knew Vince, knew he had a kind heart and a quick mind. But, his mind had been programmed by his environment and it lay barren of culture, uncultivated by art. He understood his status, and set forth to elevate it. Unfortunately, first impressions hold fast.

This was all new to Vince. He began to realize New Jersey was not the center of the universe. He began seeing things in a different light, experiencing things from an altered philosophy. His mind opened wide. Observation plowed deep fertile furrows. New experiences planted the seeds of creativity. A new intellect bloomed and a new Vince emerged.

Tiffany had no intention of changing him. Quite frankly, she wanted nothing to do with him but she was the catalyst, she was the force that transformed him. His metamorphosis was honest, he was for real and he was starting to look pretty good to her.

Tiffany would come to realize that Vince had not changed completely. She was impressed by his persistence. She was appreciative of his ability to adapt. She could feel his heart and hear his mind. He was damn good looking, too.

His sister's influence and his vast experience had combined to form a physical being the likes of which, she had never experienced before. He took her to heights of passion that made her bluenose bleed. She had found a love that satisfied her every need and he needed to love her in every way.

Unfortunately, Vince was unable to endear himself to Tiffany's family or their society, a fact that would cause many potholes in the road to happiness.

Tiffany found it wasn't just Vince who had changed. She began to find joy in simpler things, things she had considered beneath her. She began to take pity on her family and old friends for their inability to look below their elevated noses.

When Vince received orders transferring him to the Norfolk Naval Base in Virginia, he asked her if she would marry him. She would and they did. A quick trip to Las Vegas and a ten-dollar bill produced a marriage recognized by everyone except Tiffany's parents.

It was a difficult move, Tiffany's roots had grown deep and she didn't transplant well. She had never wanted for anything materialistic. Now she found herself the wife of a sailor, three thousand mile from a home that was no longer available to her.

Money was tight. Vince took on a part-time job that kept them afloat and provided Tiffany the opportunity to explore the cultural side of Norfolk. She became involved in all sorts of events and programs, which eventually led to a position on the Arts Commission.

Following his discharge, Vince hired on at a local shipyard as a welder. It was starting to bother him that he and his wife were moving in different circles. He tried to keep the separation to a minimum by attending all the cultural events he could. He now knew and appreciated art but he felt uncomfortable among its patrons. He felt inferior to them, which was not how they perceived him. They actually admired him for his ability to inhabit and survive in two diametrically opposed worlds. They enjoyed his down to earth manner, which provided a freshness to their rarefied atmosphere.

Vince and his wife were a contradiction that people in both worlds had trouble understanding. They didn't see the love. They didn't sense the total commitment. The total dedication.

Through the years, Vince advanced culturally as well as financially. His hard work and loyalty to the shipyard, brought a string of promotions that eventually earned him the highest position ever achieved by a "through the ranks, high school graduate". This did not sit well with some of his fellow executives who viewed the executive washroom as the exclusive realm of degree and pedigree. Most came to realize that Vince was no fluke. Management could no longer bluff its way around the boardroom or the shop without risking serious challenges from one of its own.

Because of his position and physical stature, Vince often found the lure of lust cast in his direction. He would not strike the artificial bait. He knew the real thing.

Tiffany's beauty became the target of the many swollen heads and bloated egos that saturates society's upper crust. A net woven by Vince's unconditional love kept her from toppling over the rim of consummation. They were opposite, they were one, but not for long.

Two children, a boy and a girl, in the span of a year and a half, seriously altered the allocation of free time. The rearing years, although chaotic, flew by and before they knew it only a few feathers littered their empty nest.

Vince worked until he was fifty-eight. His job, his wife's activities and the needs of his children left him with no hobbies or time for recreation. He always had more things to do than time with which to do them. Now he found himself with barrels of time but nothing to fill them with.

The first six months of retirement nearly drove Tiffany to drink. Vince didn't know what to do with himself. He'd fidget like a squirrel and pace like a tiger. He followed her around the house like a orphaned puppy. When he got under foot she'd try to put him out................he wouldn't go.

Mrs. Denevi decided that moving into a condo could limit her ability to throw the lavish affairs that she now found bothersome. She would still remain active in society but a condo would insure that society no longer invaded her home.

Vince was also ready for a change. He no longer enjoyed the pleasures of home ownership. He now had time for yard work and exterior sprucing but lack the spunk to spruce.

They found a condo that was not too big and not too small, it was just right. It satisfied both his need not to putter and her need not to party. The condo was located in a community in which the median age was well above the median age. It also had in residence one Dale "The D.I." Iverson

DI and Vince formed a very close friendship, something Vince had never experienced before. He had lots of acquaintances and was very close to his wife and sister but he had never had a true male friend. A bud, a brother in the testosterone fraternity. He had one now.

It was, of course, Dale Iverson who informed Vince of the wondrous virtues of golf. This in turn, provided Tiffany with hours of much needed therapeutic solitude.

It was also Dale who hatched the idea of forming the Friday foursome, which consisted of himself, Vince "The God Father" Denevi, and two other condo residents, Barney "The Deputy" Melton and Wally "The Mart" Ferguson, who was just now pulling into a vacant parking space outside Vince's kitchen window.

Vince jumped up, brushed his lips across his wife's cheek and was out the door before Wally's car came to a complete stop.

Tiffany lowered her newspaper, closed her eyes and sighed, "God bless you Wally Ferguson."

WALLY

Wally Ferguson eased his aging Cadillac into a vacant space in front of the Denevi's condo. Wally, at age sixty-seven, was the elder statesman of the Friday foursome. If he stretched he stood five foot nine. When he eyed the scale from the extreme right hand side, he weighed a mere one seventy-six. These statistics classified Wally as the medium in the group.

His once washboard abs could now be more accurately described as washtub. His buns of steel had atrophied to the point they no longer kept his pants from falling to his ankles. And the once muscular legs now protruded from his golf shorts like clapper ropes dangling from church bells.

He always felt a little cheated by his mediocre stature but he found solace in knowing he at least met the minimum physical requirements for becoming a police officer. It wasn't that he actually wanted to be a policeman but just knowing he could have been, made him stand a bit taller.

Wally grew up in a very small, close-knit rural town in Northern California. He was, naturally, the middle child in a family of three sons. Wally attended a two-room school that grouped grades one through four in one room and five through eight in the other. His graduating eighth grade class consisted of himself and five giggling girls. Although he loved his small country school, it did little in preparing him socially for his high school years.

The closest high school was twenty miles away and had a student body of over eighteen hundred. Wally found himself awash in a sea of pimply faced strangers, most of which were well into their growth spurt. Wally was not.

Shy by nature, and small in stature, Wally turned inward. He felt overwhelmed by the numbers and intimidated by their size. The first two years, he concentrated on his class work and knocked down some pretty good grades. Then, three remarkable events sent his grades plummeting and his spirits soaring. First, he got his driver's license. Second, he had a growth spurt, well, more of a growth sputter but growth never the less. Third, he met a girl..........Linda.

Actually she met him and it wasn't easy. He had become so withdrawn that he had trouble seeing beyond the inner world in which he dwelt. She sat across from him in geometry class. She found his shyness and solitary independence mysteriously attractive. She made an effort to talk to him about things other than class work but he became tongue-tied. He felt foolish, he wanted to talk to her, he wanted to impress her but he didn't know how. He tried too hard, his brain locked up, words were slow in coming and when they did arrive they were abstract and obtuse. She mistook this brain fade for profundity. She thought him deep and cerebral. He thought himself a dullard.

Although Wally couldn't understand Linda's interest in him, he certainly appreciated it. He didn't have a clue as to how or what he should do to form a closer relationship. Linda did.

They went together for the remainder of their junior year and the following summer. It was a summer of discovery. A summer movies are made from and songs written about. A summer of first love that Wally locked fast in special memory, a warm smile in a sentimental heart.

Their love was no different than any other first love. It was like no other. They had known no other so how could they compare, how could they know. They only knew it was the most wondrous of all their emotional experiences and they would be together forever............or maybe not.

Linda's father, a career military man, was reassigned to a base in Texas. This of course required the entire family to relocate. Linda and Wally contemplated running away but were mature enough to realistically evaluate the consequences of such a drastic move. They, of course, vowed to be true to one another. They would write religiously until such time as they would be reunited.

The letters quickly declined in frequency and waned in passion. The romance could not breach the barriers of distance and loneliness. Wally never heard from her again but he often thought of her and what might have been. It hurt.

His relationship with Linda had ended in pain, but it had given Wally confidence in himself. He knew he was capable of loving and being loved. He had grown emotionally and he was forming a circle of friends he could relate to. Still his lack of physical stature bothered him. In his mind he knew how trivial size was in the measure of a man, yet he could not shake a feeling of inadequacy. It wasn't a full-blown inferiority complex but a nagging feeling of mediocrity, being so damn medium.

After high school, Wally enlisted in the Marine Corps. By now you know, it was just something guys did back then. The Corps helped Wally overcome his size fetish. Unfortunately they over did it. They washed his brain with a strong solution of esprit de corps, placed a large chip on his shoulder and convinced him that no one could knock it off. They lied. A couple of very large paratroopers took exception to Wally's cockiness. Not only did they knock the chip off his shoulder, they stuffed it where the sun didn't shine, thus proving that, in some things, size does matter.

After his discharge from the Corps, Wally hired on at a large west coast manufacturing company. It was there he met Doris. Doris worked in the same department and took it upon herself to show him the ropes. They worked side by side and became very close. More like buddies at first, but inevitably their relationship evolved into the conventional male female affair. Unlike most workplace romances, theirs endured and they were married within a year.

Well before they celebrated their first anniversary, the first little Ferguson arrived. When someone did the math and questioned the timing. Wally simply claimed that Doris' gestation period was only seven months. She was a very fast gestater.

Doris quit her job at the company and became a full-time mother and housewife. It was just something women did back then. Two additional Fergusons would follow in rapid succession.

Wally advanced to the position of department head where he would remain until his early retirement. He really hadn't considered retiring early, it just kind of happened. The very day he qualified for a full pension, was the very day Wally's work ethic changed. He developed an attitude that was counter to that of the company. For years Wally had been silent about the way things were run. He seldom questioned the status quo or decisions from higher up. It wasn't that he was a yes man, quite the opposite, it was simply the time, energy and consequences of openly bucking the system was too high a price for him to pay. He developed a method of appearing to be the quintessential company man while in fact, being his own.

He had a keen sense for cause and effect so, when a procedure or company edict struck him as unworkable, he simple reworked it to achieve the desired product or effect. A change notice was never filed. In his particular position this method served him well. Seldom did Wally suffer at the hand of upper management.

Wally began to realize that the company had profited from many of his changes. But because the changes were transparent to those higher up the corporate ladder, Wally received no credit or more important, no monetary reward. This pissed Wally off but he understood it was of his own choosing, the price of anonymity. Not wanting the hassle of bucking the system may have saved him some aggravation and a few gray hairs, but it cost him a lot of recognition.

With his pension secured and his children grown, Wally became very independent. He became more vocal and argumentative. He no longer was the team player the company thought him to be, in fact he was becoming a burr beneath the corporate saddle. Within eighteen months Wally took his pension and left the company.

Ironically, salvaging a few gray hairs at work, meant very little now. Wally was now in the advance stages of male pattern baldness. The once small thin spot on the top back portion of his head was rapidly expanding and in danger of colliding with his rapidly expanding forehead.

Wally jokingly referred to his bald spot as, "The solar collector for his sex drive." He noticed, however, that the drive output seemed to be inversely proportional to the size of the collector. This inconsistency might be explained by the fact that Doris, upon learning of his collector theory, immediately bought him a hat. It became a running gag between the two of them. Any time he left the house during daylight hours, the last words he heard were, "Don't forget your hat!"

Wally would sometimes return home claiming his hat had blown off on the 18th tee and he was feeling a little frisky. Or, he might walk in, hat in hand, proclaiming, "I've been energized, come feel the power!" Doris could usually cause him to short circuit by feigning a headache.

Life was good for Doris and Wally. Financially they were pretty well set. Not wealthy but comfortable. They were also very compatible and enjoyed many common interests.

Two years of retirement flew by before Wally felt a sense of restlessness invade his complacency. He began to feel as if he and Doris had settled into a social and environmental rut. There was nothing new and exciting in their lives. They had lived in the same old house, in the same old town for over twenty-eight years. It was time for a change.

Wally was surprised when Doris told him that she too was experiencing feelings of discontent. Maybe it was time they made some changes. Maybe it was time to move, really move, make a clean break and a new start. But where? They had to determine what it was they were seeking.

Doris had an affinity for the sea. The ocean had always been near to her and she could always drive to the coast to refresh her spirit. She feared if they moved inland she'd dry up like a beached flounder. Wally, on the other hand, preferred fresh water and the serenity of the mountains. They debated the merits of both and Wally finally traded the mountains for a location with four seasons. Being a native Californian, Wally had only known two seasons, wet and dry. He wanted to see the changing colors of autumn and feel the frosty breath of winter but not a deep and lasting breath.

After many discussions, debates and a few concessions, mainly by Wally, the Fergusons narrowed the field to the Tidewater region of Virginia.

They purchased a condo in a nice neighborhood and returned to California to sell the house and tie up loose ends. They never looked back. The golden state a fading image in the rearview

23

mirror. They looked forward to a new life with new friends.

Now, ten years later, one of those friends, Mr. Vince Denevi, golf clubs in hand, approached Wally's vintage Caddy. Wally popped the trunk and reached for "The Hat" which lay on the passenger seat. This was the latest in a long line of "The Hat" that Doris dutifully purchased every spring.

Memory drew a broad smile across Wally's face as he gently tossed "The Hat" in his hands before positioning it on his bald head. It felt warm and so very comfortable.

Vince Denevi slid into the passenger seat beside Wally.

"You look happy this morning." Vince said.

"Oh I am, my friend," Wally replied, "I truly am."

FOREPLAY

Dale Iverson walked into the clubhouse and headed straight for the grill. A young man working behind the counter looked up and smiled as Dale approached.

"Well look what the cat dragged in", he said returning his attention to a chore that lay hidden beneath the counter.

"And a very good morning to you too, Tom," Dale countered. "Don't tell me you're finally washing those bacteria traps you pass off as beer mugs."

"What's the point?" The young man said not bothering to look up.

Dale threw a long leg over one of the backless stools and sat down.

"May I help you?" Tom said, still intent on whatever it was beneath the counter.

"You may!" Dale said, "How 'bout a couple of eggs...over medium...some extra crispy bacon...wheat toast...and throw on some of those mushy, tasteless things you try to pass off as hash browns."

"Tasteless!" Tom protested, "Look who's talking tasteless, why if you had any taste..."

"If I had any taste," Dale quickly interrupted, "I'd eat down at Bubba's Burger Pit rather than risk a massive coronary in this grease mill. Just bring me whatever you call 'em and I'll attempt to keep 'em down until lunch...Okay?"

"By your leave, Sire," Tom said as he spun and pushed through the swinging door to the kitchen. 'Eggs over, wheat toast, crispy bacon and some house potatoes with your super secret herbs and spices, it's for DI"

"For D.I.?" Replied a voice from the kitchen, "I'll have to go out to the dumpster for those special ingredients."

"And don't forget to wash your hands...you walking health code violation." DI hollered back.

"Up yours, you old dirt bag."

"Can you feel the love?" Tom sobbed with forged emotion.

"It just makes me break down and weep." DI moaned, wiping an imaginary tear from his cheek.

Tom returned to the counter.

"Coffee?" he asked.

"Well duh!" DI answered, "A good server would have already taken care of it."

"That's right, a good server would have." Tom said placing a mug on the counter and reaching for the coffee pot in one continuous motion.

"How's Donna?" he asked while pouring.

"Better, I think those antibiotics finally kicked in."

"Good, she sure is a nice lady. How she wound up with the likes of you......"

"Yeah yeah yeah...like I've never heard that before." D.I. cut in.!

"D.I." a voice called from behind.

Dale turned to see Kenny Martin, the head pro, rapidly approaching. Kenny was always rapidly doing something. He was one of those nervous dynamos that made D.I. tired just looking at him.

"Hey Kenny, what's up?"

Kenny gasped in a quick breath and words began pouring out faster than his mouth could form them.

"We finally got those new clubs in from Callaway if you wanna try 'em come by the pro shop and I'll let ya whack a few on the range." He gulped another breath and looked at D.I.

D.I. purposely hesitated just to watch him fidget.

"Okay," he drawled, "If I survive Tom's ptomaine kitchen I'll be over. Thanks."

"Good," Kenny gasped, "And if you like 'em I'll cut you a really really good deal. Hey even if you don't like 'em. I'll work with you, you know I always take good care of my good Buds." Kenny exhaled and anxiously awaited D.I.'s response.

"Buds?" D.I. questioned.

"Buddies," Kenny explained, "I always take care of my friends."

"Ooooh," D.I. said smiling at Tom.

"You're jerkin' me around again aren't you?" Kenny complained.

"Me?" D.I. feigned in wounded astonishment.

"Look," Kenny said, "All kidding aside, try the clubs, if you like 'em, I'll give you a really good deal."

"Yeah......Such a deal." D.I. said in an insinuating tone.

"No really, I'll do ya real good."

"That's what I'm afraid of." D.I. smiled.

"No, really D.I. you know I always treat you right."

D.I. turned to Tom,

"This is the same man who made his own mother pay retail for that cart cover."

"Hey that was a special order." Kenny justified, "Besides, she can afford it...and...and she loves me."

"Is it any wonder." D.I. said shaking his head.

Tom poured a cup of coffee and handed it to Kenny.

"On the house O' benevolent one."

"Thanks O' smart ass." Kenny countered, "Look D.I.," he continued, "No kidding you know I'll work with you."

"Kidding? Who's kidding?" D.I. said smiling at Tom.

"I give up", Kenny groaned, "I can't discuss business with a couple of immature brats."

"I'm not a brat!" D.I. pouted.

"You are a brat," Kenny persisted.

27

"Am not," D.I. whined.

"Are too," Kenny argued.

"Am not," D.I. and Tom cried in unison.

"Aw forget it," Kenny fumed, turning and beating a hasty retreat toward the pro shop, "If you want to try the clubs fine...if you don't that's fine too, it's up to you, I really don't' give a crap one way or another." He huffed.

"I'll be over in a bit Kenny." D.I. called over his shoulder.

"Yeah, whatever!" Kenny mumbled as he left the grill.

Tom and D.I. looked at each other for a moment then began to laugh.

"I don't think you should give that man any more coffee." D.I. said.

"You know," Tom stated with conviction, "I think it actually calms him down."

Tom, like most the others at the golf course, enjoyed the verbal sparring D.I. provided. Kenny, on the other hand, had neither the time nor the inclination to recognize sarcastic humor. He took it as a personal affront. It bothered D.I. that Kenny became so easily aggravated but not enough to stop teasing him. He couldn't stop, it was his nature, besides, he knew he was always able to smooth things over.

"You sure pushed his irate button didn't you?" Tom snickered.

"It's a gift...he'll be all right, I'll probably buy a new club and all will be forgiven." D.I. said, suddenly wondering who was really teasing who.

"Orders up!" came a call from the kitchen. Tom pushed through the swinging door and returned on its follow through swing without having to touch it. He placed a plate in front of D.I.

"Enjoy," He said with a sardonic voice and evil smile. "I'd love to hang around and chat but unlike you, I have to work for a living."

"What's that like?" D.I. asked.

Tom didn't answer. He turned and started stocking the cool boxes with beer.

D.I. took a forkful of potatoes.

"Garcon?" he called in his best French accent and a snap of his fingers. "Would it be possible to get some hot sauce to add a little flavor to this tripe?"

"Wee Wee Mon-sewer, will there be anything else?" Tom asked, placing a small bottle of Texas Pete on the counter in front of D.I.

"No, you are dismissed."

"By your leave, my Lord." Tom said bowing slightly as he backed away from the counter.

D.I. shook a liberal dose of hot sauce on the potatoes, stirred them with his fork, then placed a forkful in his mouth. That's better he thought as the spicy flavors aroused his sleeping taste buds.

As he cleaned his plate with the last piece of toast, D.I. felt the presence of someone on the stool to his left. He turned and looked into the smiling face of Wally Ferguson.

"Mornin' sunshine," Wally chirped.

"Yeah yeah," Dale groaned. "Where's your partner in crime?"

"Right here sweet pea," came a voice to his right.

"Oh crap, I'm surrounded by happy faces," Dale moaned as he turned to see Vince Denevi blowing air kisses in his direction. "Hey Tom, what kinda place are you running here, lettin' the likes of these two in?"

"Hey if we let you in, we have to let anything in." Came the swift reply.

D.I. shook his head in disbelief. "Where's the Deputy?" he asked looking around.

"I think we saw his car heading back toward the condo, he must of forgot something," Wally volunteered.

"What's new?" D.I. said pushing his plate away. "Well I need to see a man about a horse and Kenny about some clubs. I'll meet you all out at the carts in a little bit." D.I. swung around on his stool, stood up and headed for the men's room.

"Aren't you forgettin' something?" Tom called after him.

"Put it on my tab."

"Tab? You can't even spell tab let alone run one," Tom yelled at the empty doorway. Tom poured Wally and Vince some coffee.

"You got any sweet rolls this morning?" Vince asked.

"They just came in, they're still in the back, what do you want?"

"I'll take a bearclaw if you have one, otherwise give me a Danish.........cheese if you have it."

"How 'bout you Wally, you want something?" Tom asked heading for the kitchen.

"No thanks, I've got to watch my sugar intake besides, bikini season's coming."

Vince visibly shuddered.

The two men sipped their coffee in silence.

"You want your bearclaw heated?" Tom yelled from the kitchen.

"Please.........and put a little butter on it while you're at it."

Wally gave Vince a stern stare.

"Don't start with me Ferguson I've been good lately."

"I didn't say a word.........what's another bypass anyway, might just as well have 'em install a zipper, it'll save you time and money."

"You sure can suck the joy right out of a bearclaw you know that mother?" Vince snapped.

"That's what I'm here for son." Wally cooed.

Tom returned with the bearclaw and set it in front of Vince. Wally leaned over and looked down on the plate.

"That'll clog your pump." He said.

"So be it." Replied Vince. "Want some?"

"Sure." Wally answered picking up a fork. "Are you going to hit some balls?" Vince glanced at his watch. "Not enough time."

"We could split a small bucket." Wally suggested.

"Naa, I don't really feel up to it, besides, I only have so many good shots in my bag, I can't afford to waste 'em on the range."

"Put it on D.I's tab," Wally joked to Tom as he walked toward the pro shop. Tom was about to protest when Vince threw a twenty on the counter and followed Wally to the pro shop.

"You payin' for D.I. too?" Tom called after him.

"Take it all out of it," Vince answered disappearing into the pro shop.

"You've got change comin'," Tom yelled.

"Keep it. I've got a couple of pigeons to pluck."

When the assistant pro working the register saw Vince come through the door, he called out.

"Yo! Vinnie, come-a here, I'm-a-gonna break-a yo face."

Living in the south with a Jersey accent brought with it an inherent amount of torment. Vince took the ribbing gracefully, believing it was done in the spirit of friendship. There were times however; he heard the requited rumbling of Confederate canons.

"Yo, you wanna piece of me?" Vince answered performing a Rocky Balboa shadow box.

"You just wait, you Yankee dog, the South shall rise again."

"There ain't enough Viagra in the world to get a rise outa you julep suckin' rebs, and even if there was, YOU ALL wouldn't know what to do with it."

"Oh yeah, you......"

"Hey, Hey!" Kenny shouted leaning out of his office door. "We're trying to run a business here."

"Oops, sorry Kenny," Vince said blushing slightly. "But he started it."

"Did not!"

"Did too!"

"Did n..."

"Stop it!" Kenny screamed. "I swear to God, you all are worse than a bunch of jet jockeys at a tailhook convention. Now do what cha gotta do and get the hell outa here." Kenny withdrew into his office and slammed to door.

"Whoa, someone's got a powerful case of the grumps," Vince said.

"Yeah," the assistant pro agreed "D.I. got to him a little while ago."

"That would explain it," Wally said looking around. "Where is D.I.?"

"He's out on the range trying some new clubs." The assistant answered motioning toward the range. Wally and Vince paid their green fees and proceeded to the cart area. Each took a cart and drove to the bag drop, which was just across from the practice tee.

"Hey D.I., who do you want to ride with?" Wally hollered.

"Don't matter," D.I. answered back.

"How 'bout you Vince, who do you want to ride with?"

"Well not with Barney," Vince answered seriously, "He's beginning to worry me. You notice how friendly he's getting' lately?"

"What do you mean friendly?"

"You know, he's a lot more......touchy feely, puts his arm around your neck, that kind of stuff."

"Your sick!"

"No I mean it, I think he's lonely."

"Well of course he's lonely, his wife died four years ago."

"That's what I mean, we need to find him a woman before he turns funny."

"Turns funny, you're the one that's funny, I can't believe you're serious about this."

"Okay, you ride with him, you'll see, just watch him, you'll see."

"Okay I will. You're unbelievable you know that?"

"You'll see."

Just as Wally and Vince had loaded their bags on the carts, Barney's car pulled up to the bag drop. Barney got out to unload his clubs.

"Hey Deputy, we saw you headin' the wrong direction this morning', forget your pants or somethin'?"

"No, just my shoes," Barney replied.

"You'll be riding with me," Wally said walking over to Barney's car.

"Here, let me take your clubs and I'll meet you down in the parking lot."

"Hey you're all right," Barney said putting an arm around Wally's neck and giving him a little waggle.

Wally looked at Vince who gave him a, see what I mean look-n-nod. Wally shook his head in disgust. Barney turned Wally loose, got in his car and drove off to the parking lot.

"Well was I right or was I right?" Vince said smugly.

"Get outa town, the man's just a little more demonstrative than we are, he's always been like that, you're way off base on this one."

"I don't think so, I'd watch my back side if I were you."

33

Wally loaded Barney's bag on the cart then drove to the parking lot to pick him up. When they arrived back at the driving range, D.I. was just walking back to the pro shop.

"D.I., have you paid yet?" Barney asked.

"Not yet, I have to return these clubs to Kenny."

"Wait up, I'll go with ya." Barney said trotting after him. As he drew aside of D.I. Barney draped a hand over D.I.'s shoulder.

"So how's it going' big guy?" he asked as they walked off toward the pro shop. Wally turned to Vince and pointed his finger at him.

"Don't you say a friggin' word Denevi."

Wally pulled his cart around near the pro shop door. Vince pulled up beside him. Wally tried to avoid eye contact knowing full well Vince would continue to push the issue. He tried but he just couldn't help himself. When he looked over, Vince was smiling wiggling his eyebrows and fluttering his eyelids. Wally burst out laughing.

"You are one sick puppy, you know that?"

"Yeah, I know," Vince said as he joined Wally's laughter.

"What's so funny?" D.I. asked as he came out of the pro shop Barney following close behind.

"Oh...nothing," Wally giggled.

D.I. stopped beside Wally's cart. Barney came up beside him and leaned an arm on his shoulder. Wally and Vince lost it and burst into hysterical laughter.

"What?" D.I. asked.

Wally and Vince could only shake their heads, their laughter becoming contagious, infecting D.I. and Barney who both began chortling in puzzlement. Soon all four were heavy with laughter.

1

It was a chortling foursome that pulled up to the starter's shack. Two laughing with purpose, two by association.

"What's with you guys?" the starter asked as they approached his window. "Little early to be hittin' the sauce, ain't it?"

"Hey, I'm just laughin' at those two doofuses," D.I. said throwing a thumb over his shoulder in the direction of Vince and Wally who were just beginning to regain their composure.

"They are pretty funny," the starter agreed, "What the heck got into 'em?"

"Haven't got a clue Jim, I don't think they have either. They just kinda went goofy on us."

Vince and Wally, still snickering, handed their receipts through the starter's window. Jim eyed them suspiciously, shaking his head in mock disgust.

"You had to be there," Vince offered weakly, choking back a new swell of laughter. Jim inspected the receipts then handed them back.

"What's your tee time?" he asked scanning his list of starting times.

"9:05, same as always," Wally answered somewhat puzzled by the question. "We always have 9:05, and you know it."

"Well I'm sorry," Jim said flatly, "But I don't have anything listed under Geezers."

"Boy, if that's not the pot callin' the kettle black." D.I. retaliated, "You're the exalted ruler of

Geezerdom. By the way, does Kenny know how badly you treat his payin' customers?"

"Does he know?" Jim said, "He insists on it. What's your cart numbers?"

"26 and 19," D.I. answered automatically, "Are we good to go or do we have to wait around here and be subjected to more of your callous ridicule?"

Jim checked his watch then the tee sheets.

"You guys are a little early, I have the Taylor group in front of you, but they haven't checked in yet." He looked at the first tee where a foursome was waiting to tee off.

"If the tee clears before they show, you'll be next. Just pull your carts off to the side until I give you the okay."

"Thanks, Jim," D.I. said.

"Oh, and guys," Jim injected, "Please keep the merriment to a minimum, we wouldn't want folks thinkin' you actually enjoy playin' golf."

"Hey, you can't help but laugh playin' with these yahoos." D.I. explained.

"Well just try to keep it down, we're tryin' to run a serious golf facility here."

"Since when? If that were true, Kenny would've fired your sorry ass years ago." Vince exclaimed.

"You gentlemen, and I use the term in it's loosest and lowest possible connotation, seem to forget who has jurisdiction over your tee time."

"Seig Heil, Mein Fuhrer?" D.I. shouted crisply and thrusting an arm into a nazi salute while at the same time clicking the heels of his size twelve Foot Joys.

"That's better schweinhund, now get over there and wait 'til you're called."

The merry foursome returned to their carts and drove them to the side of the cart path. Wally and Vince headed for the practice green. Barney and D.I. began performing their pre-round checklist. Tees, balls, ballmarks, divot repair tools, towels, water bottles and various and assorted golf paraphernalia were removed from the many zippered pockets of their golf bags. Rings, watches, wallets, keys, anything that might in anyway, hamper their ability to swing a golf club, were zipped into the many pockets of their golf bags. There was a whole lotta zippin' going on.

The diverse demographics of the foursome, necessitated certain ground rules be set regarding conversational topics and subject matter. These rules were established in order to form a more perfect union and provide the common defense of an amicable round of golf.

Geographically, the group consisted of, one Confederate, one Southern Gentleman, one Yankee Dog and a West Coast Carpetbagger claiming neutrality. Therefore, any talk of geographic superiority was forbidden.

The political spectrum of the foursome ranged from, a staunch right wing Republican, to a bleeding heart left wing liberal. In-between, lay a moderate conservative and a middle of the road fence straddler who leaned and fell in the direction of the prevailing political winds. To this end, politics could only be discussed in the most general of terms. Specific political ideals or party affiliations could not be mentioned.

The group members' religious penchant was, one practicing southern Baptist, one Special Event Baptist (Easter and Christmas), one non-practicing Catholic and one Believer in something and at times, anything. Thus, the topic of religion was strictly taboo.

Because of these restrictions on conversation, most discussions within the foursome tended to be on the bland and mundane side. But not always.

"Oh crap," D.I. said looking toward the starter's shed.

"What?"

"I sure hope that's not the Taylor group."

Barney looked up and saw a foursome of ladies talking with the starter who was motioning toward the first tee.

"Oh man," D.I. groaned, "We'll be out here all damn day."

The ladies returned to their carts and headed down the path toward Barney and D.I.

"Iverson group?" One asked as they pulled along side.

"Yeah." Barney and D.I. replied in unison.

"Starter said we're ahead of you but if it's just the two of you why don't you gentlemen go ahead."

"Well, we've got four but if you wouldn't mind we........."

"No no, if you've got four we'll just stick to our tee times. We won't hold you up too much, will we girls?" She said driving off to the tee box before the others could respond.

"Bitch!" D.I. mumbled under his breath.

"Hey that's all right," Barney said, "We don't have anyplace to go. Do we?"

"That's not the point, you can't get any kind of rhythm goin' if your waitin' all day on a bunch of cacklin' hens."

Vince and Wally returned from the practice green as Barney and D.I. continued to debate the gender effete on the speed of play.

"What's all the hub-bub?" Vince asked.

"Do you see what's in front of us?" D.I. complained.

Wally and Vince looked down to where the first lady was placing her tee in the ground.

"Yeah? So?" Vince said knowing full well how D.I. felt about women on the golf course.

"So? You mean that doesn't bother you?"

"No...should it?"

"Here we go!" Barney complained. "We're gonna have a dissertation on male, female incompatibility."

Wally hadn't said anything but he saw an opportunity to have a little fun at D.I.'s expense.

"Hey D.I.?" Wally said, "You telling us you don't like women any more"

Vince's eyes brightened as he realized what Wally was up to.

"Oh oh, you mean there might be reason for concern here?"

"You needn't concern yourself you ugly troll, you're not my type," D.I. huffed, "Besides, I like women just fine, thank you very much, in fact I love 'em......I just don't..."

"You love 'em in their place, right D.I.?" Wally goaded.

"That's right, and their place is not on the golf course......at least not at the same time men are on the course. They need a special day or maybe special times, preferably after all the men go off.

"Well Geeze, D.I., maybe they should just have their very own golf course." Wally suggested.

"Now that's not a bad idea," DI agreed. "Yeah, a nice short course, pink flags, no water, no sand, nothing to cause emotional trauma. You might be on to something, Ferguson."

"Sure and the cups would all be bigger...say, maybe a ...D cup or even a double D." Wally continued.

"Mmmmmm! Those are nice cups." Vince murmured.

"Why you sexist pigs, you." D.I. said, in a high pitched tone and limp wrist wave.

"There could even be a salon at the turn so they could have their hair and nails done while pondering the meaning and emotional significance of their front nine," Vince added.

"And maybe an outlet mall adjoining the 18th green so they could take their frustrations out on their credit cards," Wally offered.

The three men went into a verbal frenzy. Barney preferred not to participate.

"Oh yeah," D.I. suddenly said. "Did you see that?"

"What?"

"She just dribbled one about ten yards off the tee," he said pointing to the ladies tee.

"Oh, and you've never done that before, have you D.I.?" Barney said sarcastically.

D.I. didn't answer. None of them did. They all knew they had the same shot in their own bags.

The ladies left the tee box, one walking the short distance to her tee ball, which appeared to be deep in the rough between the tee and the fairway. Her second shot struggled to make the fairway which, considering the lie, was not that bad a shot, but it produced a groan deep inside Dale Iverson.

The men pulled up beside the white tees.

"You want me to keep score?" Vince asked as he positioned a scorecard under the clip on the steering wheel.

"Sure," D.I. said, "You can practice your 'rithmatic."

"The usual game? Fifty cents skins, birdies, sandies and greenies?" Vince asked.

"Yeah, the usual." D.I. affirmed.

"Carryovers?"

D.I. gave Vince a look of exasperation.

"What did I just say?"

Vince thought for a moment.

"The usual." He answered.

"Well?" D.I. prompted.

"Carryovers." Vince concluded, "Right?"

D.I. threw his hand up in frustration.

"Yes Vince, carryovers, just like we played last week and every week for the last umpteen years. The usual."

"Just wanted to make sure we're all on the same page," Vince explained.

"Your not even in the same book." D.I. quipped.

The four men selected their clubs and ambled to the tee box. D.I. tossed a tee for honors, which wound up pointing to Wally.

"Ferguson you're up first," D.I. said stooping to retrieve the tee, then tossing it in the air again. The tee fell and pointed between Barney and Vince. D.I. made a snap executive decision.

"Melton's second up." He stated with unquestioned authority. D.I. repeated the procedure one more time, the tee ended up pointing directly at him.

"I'll bat clean up," Vince said before D.I. could speak.

"Well at least I'll get to hit first once today." Wally mused.

"Better make it a good one Wally-Mart." Vince teased.

The four men fell silent, eyes trained down the fairway where the four women waited for the green to clear.

"Say what you will," D.I. said, breaking the calm. "But I think things ran pretty well before the first bra was burned back in the sixties. I think society has paid a heavy price trying to balance the sexes. The feminist movement has created a no man's land. Oops, I mean a no person's land between men and women. Let's face it, women and men are about as contrary as dogs and cats, but that doesn't mean they have to be rivals. Women, by nature, are more nurturing and children, naturally need nurturing."

41

"Well, I need a little nurturing myself." Vince whined.

"Case in point," D.I. said, rolling his eyes and nodding in Vince's direction. "And I'll tell you what," he continued, "As hokey as many people think the fifty's were, I think things ran pretty darn well. Ozzie and Harriet, the Cleavers and Father Knows Best, they might have been corny; but they were about as good a role models as you could want."

"So you think women should be barefoot and pregnant in the kitchen?" Barney questioned.

"Of course not! I'm talking family values here," D.I. answered.

"Times change," Vince offered.

"But not always for the better," D.I. countered, "Morality should remain constant."

"As defined by who?" Wally asked, "You?"

"Ah, there in lies the rub," Barney imposed. "Who's morality do we follow?"

"Oh man, this is getting a little too deep for my philosophical and theological bent." Vince complained, "I just want to play a little golf."

"Look," D.I. persisted, "All I'm saying is, when a woman decides to have children, she should be there for the duration. In my opinion, this whole idea of day care really sucks."

"You don't think women should be able to pursue a career?"

"I'm not saying that, I'm saying they have to make a choice."

"You mean it's either or?"

"In a way, yes. At least during the rearing years. A child should have a full-time mother. If a woman wants a career that's fine; but if she has children, her first career must be her children.

When they're grown and gone, she can start a second career if she so chooses. I know this doesn't exactly seem fair but to me it's how the system was designed and it worked quite nicely prior to the feminist movement."

"So, you think the feminists are to blame for all our woes?"

"I think the feminists had some legitimate gripes. Equal pay for equal work, sexual harassment and things like that; but the movement when beyond that. It declared all out war on the male oppressor and created an even larger rift between the sexes than had existed before."

"Well, when you think about it, D.I. men were definitely in control."

"We were, and we were in no particular hurry to change things. We had it pretty darn good."

"Then why are you pointing the finger of blame at the feminists."

"Because of the way the whole thing came down. The anger, the hatred, the extremism. The American male was fat, dumb and happy, all of a sudden he's the root of all evil. He was sucker punched and he lashed out in self-defense. Women countered and we have stood toe to toe ever since. The sexes have become polarized and intolerant. divorce has become the solution for even the most trivial disputes. We have lost our ability to compromise, flexibility is viewed as weakness."

"Are you blaming the divorce rate on the feminist movement?"

"Hey, the male/female relationship was difficult enough before Mizzz Gloria hit the scene, now it's damn near impossible. I think if it wasn't for the actual sex act, singles today wouldn't even deal with each other. Look at the number of single parents out there, not all of them are the result of divorce. A woman wants to have a kid, she simply has a few one-night stands and bingo bango bongo, she's a mommy. If she has a real aversion toward men, a quick withdrawal from a local bank and a date with a test tube can do the trick. I tell ya, the whole thing makes me sick. I'm just glad I don't have to worry about the singles scene."

"Hey D.I., I'll bet every single woman in American is equally delighted," Vince said, as he took a practice swing at a cigarette butt.

"I'll tell you something else," D.I. continued, "The sexes have become so alienated that more and more are turning to their own, if you get my drift."

"What! You're blaming homosexuality on the women's movement, too?" Wally said in amazement.

"Hey!" Vince interrupted, "Put a sock in it, it's time to play some golf...Mr. Ferguson, I believe you have the honors."

The first hole, a lengthy par four, plays slightly down hill then drops off into a rough, infested low area with a drainage ditch running through it. The green resides on the uphill slope on the other side. A good drive still leaves a hazardous shot across the ditch and rough.

Wally's head was still shaking in disbelief as he teed up then faded one down the right side of the fairway.

"Nice ball," Barney said, bending to tee up his ball.

"Thanks"

Barney sent his tee ball right down the middle and fairly long.

"Ho hum, ol' boring Barn," D.I. yawned.

"I'll take that as a compliment," Barney said eyes still tracking the ball's flight.

D.I. teed his ball then stood behind it to select his line.

"You can take it anyway you want but if you ask me, constantly playing from the center of the fairway kinda takes the challenge out of the game."

"Envy doesn't become you."

D.I. addressed his ball. "I'll give you something to be envious about," he snorted, taking his driver well beyond parallel. The club hung there momentarily before DI made a mighty swing. The club struck the top of the ball sending it hopping along the ground like a jackrabbit on speed. The ball ran a few yards past the ladies tee then came to rest in some short rough. The momentum of his swing caused D.I. to stagger back as he fought to remain upright.

"Well look at her," Wally snickered.

"Maybe if you swung just a bit harder," Barney offered.

"I thought we might have to evoke the "Alice" rule," Vince remarked.

The Alice rule, which is not found in the USGA'S Official Rules of Golf, is invoked when a stroke played from the men's teeing area does not advance beyond the ladies tee. The rule requires the player of said shot, to play the remainder of the hole......... well, to avoid being crude, let's just say......... exposed. This is not a penalty per se, but more a proof of gender. Although the rule is often called, it is seldom if ever enforced.

DI ignored the bantering of his playing partners and quickly declared a Mulligan. He teed up another ball, made another violent pass, which sent his ball rocketing toward the woods on the left.

"Kick it out," D.I. pleaded as the ball disappeared into the foliage. A crisp wooden knock was heard and the ball magically reappeared and bounded safely toward the center of the fairway about 180 yards off the tee.

"Clean livin'," D.I. proclaimed proudly.

"Dumb luck," Wally corrected.

Vince teed up, made a nice smooth swing and sent his drive a few yards beyond Barney's.

"I like it," Vince said, holding his follow through pose.

"And well you should," Barney agreed.

"You gonna stand there like the top of a trophy all day or can we get on with it!" D.I. complained as he walked towards the ladies tee to fetch his first ball.

"Let him enjoy it, probably be his only decent shot all day.'

"Thanks for the vote of confidence," Vince said walking towards the carts, eyes still focused down the fairway.

The four men drove to D.I.'s ball, which was a good 230 yards from the green. Not wanting to flirt with the green side bunkers, D.I. chose to lay up. He made a nice pass with an eight iron, which left his ball dead center at the 100-yard marker. Wally and Barney proceeded to Wally's ball and Vince and DI stopped nearby. The ladies had just pulled the pin and were beginning their final assault on the cup. Vince and D.I. walked over to where Wally and Barney stood watching the green.

"Hey Barn, that gal in red is kinda cute, don't cha think?" Vince asked.

Barney didn't answer. Fact was he had noticed, which surprised him. He had had very little interest in women since Barbara's death, but there was something about this one that got his attention. She had made direct eye contact with him while D.I. and the other ladies were discussing the first tee batting order. Barney liked what he saw in those eyes. A warmth and caring he had not seen since Barbara's eyes were forever closed. He felt the stirring of sleeping emotions as he watched the woman move gracefully about the green. A pleasant ache invaded the pit of his stomach and a hollow whisper of longing echoed through the empty chambers of his heart.

"What cha think Barn? Nice huh?"

"Yeah, she seems nice, probably married though," Barney said trying to conceal what was going on within.

"Bet she's not," Vince said, "Bet she's looking for someone just like you, Barn."

"Yeah, right."

"I'll bet cha Barn, how much you wanna bet?"

"What's the point, we'll never be able to prove it one way or another."

"Hey, I'll find out if you make it worth my while," Vince challenged.

Barney thought for a moment, he could play this to his advantage. He knew that for the price of a five-dollar bet, he could hire Vince's easy way with women to gain information, something he himself found difficult to do.

"Five bucks says she married," Barney stated flatly.

"You're on lover boy," Vince shouted firmly pumping Barney's hand to seal the wager, a wager Barney Melton was more than willing to lose.

The last lady dropped her putt and the lady in red placed the pin in the cup. As they walked off the green she turned and looked toward Barney and smiled. At least he thought she smiled, he hoped she smiled but at a full nine iron distance he couldn't be sure.

"Did you see that!" Vince whooped. "Oh man, she wants you, Barney boy. Man, this is going to be the easiest five bucks I've ever won."

Wally hit his second shot to the back left portion of the green. Barney and Vince both hit the green but on opposite sides of the pin. D.I.'s wedge was right on the stick but released to about 10 feet above the hole. Wally two-putted for par, as did Vince. Barney rolled in a 15-foot birdie putt to win the hole and a fifty-cent birdie. D.I. missed his downhill 10 footer and had to settle for a mulligan, barky, bogey five.

HOLE	1	2	3	4	5	6	7	8	9	OUT
PAR	4	4	5	4	3	5	4	3	4	36
YRDS	385	359	488	334	168	499	396	163	384	3146
D.I.	5									
Vince	4									
Wally	4									
Barney	• • 3									

2

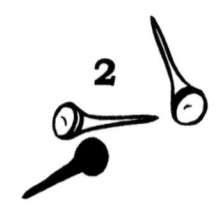

"I knew it," D.I. protested as he pulled up to the second tee.

"Knew what?" Barney asked knowing full well what was coming.

"They're just now getting off the damn tee."

"Well have you bothered to look beyond them? Can you see far enough to see the foursome on the green? Those four GUYS on the green? I swear D.I., you're the biggest sexist pig this side of the Omaha stockyards."

"Must be another group of women up ahead somewhere," D.I. muttered.

"Yeah that's probably it, couldn't be a group of men could it?"

"Hey D.I.," Wally said. "Tell me more about this feminist homosexual theory of yours."

"It's not a theory, more of an observation."

"Well what's your observation then?"

"Well, it just seems that since the feminist movement started, homosexuals have been coming out of the woodwork."

"Closet!" Wally corrected.

"Whatever," D.I. conceded grudgingly.

"I don't think we have a higher percentage of gays," Barney said, "I just think they've become more visible."

"And that's another thing," D.I. protested, "Where did they come up with this Gay crap? Should be Sads as far as I'm concerned, I feel sorry for them."

"What bothers me most about the Gays," Vince added, "is when they flaunt it, their in your face attitude. You ever see one of those Gay pride parades? I gotta tell ya, that's nothin to be proud of."

"Yeah," D.I. agreed, "they think the more they prance around, the more we're going to accept 'em. They're takin' something that goes against the laws of nature and tryin' to legitimize it. Well that dog just don't hunt."

"I think that's just the lunatic fringe," Barney said, 'Except for their sexual preference, most gays are pretty normal folks."

"Well there in lies the rub Barney Boy, preferring the same sex is not normal. There's something wrong with their plumbing. You can't plumb a house using only male connectors, it just don't work," Vince argued.

"Plumbing's not the problem," Wally said, 'it's in their wiring, got a short circuit or they're a hundred and eighty out of phase. Maybe they just need to be polarized or somethin'."

"I agree," Barney admitted, "But they're still human beings, I mean I don't know what caused them to be the way they are, I really don't think they chose to be that way."

"Oh, I think it's a choice," D.I. stated.

"No, I don't think so," Vince said, "I think something happens early in life, maybe a dominant parent, incest or something that turned them off to the opposite sex."

"Your full of it Denevi," Wally argued, "I think they're born that way, something missing in their gene pool."

"Oh there's nothing missing in their jeans," D.I. countered, "They just don't know how it's supposed to be used."

Even as offensive as that sounded to Barney, he couldn't help but laugh along with the others.

51

"Okay, okay," he said, "We don't know what causes it but don't you guys think gays have rights, too?"

"Here we go again," D.I. moaned, "Of course they have rights but here again the militants aren't satisfied with basic rights, they want special rights and special protection and that's where I draw the line."

"Yeah me too," Vince concurred, "I mean they're protected under the anti-discrimination laws and they have extra protection from the hate crime statutes."

"You saying they shouldn't be?" Barney asked.

"No, I'm saying they should be, they have to be with all the ignorant thugs out there. But, when they want to legalize same sex marriage and adoption by same sex couples, well call me old fashioned but I don't think that is morally acceptable."

"Not only that," D.I. added, "Some states require companies to provide fringe benefits to their partners. Listen Barn, do I think the gays have it rough? You bet, but don't ask me to lower my moral standards to support a deviant lifestyle. I'm a firm believer in live and let live and I have no problem working with, socializing or even living with anybody, I mean look who I play golf with, just don't expect any special favors and stay out of my face."

"Well if you think all the existing laws are sufficient to protect gays, how you explain what happened to Ellen the TV show. It got canceled after Ellen came out of the closet."

"That's a bunch of B.S. Barney and you know it. Ellen was canceled because of ratings not because she was gay. I have to give ABC credit for hanging in there as long as they did, after all, they're running a business not a gay telethon. I used to watch Ellen, I thought she was funny but when the show's content turned to gay themes, well I'm sorry, it was no longer entertaining to me. She had the right to air the show and I had the right not to watch it. Sounds like equal rights to me."

"I feel the same way," Vince agreed, "It's a matter of economics. If the product doesn't sell, you have a poor product, plain and simple."

"Hey guys," Wally interrupted, "Let's quit bashin' gays and bash some golf balls. It's clear to hit."

The second hole, a short dogleg left par four, plays up hill from the tee then flattens out to the green. Longer hitters aiming up the left side can carry the bunker at the corner and have only a short wedge or chip shot to the green. If they hit a push or fade, they are in danger of hitting through the fairway and into the woods on the right.

"Anybody beat a birdie?" Barney asked facetiously.

"Oh, listen to Mr. Humility here," D.I. said gesturing toward Barney who was already planting his tee.

Barney wasted little time with preshot routine, he made another smooth pass duplicating his first hole tee ball.

"Ho hum," Vince yawned as Barney's ball once again split the fairway.

"Down right disgustin' ain't it?" Wally said moving up to hit next. Wally's ball faded right again, just finding the first cut of rough. Vince's drive went straight and long, out distancing the others by thirty yards.

"Where the hell did that come from?" D.I. asked in amazement.

"Talent, pure talent," Vince boasted, retrieving his tee.

"Law of averages is more like it."

D.I. attempted to take a little off his swing and wound up slicing it in the rough just short of the tree line.

"Looks like it's gonna be a long day." He said retreating to his cart.

The four men gathered near Wally's ball, as he would be the first to play his second shot. One of the ladies ahead was blasting out of a green side bunker while the others surveyed their putts.

"Looks like your lady friend has a good chance for birdie," Vince said walking toward Barney.

"No, I think she's layin' three," Barney answered before realizing his faux pas.

"Been watchin' huh?"

'Barney's got a woman?" D.I. quizzed. "All right Barn! Which one is the chosen maiden?"

"The lady in red," Vince answered, "I think she's kinda sweet on the deputy here."

"Aren't you guys jumpin' the gun here?" Barney said, his face blushing slightly. "She's probably married to a millionaire kick boxer or somethin'."

"Well we're gonna find out, aren't we lover boy?" Vince teased.

"How?" D.I. asked.

"Oh me and Barn gotta little bet going, I'll find out first chance I get, don't you worry 'bout that."

"Well I'm glad to see ol' Barn finally showing a little interest, I say we do everything in our power to cultivate this budding romance," Wally suggested.

"I'm dead," Barney said wearily, "someone call Dr. K. and put me out of my misery."

"Look Barn, you may be old, but you ain't dead," Vince explained, "you need a little spice in your life and that there lady in red just might be able to pepper your soup."

The lady in red was the last to putt and when her ten-footer found the bottom of the cup she did a little dance of delight. She also looked back to where the four men stood watching and gave a little wave.

"Hot dog," Vince whooped placing an arm around Barney's neck and shaking him gently. "You da man!"

Wally looked at Vince with an accusing,"What's this," expression. Vince quickly withdrew his arm from around Barney's neck.

"Aw, bite me Ferguson," He said in annoyance.

"Hey, you started it."

"Started what?" D.I. asked.

"Aw nothin'," Vince answered.

"Yeah, it really was nothin' wasn't it Vince?" Wally said.

Barney was in a bit of a quandary. He was interested in this lady in red, but he feared his three playing companions might make it difficult if not down right embarrassing to pursue the matter any further. He knew Vince could be a valuable tool in gathering information but he also realized, each of his three playmates were capable of overzealous assistance which, could also be defined as inadvertent sabotage. Subtlety was not their strong suit. They were prone to over exuberance in the advice and assistance department. They often breached the bounds of tact and diplomacy. If he so much as intimated an interest in this lady, it would be akin to dangling her as well as himself, above a school of hungry piranhas. He feared it might be too late. He saw their eyes brighten as they locked onto their prey. He could sense their titillation quotient multiply. If he didn't act, they might go all giddy on him. A dark cloud of gloom and doom enveloped him.

"Look guys," Barney said, "I must admit, I am interested but let's not rush anything. Okay? I don't get many chances so please don't do anything that might put her off...pleeeeeeeease."

"Barney, you cut me to the quick," Vince said, feigning emotional pain, "We're your friends, we want only the best for you. We're here to help and support you in any wa........."

"Put a sock in it Vince, I know how you guys operate and I'd really appreciate it if you all would just cool it... Okay?"

"You can count on us Barn," Wally said, pulling a seven iron from his bag. "I think it's great seeing you back in the hunt." Wally took a practice swing before addressing his ball, which was nestled down in the first cut. The ball came out hot, landing just short of the green and running all the way to the back fringe. D.I. played a seven iron off a hardpan lie near the base of a large oak. The ball landed short and ran to within ten feet of the pin.

"Great shot!"

"It was wasn't it?" D.I. agreed proudly.

Barney played an eight iron that bounced once then spun back to about three feet of the hole.

"Geeze," D.I. groaned, "If this is what a woman does to him, we need to end this little romance right now."

"He's never had a ball back up in his whole life," Vince said walking to his ball, 'Must be something to this love stuff."

"Will you guys please cool it with the love crap." Barney pleaded.

"Sorry Barn, just too good to pass up."

Vince hit his wedge a little heavy and it stuck to the front fringe like Velcro. As the men neared the green, Vince noticed a club laying just off the green.

"Looks like one of those ladies left a club," he said.

"Figures," D.I. mumbled. Vince stopped the cart and retrieved the abandoned club.

"Hey Barn," He called, "Looks like your woman left you a sign."

"What do you mean?"

"Look here," Vince said holding the club aloft, "She's given us an opportunity to get up close and personal, hop in and let's get to the bottom of this thing."

Barney could feel his pulse quicken. Butterflies began to flutter in his stomach. His heart was ready but the rest of his being balked.

"Well come on!" Vince ordered, "We've got to strike while the iron is hot!" Vince sat for a moment, before being struck by the irony of what he had just said. "Hey that's pretty good, strike while the iron's hot. Get it? Iron," He held the lady's eight iron out to Barney.

"I got it, I got it," Barney said taking the club and reluctantly getting into Vince's cart, his emotional blender trying to frappe' feelings of dread and excitement.

"Hey are we going to play golf or footsie?" D.I. protested.

"You guy's hole out, we'll be right back," Vince said driving off with a somber Barney at his side.

The ladies were standing on the tee, once again waiting on the group ahead. As Barney's eyes locked on the lady in red, his mounting anxiety induced a total brain fade. His mouth slowly filled with Styrofoam popcorn, he was in the midst of a full tilt panic attack.

Vince pulled the car along side the tee. The ladies turned when they heard the parking brake set. The lady in red gazed softly at Barney who sat motionless, momentarily paralyzed.

"Did one of you young ladies leave a club back on number two?" Vince asked giving Barney a nudge. Barney held out the club in a robot like manner.

"That would be mine," The lady in red answered walking toward Barney. Vince gave Barney a more persuasive bump knocking him out of his trance and nearly out of the cart. Barney got out of the cart and walked towards her still holding the club extended. When she reached out their hands touched briefly and suddenly Barney's senses began recording every sensation. Her hand was soft, gently, warm and dry. His, he knew, was clumsy, clammy and trembling.

"Thank you so much," she said in a satin voice that slipped easily into his ear.

"Your welcome," was all he could offer as he stood looking into her eyes, eyes that shown brighter and clearer than their years. Eyes of hazel intensity, of life, of passion. She smiled and Barney reciprocated, he could see the years crinkle beneath a light veil of make up. She had a pleasant face with petite features, a kind face that eased Barney's apprehension. Barney heard Vince's voice behind him.

"You ladies from around here?"

"Yes we are," she said diverting her eyes momentarily from Barney.

"I thought you looked familiar," Vince continued, "Aren't you married to Joe Harris?"

"Who me?" she said pointing to herself.

"Yeah," Vince continued, "I'm sure I've seen you somewhere but I can't put a name with the face. What's your husband's name? Maybe I know him."

Barney wondered what the heck Vince was up to, he really didn't appreciate his interruption.

"I'm not married," she answered, "...... Well I was but my husband died two years ago."

Bingo! Barney thought as a flame of hope ignited within him. "I'm sorry," He said automatically.

"Thank you," She said as her eyes returned to his.

He was, genuinely sympathetic. He knew well, the pain of loss and a breath of guilt nearly extinguished his flame of hope. "I lost my wife four years ago." He said without hesitation. She said nothing, her eyes softened and her face saddened.

"My name's Vince and this is my good friend Barney." Vince interrupted again.

"I'm Stella," she said extending her hand to Barney.

"Pleased to meet you Stella," Barney said taking her hand and shaking it gently, all the while repeating Stella silently in his mind, hoping the name would find permanent residence in his memory.

"Barney Melton," He said, anticipating a like response.

"Stella Stearns," she replied quickly. Stearns, Stella Stearns, he repeated to himself still trying to locate fertile memory in which to plant her name.

Vince was busy introducing himself to the other women who came over and introduced themselves to Barney but his ears heard but one name, Stella Stearns.

"Looks like you ladies are free to hit," Vince said, breaking Barney's concentration, "we best be getting' back before they send out the hounds. Nice meeting you!"

"Nice meeting you, too," they chimed together as Vince and Barney returned to their cart. Barney sat in the cart looking back at the lady in red as Vince drove back to the second green. She was following them with her eyes and Barney's mind went blank.

"Damn!" he said in frustration, "I forgot her name already."

"Stella, Stella Stearns." Vince remembered.

"Stella, yes Stella Stearns, Thank you."

It's about time!" D.I. scolded as Vince and Barney walked to the green putters in hand.

"Hey we're not going anywhere," Vince said, "It's pretty backed up ahead.

"Well the guys behind us are gettin' a little restless."

"Well they can bite me," Vince said a little perturbed, "You guys hole out?"

"Well duh!"

Barney marked his ball while Vince lined up his putt from the front fringe.

"You make your putt DI?" Vince asked standing over his.

"Hell no!" Wally answered, "He wooshed it." Vince struck his putt three feet past the cup. He hurried the return, which, to D.I.'s delight and Vince's chagrin, lipped out. Barney calmly placed his ball, took one quick look then stroked the three-footer into the center of the cup for back-to-back birdies. The putt also won him his second hole.

This is going to be a really long day," D.I. whispered under his breath.

"Easy money," Barney answered.

HOLE	1	2	3	4	5	6	7	8	9	OUT
PAR	4	4	5	4	3	5	4	3	4	36
YRDS	385	359	488	334	168	499	496	163	384	3146
D.I.	5	4								
Vince	4	5								
Wally	4	5								
Barney	•• 3	•• 3								

3

The four men gathered on the tee of the par five third hole. The third hole is not long but ball position on the first two shots is crucial if a player hopes to reach the green in regulation. It requires a little ego control to keep the ball in play. This posed a challenge to two members of the foursome. The double dogleg with a creek bisecting the fairway between the bends dictates the precise club selection and shot making. Hitting driver off the tee usually puts the ball through the fairway or in the creek. A nice five wood or long iron should put a ball at the first turn. From there, another fairway wood or long iron would fly the creek and position the ball a the second turn leaving only a wedge or short iron into the green.

The ladies had reached their tee balls and were evidently waiting on the group ahead to hit their third shots.

The men stood in momentary silence, each occupied by profound and meaningful inner thoughts. Or possibly not.

D.I. scanned the three faces around him and a broad smile crossed his face. Barney looked at him with a question mark stare.

"What?" he asked.

"I was just thinking," D.I. answered.

"Don't hurt yourself," Vince cracked.

" 'Bout what?" Barney asked.

"About fate, happenstance. Whatever you want to call it. About how we're all together at this place at this very point in time."

"How profound," Vince groaned.

"I know what you mean," Barney agreed, "We all came from different places and varied circumstances yet somehow we all wound up here.........together."

"I think I'm being punished for past sins," Vince stated flatly.

"You've never had it so good, you dumb Wop," D.I. chided, "I think we're probably closer than most brothers."

"How would you know?" Vince countered, "You don't have any."

"You know what I mean don't you Barn?" D.I. prompted.

"Yeah, I think we all do, it's just something we never expressed before. I think we've grown pretty close, don't you Wally?"

"It's understood," Wally stated, "it's a feeling, a trust. It doesn't have to be verbalized."

"As much as I hate to admit it," Vince said, "I do think more of you guys than I do of my own brothers. But, I don't really think much of my brothers so it's really not a glowing endorsement. Please don't go jumpin' to any conclusions and whatever you do, don't you dare think about calling a group hug......... I swear, if you do, I'll pound you."

"Ah that Yankee machismo, that Jersey sentimentality. It just brings a tear, don't it?" D.I. said brushing away imaginary tears.

Vince struck D.I.'s upper arm with a sharp jab. "Here's a Jersey kiss to help keep those tears a flowin'."

D.I. flinched and grabbed his arm. "Oh, he does love me." He gushed, extending his arms toward Vince and stepping forward.

"Come'ere you big lug, give daddy a big hug."

"Getta way from me you dixie-dandy," Vince shrieked backing away. D.I. locked him in a bear hug and momentarily lifted him off the ground. Vince struggled briefly then quickly secured his freedom by planting a big kiss on D.I. cheek. The two men stared at each other for a few moments then embraced warmly.

"You son of a gun," Vince said slapping D.I.'s back firmly, "I do love you. I love all you guys." He released D.I. and turned to Barney and Wally who stood somewhat dumbfounded. "Come on guys, group hug."

"That's okay," Wally shrugged.

"Maybe some other time," Barney offered.

"Don't you leave me hanging here," Vince pleaded.

They did.

"Birdie man's up," D.I. said after noticing the ladies were out of sight around the dogleg. Barney pulled the head cover off his driver and casually tossed it on the cart seat.

"You hittin' driver?" Wally asked.

"I cut corner, carry creek with big stick," Barney answered confidently.

"He's lettin' those two birdies go to his head," D.I. remarked with a grin.

Barney strutted to the tee marker, tipped his Titleist hat to his gallery of three and bowed slightly.

"Such humility," Wally cooed sarcastically.

"A real scuz," D.I. added, "Hit the damn ball, Maynard."

Barney, wanting to really impress his playmates, abandoned his normally smooth stroke and tried to really rip one. It didn't work. He sent a worm burner skittering about seventy-five yards off the tee.

"Right down the middle," D.I. offered. "But short."

Barney couldn't help but laugh.

"After birdie blues?" Vince asked.

"Slice of humble pie," Barney admitted.

D.I. searched for the perfect location for his tee placement. He settled on the extreme right hand side of the tee box, planted the tee and topped it with his ball. When he stepped back, he decided the ball was teed too high for an iron shot so he repositioned it so that the bottom of the ball just cleared the top of the grass.

"Now here's how it's supposed to be done," he said taking a practice swing with a three iron. He checked his alignment before sending the ball in a lazy draw to the center of the fairway right at the corner, in perfect position.

"Ooooo!" the others uttered in mocked admiration.

"Impressive huh?"

"Very," Wally agreed as he prepared to hit his tee ball, "You couldn't walk it out there any better."

Wally's tee shot, although not perfect, was safe and playable.

Vince stepped forward with his driver in hand.

"Now on the tee," D.I. announced, "Maxilla Gorilla."

"Driver?" Wally questioned, "Will you never learn?"

"Nope!" Vince stated stubbornly.

"Well than Vince, let the shaft out," Wally acquiesced.

"Yeah," D.I. egged on, "Hit it really, really hard."

Vince obliged with a powerful swing that produced a small grunt and a loud crack. He caught it right on the screws and they could hear a swoosh as the ball bore through the air.

"Whoa Nelly!" Wally whooped, "You knocked the snot out of that one."

"I think you might have flat spotted it." Barney said.

"You defiantly knocked it out of round." D.I. added.

They all stood watching as the ball cut the corner and disappeared.

"Didn't catch it all," Vince said striking a body builder's pose, "Think it cleared the creek?"

"I think it cleared Richmond," Barney mused.

"You get a little last night?" Wally asked in amazement.

"Nope, I don't do that any more."

"Yeah and you don't do it any less either, right?" Wally quipped.

"No I mean it, I don't bother any more, it's like tryin' to put a raw oyster into a parking meter."

"You know, they've got pills for that little problem," Wally said returning to his cart.

"What do you mean, "little" problem?" Vince complained.

"Oh my, he's sensitive to the size thing," Wally teased, "Well I have to tell you Vince," Wally continued, "pills can't change the magnitude but they can alter the angle of the dangle."

"Oh no?" Vince said sternly, "I'm very particular about what I put in this temple of hunkdom, besides, I don't have a whole lotta faith in the FDA, they have no idea what the long term effects of those pills are gonna be."

"Why should an old fart like you worry about long term effects?" Wally asked in wonderment. "Long term is a term that no longer applies to you."

"Oh you're a real riot Ferguson." Vince snorted, "I'm trying to be serious here. I wouldn't take any of those things if they paid me. Have you ever read all the disclaimers and possible side effects associated with some of those drugs?

"You mean like hardening of the arteries and stiff joints?" Wally joked.

"No! Smart ass, I'm more concerned about premature rigor mortis," Vince answered, "Guys are dropping dead after using that stuff."

"Yeah but they're going out smilin'," Wally said as he and Barney drove off in their cart.

"Stick it in your ear Ferguson," Vince yelled after them.

"You're really serious about this aren't you Vince?" D.I. asked as he got in the cart. Vince put his driver in his bag and got in the cart.

"Yeah, it's beginning to bother me. Tiff thinks maybe something's wrong with her, like she's no longer attractive to me."

"You mean nothin's happening?"

"Well I have my moments but they're not on demand, not on cue."

"Well when then?"

"You know, like when I wake up in the morning...............sometimes."

"Well if he still stands at attention for reveille, I don't think the problem's physical."

"No?"

"No! Remember those Bob Dole ads on TV about E.D.?"

"What about 'em?"

"Well it seems they're learning a lot more about it. There are many causes and many treatments, you should get checked out."

"Oh man, that would be totally embarrassing, I don't think I cou......"

"Hey, Vince, don't let your ego strangle your libido, you're too young to go celibate, besides, I think Tiffany might like to have a say in this."

Vince's face screwed into an expression of guarded resignation. He pressed the accelerator and the cart moved forward.

"Yeah......your right," he acknowledged grudgingly, "but......"

"But nothin'! You call somebody and get checked out before it turns into a bigger problem."

Vince didn't answer. He knew D.I. was right and he cursed him silently for forcing him to confront his dilemma. He also thanked God for having friends like D.I.

Barney couldn't hit a full shot without flirting with the creek so he poked a nine iron to within a couple of yards of D.I.'s perfect tee ball. The men congregated in the fairway and waited until the ladies had hit their approach shots. Wally, once again had a slight case of the rights and his ball settled in the right-hand rough just at the corner about a hundred and forty yards out. Barney hit a three wood that got a lot of roll and left him only a hundred and twenty from the stick.

Wally walked over to Vince who was sitting in his cart while D.I. prepared to hit his second shot.

"Sorry," he said softly, not wanting to distract D.I. from his routine. Vince held up a hand in a hush motion as D.I. started his back swing. The club slashed downward and propelled the ball in an arching fade that worked it's way around the second dogleg to within fifty yards of the green.

"Nice ball D.I.," Vince said turning to face Wally, "Don't worry about it Wally, it's my problem."

"I was only kidding," Wally explained, "if I thought you were really serious I would nev..."

"I know, forget about it, we're out here to have fun."

The two carts returned to the cart path and drove across the bridge spanning the creek. Vince's ball lay thirty yards beyond.

"Great tee ball," Barney complimented, "You gonna go for it?"

"Damn straight!" Vince said with certainty.

"You think you can carry those trees?"

"I got this far didn't I?"

"Yeah but you'll need to get it up real quick."

"Vince frowned and eyed Barney suspiciously."

"You're not gonna start on me, are you?" He groaned.

"No, no to clear the trees......you'll need to get......the ball up...really quick......and high in order to clear the trees." Barney stammered.

Vince peered through the trees to the green.

"As soon as your girlfriend clears the green..."

"She's not my..." Barney started to protest, before thinking better of it. He knew the level of harassment was directly proportional to the intensity of his denial. He looked toward the green and his eyes locked on a splash of red that seemed to twinkle through the trees and distance. From this distance, age was not discernible but her gender sure was. She moved with a lightness, carefree but not frivolous. She had a true dignity about her and he was truly smitten by ......Stella... yeah that's it Stella.

The four men waited in silence. The ladies holed out and quickly cleared the green. Stella once again glanced in their direction inciting a mini banter riot on the other side of the trees. After the jesting had run its course, Vince lifted a beautiful five wood up and over the trees right online with the pin. But his shot fell short, plunging into a bunker guarding the right front portion of the green.

"Oh man! I can't hit it any better than that," Vince sighed tossing his club lightly into the air and missing the catch. "I really hit that sweet."

"It was a pretty shot," they all agreed, "but."

Wally played his seven iron to the middle of the green leaving him with a testy cross slope birdie putt.

putt. Barney selected a nine iron that came up a good ten yards short of the green and laying four.

"Looks like the end of the birdie train," D.I. said as Barney looked at the sole of his club as if to question its designation.

"I can't believe it, I hit it good, should have been plenty of club to get there," he said looking up at D.I. for some kind of explanation. D.I. shrugged his shoulders.

"That's golf!" was all he said.

D.I. walked to his ball carrying his putter and sand wedge.

"I hate these little half swing shots," He complained, dropping his putter and placing the lofted blade of the wedge behind the ball. With little hesitation, he struck the ball smartly to within eight feet of the flag.

"You should hate all your shots that much," Vince called from the cart as he returned it to the cart path. D.I. walked to the green, marked and repaired the ball mark. Barney's chip left him with a ten-foot bogie putt.

"Oh man look at this," Vince moaned as he peered into the green side bunker, "plugged right up under the lip."

"Piece of cake for a player of your caliber," Wally said with a smile, "Hey you even gotta chance for a sandy."

"Not with this lie," Vince said stepping into the bunker. He muttered something the others could not decipher but from his tone they determined it was better that way. Vince had to take an awkward stance in order to address the nearly buried ball. He closed the blade of his sand wedge a bit and took a full swing. An explosion of sand filled the air around him, his ball caught the lip of the trap and bounced up and over his head, landing in the center of the trap behind him. This time, they had little difficulty hearing what was being said. Vince utilized his full and rich vocabulary as he shook sand from his hair and brushed it from his face and clothes. He hit the next shot thin sending it a good thirty feet past the hole. D.I. tossed him a rake and as he began raking, Vince struck up another conversation with himself that wasn't very complimentary.

While Vince raked and ranted, Wally played ready golf. His fifteen foot cross slope birdie putt missed on the low side and he tapped in for par. Vince two putted for bogey six and left the green questioning his abilities, his intellect, his lineage and the merits of the game of golf.

Barney missed his ten-foot bogey putt and had to settle for a double bogey seven. D.I.'s eight-footer lipped out causing him to strike up a brief conversation with himself while walking back to the cart.

It was not a happy group that headed for the fourth tee.

HOLE	1	2	3	4	5	6	7	8	9	OUT
PAR	4	4	5	4	3	5	4	3	4	36
YRDS	385	359	488	334	168	499	396	163	384	3146
D.I.	5	4	5							
Vince	4	5	6							
Wally	4	5	5							
Barney	3 ••	3 ••	7							

4

"Man! I'm sure glad that's over with," Vince said referring to the play on the previous hole. "What a way to waste a great drive."

"Yeah," Barney concurred, "I sure hope we got it all out of our system and we can get down to some serious golf."

"Not likely," D.I. said looking down the fairway of the straight away par four fourth hole, "not at this pace anyway."

The women stood talking in the fairway waiting for the group ahead to clear. Stella glanced back but this time only Barney seemed to notice. He felt a warm tingle and his hand produced an involuntarily shoulder high mini wave. A wave that missed Stella who had turned back to her playing partners. Barney glanced at Vince whose eyebrows did a hubba-hubba dance. Barney's heart sank. He looked at Wally who just smiled and nodded his approval. D.I. wore a look of condemnation. Barney could only smile sheepishly.

"You know," D.I. said suddenly, "For the life of me I can't figure out what the heck women want. I mean they already control seventy five percent of the nations wealth and a hundred percent of sex. How much more power do they want?"

"You just don't give up do you," Wally protested, "What is it that bothers you so much about women anyway?"

"Oh please, not again," Vince groaned.

"My problem," D.I. continued, "is they're never satisfied."

"Sounds like a personal problem to me," Vince cracked.

"No, I mean it, I can't think of a single all male institution that hasn't been invaded by women."

"Invaded, you make it sound like a war."

"Well isn't it? It's been called the battle of the sexes for as long as I can remember and the American male is losing his butt. We haven't won a battle, we've been in full retreat since day one."

"What exactly have we lost?" Wally asked.

"What have we lost?" D.I. repeated in a raised voice. "Where the heck have you been? We've lost the military, the Citadel, VMI, why there isn't a single male bastion that hasn't been penetrated by a She Storm Trooper. Why? Why do they want to go into an all-male institution anyway? You don't see a bunch of guys going to court to get into Vassar do you? I think a lot of these women just want a little notoriety, get themselves on TV, maybe write a book and make a fortune. The killer is that when they do get in, they last about two weeks then run off crying."

"D.I. you're a classic example of selective knowledge or lack of," Wally countered. "You failed to mention that a high percentage of males drop out of those institutions, too and I don't think they have to put up with near the harassment the women do."

"Here we go, the big H card falls again," D.I. snorted sourly, "I swear you can't look at, talk to or touch a woman without fear of being charged with harassment. I tell ya it's gotten completely out of hand."

"Well, as much as it pains me, I hafta agree with D.I. on this one," Vince said, "Women have become way too sensitive and defensive. You hafta be real careful in what you say and do. You can't be spontaneous, you're always under a microscope. You're simply not taken at face value."

"Lucky for you," D.I. quipped.

Vince continued on.

"Everything you say and do is scrutinized for hidden meaning or intent. If I were single today, I'd either be up to my neck in legal fees or in jail."

"Probably both," Wally figured.

"Amen to that brother," D.I. agreed.

"Geeze just listen to these two sexist pigs," Wally said turning to Barney who remained silent, "talk about sensitive and defensive."

D.I. sighed heavily, "Look," He said in a composed tone, "I'm not being sexist, I'm simply voicing an opinion about carrying things to excess."

"Testify, Brother," Vince shouted in his best evangelistic inflection.

D.I. smiled and shook his head, "I'm not denying that women have been harassed, I have seen it myself and it's embarrassing. There's some real scuzzes out there but don't punish all of us for the behavior of a few. I mean it's like speed bumps."

"Speed bumps?" Wally questioned.

"Yeah, you have a small number of speeders but because you don't want to expend the time, money and energy to catch and punish them, you install speed bumps and punish everybody by making them go over those friggin' things. It just seems that whenever we try to legislate behavior, we do it with a speed bump mentality. We need to be more offender specific and quit punishing all the law abiding citizens."

"What exactly constitutes sexual harassment anyway?" Vince asked, "I mean everybody knows you don't just walk up and grope someone, or require sex for a job or promotion. That's just common sense and that kind of behavior should be punished. I just don't know at what point a look becomes an ogle, a touch becomes a grope, or innocent flirtation turns into a seduction. There has to be a little more give and take if you ask me."

"Who asked," Wally said, playfully punching Vince's shoulder.

"Oh! Harassment! Harassment!" Vince wailed holding his arm and staggering around.

"Oh shut up, I get your point." Wally conceded. "Unfortunately," Wally went on, "when the pendulum swings, it swings fastest through the middle, and only stops at the extreme. It never stops in the middle unless it's broken."

D.I. looked at Wally, "Well I'm not sure but I think we are in agreement."

Wally nodded, "Yeah, now that I know where your comin' from. It's just your initial statement misled me."

"I hafta work on that," D.I. confessed, "It gets me in a lot of trouble on the home front, too."

"Whoa I'll bet. Donna probably punishes you pretty good when you come off the wall like that."

"Let's just say I've served some time."

"Is there a lot of leather and spanking involved?" Vince asked in playful enthusiasm, "Whips and chains things like that?"

"You're one sick pervert," D.I. said looking down the fairway.

"Crap!" He muttered.

"The others looked down the fairway to confirm the source of D.I.'s discontent. The women were still waiting."

"Hey D.I.," Wally asked, "what's your hang up with women in the military anyway?"

"Got no hang up, women weaken the military, that's all."

"How you figure that?"

"Look, anytime you put men and women in close proximity you create problems. With an all male military, or for that matter an all female military you eliminate all those conflicts that make up the war between the sexes. On top of that, you have another set of battles involving 'The Green Eyed Monster' and who's doing what with who. There should only be one objective in the military and that's get the job done."

"Oh you're saying women can't get the job done?"

"No I'm not, I'm saying a uni-sex military is stronger than a sexually mixed military. With today's high tech weaponry I have no doubt that women could run a war just as effectively as men, in fact, with their current militant attitude, they just might be better at it, especially if they go up against a male enemy."

"So what's the problem?"

"Wally, turn up your hearing aid, read my lips, the problem comes when you mix the sexes. Look what's happening in the Navy. They throw some women on an aircraft carrier and all hell breaks loose. Used to be all hands on deck, now hands are roamin' all over the place. Used to be but one objective, launch and retrieve airplanes, now you have the male sailors fightin' to score on the females and probably visa-versa. This doesn't create a cohesive fighting force if you ask me."

"Don't you think you're exaggerating just a little bit?"

"Am I? Have you read how many pregnant sailors they've removed from just the carriers alone? They're doing more than launchin' aircraft I'll tell you that. Next thing you know they'll have maternity wards on board. Shoot! we don't have a Navy, we've got a bunch of friggin' Love Boats."

"You know what I think?" Barney said breaking his silence, "I think this whole discussion smacks of sour grapes. Men our age have been spoiled by stay at home moms and wives from the old school. Times have changed radically in the last couple of decades and we feel threatened by it. No one likes to lose power and that's exactly what's been happening. Women have been moving up in all sectors of American society, the all male bastions have been crumbling like a stale muffin and we don't like it."

"Including you Barn?" Wally asked.

"Yeah, including me. I mean we had it good...... hell the fact is, we still do. Our lives haven't been affected all that much by the changes we have witnessed. It's the comparison from then to now that makes it all seem so foreign to us. This new generation has nothing to compare to so it's all quite normal to them."

"Don't that bother you?" D.I. asked.

"Not really, I mean it doesn't make me want to blame women for all the ills in the world like some people I know."

"Who? Me?" D.I. asked in false amazement, "Look I really don't blame them, I don't hate 'em either. And, I don't begrudge them an equal piece of the pie. It just seems they're pushin' it to the limit. Don't you think they're pushin' it?"

"Unfortunately," Barney said, "In order to facilitate change, you have to push hard and that tends to put people off."

"You got that right."

"I think your concern of additional problems stemming from a mixed military is valid. I've seen the same thing happen when women first broke into a previously all male work force. The men resent the intrusion which in turn instills an attitude in the women and now you have an adversarial work force."

"Exactly my point," D.I. agreed.

"But that's not all," Barney continued, "There are other forces at play here. The id, the libido, the ego."

"Oh crap!" Vince complained, "Dr. Sigmund's got his couch out again."

"Lord help us," Wally prayed, looking skyward.

"Let the good doctor speak," D.I. commanded, "You two nimrods just might learn something."

"I tell ya, the more I think of this stuff, the more it amazes me," Barney said, lightly shaking his head. "It's great, I mean how do you explain it? You have all this turmoil, this hostility going on in the conscience mind while in the subconscious, the id, the libido and the ego are churning out basic instincts, which are contrary. Its like having two sets of magnets, one set with like poles repelling each other and the other set attracted to each other by their difference. But, the old adage, 'opposites attract', doesn't really work outside the physics of electricity."

"What do you mean?" Vince questioned, "Women and men have always been attracted to each other and as we well know, you can't get more opposite than that."

Barney hesitated momentarily. "This is true," he said, "At least on the surface but the male/ female attraction is very complex and each one is unique in it's power and mystery. I'm not talking physical attraction here, that's a given, it's the only constant in an equation teeming with variables."

Vince massaged his temples, "Variables? What variables? Man, this is starting to give me a headache."

Barney glanced down the fairway. The women were still waiting to hit. "Well let's take a look at what we've been discussing here. Let's examine the male magnet."

Vince turned away shielding his private area, "You're not looking at my magnet?"

"Now there's a variable right there," Barney said pointing to Vince, "Each man places a value on the importance of his... man thing... and, that value varies from man to man and changes from time to time but that's not what I mean by the male magnet."

Vince turned and looked down. "My man thing?"

"Call it what you will but that...... thing...... can be a major complication in any equation or relationship."

"It's only a minor complication in Vince's case," D.I. jabbed.

"Aw bite me Iverson," Vince snipped.

"Boys, boys, calm down and let Barney finish," Wally pleaded.

All four looked down the fairway where the first lady was hitting her second shot.

"We'll have to pick this up later," D.I. said fetching his driver. "I believe I have the honors."

"More by default than good play," Vince complained walking to the back of the tee box.

"Green is not your color Vinny," D.I. countered lining up his ball from behind.

"You better enjoy hitting first because it will be your last time today."

"That could very well be, but tell me Mr. Denevi, how many times have you had the tee today?" There was no answer other than a chortle that escaped Wally's throat. The last woman sent her ball green-ward and the fairway finally cleared.

D.I. lashed at this ball, which responded by soaring skyward at an abrupt angle.

"You'll have to de-ice that one." Wally offered stepping forward to hit next.

"Well it's in play," Was all D.I. could say as the ball finally hit the ground a mere hundred and twenty yards from the tee.

Wally's tee ball started left then faded nicely to the center of the fairway.

"Now that's more like it." He said walking from the tee in a semi-strut.

Barney had an urge to instruct Wally on how to correct his fade rather than adjusting to it but decided better to let Wally enjoy finding the fairway.

"Nice ball," Vince said as he surveyed the tee for a level spot.

"Thanks."

Vince drove his ball slightly left and just short of Wally's. Barney returned to his smooth natural swing and sent one a good thirty yards past Wally's.

"Whoa, a Linda Ronstadt", Vince crowed as he turned and faced Wally.

"A what?" Wally questioned.

"A Linda Ronstadt...... you know, Blue Bayou... ... blew by you."

"Oh really funny Vinny," Wally croaked, unable to contain a snicker.

Vince and D.I. proceeded to D.I.'s ball while Barney and Wally continued down the cart path.

"You gonna go for it D.I.?"

"I don't think I have enough club to get it there, I'll just try to lay it up to the hundred yard marker. What do ya think it is, about a hundred and seventy from here?"

"To the hundred marker? Yeah, maybe one eighty, you got a little wind comin' at ya."

"I gotta one eighty club right here," D.I. said pulling a three iron from his bag.

"Looks good!" Vince said, eyes following the flight of D.I.'s ball.

"I like it!" D.I. agreed, stepping into the cart. "Should be a nice full wedge to the pin."

The men gathered in the area between Vince's and Wally's tee balls. None of the women had found the green on their second shot and it was obvious there would be a rather lengthy delay.

"So Barn, tell me more about his animal magnetism theory of yours," D.I. asked, throwing his feet up on the dashboard of his cart and reclining back in his seat.

"I was really trying to explain why the old adage 'opposites attract', doesn't really apply to human sexuality. Trying to compare human attraction to magnetic attraction is an over simplification. True, magnetism is probably the classic confirmation that opposites attract and if physical attraction was all there was to human sexuality then I would be inclined to accept the correlation. But there is much more to it."

"That's what I was afraid of," Vince said plopping down on the cart seat.

"It's really more like an electro magnet," Barney continued undaunted, "Yeah that's it! A variable electro magnet, controlled by a set of preset resistors that are switched in and out of the circuit. These resistors, are set by one's personality and individual likes and dislikes. For example, if you saw a blonde and you have a low resistance to blondes, your blonde resistor would allow more current to flow through your magnet thus producing a greater attraction. Likewise, if I had a high resistance to blondes, less current, less attraction. Now, there are all kinds of physical resistors, such as ......eye color ......big hooters, nice pooper, long legs, things like that. Now, besides these physical resistors, we also form resistance values for personality traits ......happy .....giving......sense of humor etc., etc.

Now, when you first see someone, all your applicable physical resistors are cut into your magnet's circuit and you have your own physical attraction toward that particular person. As you get to know that person better, the personality resistors are cut in or out, either enhancing the overall attraction or weakening it. The more you get to know a person the more your magnet may vary. Remember everybody's resistors have different values and a set of male resistors is generally not interchangeable with a set of female resistors."

"Barney?" Vince asked.

"Yeah?"

"You've been spending way too much time by yourself."

"I don't know," D.I. disputed, "I think it's a real intriguing concept."

"Yeah," Wally agreed, "Very insightful, but what about behavior traits, wouldn't they effect attraction?"

"Oh very much, but I think behavioral traits would act more like a set of diodes and transistors and could, under certain circumstances, completely reverse the current flow producing a repulsive force. This to me is a very baffling area of human relations. A behavior as trivial as how one squeezes a tube of toothpaste or whether the toilet seat is left up or down can completely offset an otherwise powerful attraction. Why such a seemingly minor faux pas can create such a major dilemma has been a real boon to the field of psychology, not to mention the field of matrimonial litigation."

"Barney, where in the heck do you come up with all this crap?" Vince wondered.

"Well, like you say, I spend a lot of time alone..., but don't you think it illustrates just how complex human relationships can be? I mean if you think of the infinite number of traits there are... why it staggers the imagination. There's only one slight problem."

"What's that?" D.I. asked.

"The man thing," Vince interrupted. "It has no resistance at all. It can short circuit the whole system and take total control of your magnet, and if you don't believe me just ask ex-president Clinton."

"This is true," Barney conceded, "The man thing has laid many a man to waste."

The four men laughed as they each weighed the validity of what had been said. They also pondered the futility of their understanding.

"Hey! We can hit," Vince said jumping from his cart.

"Oh, one more thing." Barney said.

"Will it never end?" Vince pleaded, looking heavenward.

"This is all a bunch of horse hockey," Barney stated, "We shouldn't question the differences between men and women, we should rejoice in them. We should take pleasure from them."

"Oh I do!" D.I. said, "I really do!"

HOLE	1	2	3	4	5	6	7	8	9	OUT
PAR	4	4	5	4	3	5	4	3	4	36
YRDS	385	359	488	334	169	499	396	163	384	3146
D.I.	5	4	5	5						
Vince	4	5	6	••4						
Wally	4	5	5	5						
Barney	••3	••3	7	5						

5

"I can't believe I three putted from twelve feet," Barney said dejectedly as the foursome walked off the fourth green.

"I think your magnet might be in a state of flux," Vince offered, patting Barney lightly on the shoulder. "Could be the Stella effect."

"Oh please."

"No I mean it. I think she's a Godsend. She's here to cut into some of that conjuring time you have on your hands. She's gonna save us from future episodes of the "World According To Barn."

"Yeah, shut the Barn door, so to speak," D.I. added.

"Hey, I can only offer these things up as entertainment. Heaven forbid they'd cause a brain wave in you three flat liners."

"Get in the cart and shut up!" Wally commanded.

"Yeah, you know better than to ask us to think," D.I. said in feigned agitation, "What the hell's gotten into you anyway?"

"I'm sorry, I really shouldn't expect you to do something your incapable of."

"Okay, enough already," Wally said, driving off to the next tee.

The path between the forth green and the fifth tee, cuts through a stand of trees which contained a large and essential pecan tree. D.I.'s fondness for coffee combined with a daily diuretic and weak bladder, mandated he pay homage to said tree. It was not optional and for this reason, D.I. dubbed it, The Pee-Can tree.

Today, because of slow play, the tree had two additional devotees.

The fifth hole, a hundred and sixth-yard par three over water, had one group on the green, a foursome of men on the tee and the ladies were waiting back on the cart path.

"Good Lord," Wally uttered. "What's the hold up?"

The men parked their carts about forty yards behind the ladies. Stella turned and shrugged her shoulders. Wally let the cart creep forward.

"Hey, what the heck's wrong with this cart?" Wally said in near panic, "I can't stop it, there's like a strange force drawing it toward that lady in red!" Wally pretended to pump the brakes while at the same time keeping pressure on the accelerator. The cart rolled on.

"Barney, curb your magnet, quick!" Wally ordered, before bringing the cart to a halt.

"Phew! That was close." Wally said wiping his brow in relief.

"What happened?" D.I. asked walking up beside the cart.

"It's the darndest thing I've ever seen... I couldn't stop the cart, Barney's magnet locked onto that lady and I tell ya, I couldn't hold 'er back."

Barney didn't say a word, knowing that to do so would only incite further torment. Wally and D.I. walked back to where Vince sat recording the scores from the fourth hole.

"Three fives and a four... Right?" he asked.

"Yeah I think so. Hey Barn? What did ya have on the last hole?" D.I. asked. Barney didn't turn, he held up his right hand with all five digits extended.

"Yeah, Barney had a five," D.I. confirmed.

"Hey, I get a carryover," Vince said delightedly as he marked two dots above his par. "And......I get the tee."

"If we don't all die of old age in the mean time." D.I. complained.

Barney sat mute watching the ladies. They appeared to be having some kind of disagreement. He could hear their voices but couldn't make out what the dispute was about. Stella kept shaking her head and was becoming more and more animated in her disagreement. Suddenly she turned and walked toward him. Barney got out to the cart and walked to meet her.

"We're having a slight difference of opinion regarding the rules of golf," She said, as she neared Barney, "Maybe you can help us out."

"I'll try, but everybody has trouble with the rules of golf. What's the problem?"

"Well, on the last hole, my ball was just off the green by about five feet and the other three were on."

"Uh huh."

"Well, I decided to putt the ball. The other three balls were not in my line and no one had marked yet. I hit a really lousy putt, which struck Sally's ball and bumped it about five feet closer to the pin. Judy says that I should take a two stroke penalty for hitting Sally's ball."

"Well she's wrong. If your shot was played from off the green, there's no penalty."

"Thank you, that's what I thought. Now the next questions is, from what point does Sally play her next shot?"

Barney, knew the answer and was about to dazzle her with his knowledge, but, Stella continued on.

"I say she has to place it where it was before being hit by my ball. Sally thinks she gets to play it where it is."

Barney allowed a courtesy pause to ensure that Stella had finished.

"No, you're right again, the ball must be placed as near as possible to it's original position, so in effect there's no harm, no gain, no foul."

"Thank you......Barney," She said with honeyed voice and a warm smile that tickled his spirit.

"You're welcome, Stella," He said, eyes brightening at the sound of her name. They stood momentarily savoring the recognition. Barney was thrilled that she had remembered his name and astonished that he had recalled hers so effortlessly. As the seconds passed, the euphoria he felt faded into panic. His mind raced wildly trying to come up with something clever to inject into the rapidly expanding void. He could feel himself beginning to shut down.

"Well thanks again, Barney," she said with a hint of disappointment.

"Oh every time...... I mean ...... any...any...time...anytime," he flustered. She turned back to her friends. Barney cursed his brain for such a feeble effort and its inability to coordinate with his mouth. He watched as Stella began walking away. You idiot! He admonished to himself. How can you screw up such a simple encounter? You're pathetic.

"Stella?" He heard himself say.

"She stopped and turned toward him.

"Yes?"

"Would you like to play a round with me sometime?"

"Play a round or play around?" she asked, "How exactly did you mean that?"

Barney stood stunned by the implications of what he had just said. The harassment discussion replayed in his mind. Damn you brain he cursed.

"Oh Geeze, that didn't come over very well, did it?" Barney said quickly.

Barney struggled to compose himself. "What I meant to say was, maybe, if you'd like, we could play a round of golf...... sometime...... if you'd like maybe."

"Oh... is that what you meant?" She said with a disappointed pout.

"Well, ah...I..."

"Barney, relax, I'm just yankin' your chain a little, I knew exactly what you were sayin', I'd love to play a round...... of golf...... sometime."

Barney exhaled a heavy sigh "You'll have to excuse me, I'm really not very good at this sort of thing. It's been a long time since I've talked to a woman like this."

"I'm sorry Barney," She said, "I didn't mean to make it hard on you. I sometimes kid around to cover my own nervousness. I hope I didn't put you off any."

"You're nervous?"

"Oh yeah! You're the first man I've talked to since... ...well since Joe died... ... Oh I've talked to other men but you're the first one I actually wanted to talk to."

Barney felt a huge burden lift from his shoulders. His mind slowed to a jog, switching from damage control to actually processing rational thought. He noticed Stella's eyes soften and a calm peace settled upon him.

"Aren't we a pair to draw to?" Barney said shaking his head.

"Pitiful!" She agreed. They both laughed lightly at what they had just experienced.

"That was really awkward," Barney continued. "I hope it gets easier from......"

"Hey Stella!" One of the other ladies called. "Times up, let's go."

"Coming!" She answered, not breaking eye contact. "We'll talk later," she said, extending her hand. Barney's hand reached out instinctively, found hers and squeezed it gently. She smiled sweetly, turned and walked away. Barney watched her intently as emotions, he believed long dead and buried, were resurrected in his heart. Stella glanced back when she entered her cart. A jolt of delight ran up his spine. The ladies drove off to the tee. Barney turned to face two grins and a question mark.

"Way to go Barn," Vince cheered.

"This looks serious," Wally added.

"What the hell was that all about?" D.I. demanded.

Barney smiled, "She had a couple of questions about the rules of golf."

"What, like how to score, on the golf course?" Vince teased.

"I think she's way out of bounds," D.I. quipped. "She might want to hit a provisional."

"Oh, she's not out of bounds," Wally countered, wrapping an arm around Barney's neck and giving him a brisk noogie. "She's right on the pin! Right Barney ol' boy?"

Barney flushed as he bent to retrieve the hat that had been noogied from his head. "You know," he said, running his fingers through his thinning hair, "I couldn't ask for better friends...... I should...... but I just couldn't." Barney adjusted his hat and looked to the ladies' tee. Three ladies were engrossed in conversation, the other was looking back to the white tee.

The white teeing area extends a short distance into a lake and is elevated slightly behind a railroad tie bulkhead. The lay out of the hole is such that it places Wally and his perpetual fade at a grave disadvantage. The further right a ball travels, increases the distance needed to clear the water. This is due to the angle at which the lake passes in front of the green. A draw or pull provides the shortest distance to dry land. Unfortunately, neither shot can be found in Wally Ferguson's bag.

Wally's percentage of successful crossing had been well below fifty percent. But that was before he began performing his fifth hole sacrificial offerings. Today's ceremony was about to begin and a solemn hush fell upon the tee. Wally removed a ball from a small velvet bag he carried just for this purpose. This was a new ball that had never been struck. A holy ball of divine purity. A Sacrificial Virgin to appease the Water God. Wally walked to the front of the teeing area, the ball cradled in his outstretched palms. He stopped and stood atop the bulkhead, the ball held above the dark cold water. He raised the ball slowly toward the heavens and began speaking in tongues.

"Molitor Ultra Maxfli Strata," he moans, "Slazenger Precept Titleist Pinnacle."

He lowers the ball slowly and blesses it with a blessing he borrowed from a well-known San Francisco radio personality.

"In the name of Arnie, Jack and The Great White Shark. Amen!"

Then Wally reared back and threw the ball as far as he could into the lake.

Wally turned to the other three, "Can I get an Amen?" he appealed.

"Amen!" They answered.

The green cleared and Vince casually tossed a ball near the right hand tee marker. Then, using the blade of his six iron, he bumped it until it rested lightly on a tuft of grass. Eight eyes followed the ball's flight as it drew toward the pin.

"Oh be the stick," Vince pleaded.

"Get in the hole!" Wally urged.

"Better get up," D.I. said flatly, as the ball plugged under the lip of the pot bunker guarding the front of the green.

"Oh man, I thought that was good," Vince whined.

"Game of inches," D.I. said matter of factually. "What'd you hit?"

"Six, and I hit it sweet too."

"Well if that's a sweet six, I guess I better hit a tart five."

Vince stomped down the divot area and moped his way back to the cart where he forcefully deposited the sweet six into his bag.

D.I. pulled his shot slightly, winding up pin high on the left fringe.

Wally hit one dead straight on the pin, the ball landing on the green and stopping about fifteen feet short of the hole.

"This is spooky" D.I. said, "Ever since you started performing your little ritual you haven't gone in the water once."

"I did once." Wally corrected, "But I tried to use an old ball. The Water God demands a virgin."

"Doesn't it get a little expensive?" Barney asked.

"Worth every penny," Wally said brightly, "saves me two strokes a round." Then whispering so the Water God could not hear, "Besides they're really cheap balls."

Barney bladed his tee shot and the ball ran a good ten yards beyond the green where it quickly hid in the long rough.

"You came up and out at that one," D.I. advised.

"Yeah," Barney conceded. "I'm not concentrating."

"Oh you're concentrating all right, it's just not on golf." Barney did not respond openly but he had to agree with D.I.'s assessment. His thoughts were one hole ahead.

"So what did you two really talk about?" Wally asked as they drove toward the green.

"The rules of golf." Barney answered flatly.

"No, No, really?"

"Really, they were having an argument and she asked me for a ruling."

"A ruling? That's it? It looked a little more involved than a ruling."

"Well that's the gist of it," Barney said indifferently. Wally peered at his friend who smiled knowingly.

"You S.O.B.! you better spill your guts and spill 'em right now...or... I swear I'll run this cart into that big oak tree over there," Wally threatened, directing the cart toward a large tree just to the left of the cart path. Barney folded his arms across his chest, leaned back and closed his eyes.

"My life is complete," He said solemnly. "I'm prepared to die!"

"Yeah? Well I'm not!" Wally admitted, swerving the cart back to the cart path, "Besides, we're only on the fifth hole and I haven't had a chance to get into your wallet yet."

The two carts pulled up beside the green. Vince, still protesting the injustice bestowed upon him by the game of golf, slumped off toward the front bunker dragging his sand wedge in one hand and his putter in the other.

"Nice bit of driving Mario," D.I. said, walking past Wally.

"Thanks, I was just having a little fun with Romeo here."

Barney stood inspecting the face of his pitching wedge. "The man's a menace," he commented, while nonchalantly cleaning the grooves with his thumbnail.

"He's holding out on us," Wally complained. "He's acting like nothing's going on between him and that Lolita of his."

"Well maybe nothin' is."

"Oh crap, D.I., you're about as observant as a stump. I'm telling you something's going on."

"So? What if there is? Who gives a fig?"

"Well I do, and if you were any kind of friend you would, too."

"Hey, if the man doesn't want to tell us anything, that's his prerogative."

"Thank you D.I.," Barney said, walking off to locate his ball.

"Well I just think as friends, we should know what the scoop is... you know...... so we can be supportive...... and offer advice."

"Wally?"

"Yeah."

"I think you just validated his silence."

Vince muttered and mumbled over his predicament in the sand trap. His ball was deeply embedded at the base of the lip and he stooped hoping that closer inspection might reveal a glimmer of hope but it only confirmed the severity of his situation.

"This is the exact same shot I had back on number three," he protested.

Receiving no sympathy from his cohorts, he glumly accepted his fate, dug in and steadied himself over the ball. An explosion of sand all but obliterated him from view and the telltale thunk of ball meeting earth confirmed the inevitable. Vince looked around, hoping to find his ball resting on the putting surface. It wasn't. Wally grimly pointed. Vince turned to find his ball resting ten feet behind him in the center of the trap.

"Well as that great philosopher, Yogi Berra used to say, 'It's déjà vu all over again'," Wally said, trying not to laugh too heartily.

"Man!" D.I. said lightly. "I haven't seen that much sand moved since Hurricane Hugo."

Vince was not amused. He wasted little time in preshot routine and promptly blasted out to within eight feet.

"Nice out," Wally offered sympathetically. Vince did not acknowledge, he began a vigorous raking of the trap.

Barney's circumstance, although different, was none the less grave. His ball was nestled in the deep grass. His shot would have to carry thirty feet of rough. The green sloped away from him and if that weren't bad enough, there was less than fifteen feet of green to work with. Numerous practice swings sent a shower of grass blades flittering on the morning breeze. Barney laid the blade of his wedge wide open and took an overly open stance. Then with a full back swing and aggressive pass that produced wide eyes and muffled gasps from his playing partners, Barney popped the ball high into the air. It hovered momentarily at its apex then lightly fell in the first cut where it released onto the green and trickled in the direction of the hole. The four men stood in frozen amazement as the ball rolled ever so slowly on its path toward the hole, each rotation slower than the previous and destined to be the last. But, fed by gravity and nudged by fate, the ball staggered on like a drunken sailor returning to his ship, its track altered by invisible spike marks and minute indentations. At the edge of the cup it hesitated as if asking permission to come aboard then it crisply saluted and toppled into the hole.

There was a moment of silence while the significance of the event registered. Then, all hell broke loose.

"Great shot Barn!"

"Wow, not even Phil 'the flop shot' Mickleson could top that."

"I am duly impressed."

Barney knew that true compliments were a rarity in this group. Most were shrouded in sarcasm or tempered by envy. These were probably no exception but he accepted them as genuine. As he walked to retrieve his ball he accepted two high fives and a pat on the back.

"Thank you, thank you," Barney acknowledged with a tip of his hat. "I'll be available for autographs and lessons following play."

"You could use a lesson in humility," Wally suggested.

"The only autograph I want from you is on a big loser's check." Vince added.

D.I. squatted behind his ball to assess his line. "That's a pretty tough act to follow," he said, rising out of his crouch, his eyes never leaving the spot he had chosen. "Man," he muttered, positioning himself over the ball. "This is going to be a real speed putt." He was right. The ball came out of the fringe with insufficient pace to hold the line let alone reach the hole.

"Nice lag, Alice," Vince chortled.

D.I. spanked his putter blade in disgust before casually one handing the ball into the cup from two feet.

"Maybe you should putt that way all the time," Wally said.

"Couldn't hurt," D.I. agreed, snatching his ball from the cup.

Wally's putt marched right up to the edge of the cup, came to an abrupt halt, retreated a quarter of a turn and came to parade rest.

"Dad burn it!"

"That was a good putt, Wally," Barney said in a consoling tone.

"Not quite good enough," Wally said, tapping in for par. "But I did manage to get the greenie."

Vince's eight footer was on the exact same line as Wally's, straight up and in and that's how he hit it.

"That's a good bogey from what you had to work with," D.I. complimented.

"Yeah, I'll take it and go happy."

Barney placed the pin in the cup. Wally walked over and patted him on the back.

"That was the prettiest ugly I've ever seen," he said.

"Hey that's right, I get an ugly too!" Barney called to Vince, "Three dots if you please Mr. Tallyman."

"You're getting' a little greedy aren't you Melton?" Vince shot back.

Wally got in the cart and looked over at Barney.

"Okay Barn," he said, "Tell your ol' pal what's going on between you and Stella."

"No!"

"Aw come on!"

"No!"

HOLE	1	2	3	4	5	6	7	8	9	OUT
PAR	4	4	5	4	3	5	4	3	4	36
YRDS	385	359	488	334	168	499	396	163	384	3146
D.I.	5	4	5	5	3					
Vince	4	5	6	4	4					
Wally	4	5	5	5	3					
Barney	3	3	7	5	2					

99

6

When they arrived at the sixth tee, three were delighted to find it open. Barney was not. The ladies, miniaturized by distance, were already hitting their approach shots on the long straight away par five. A mere crimson smudge upon his aging retina was all Barney had to differentiate Stella from the rest of humanity. A hollow ache filled his belly as he realized he might not see her again. Maybe it would be better if he didn't. Maybe he was better off the way he was, he was comfortable with it. Maybe it was best not to risk the emotional turmoil that accompanies love and loss. Maybe it was best not to tempt the fickle finger of fate and the delicate uncertainty of life. Maybe......but, maybe it was too late.

"Wow, what happened?" D.I. said, in a near state of ecstasy. "We can actually walk right up and hit it. Come on birdie man, times a wastin'."

"How could they get so far ahead of us?" Barney asked, in a tone of urgency.

"Things usually spread out after a par three," D.I. answered.

"Yeah, but that much?"

"Hey don't question it, just enjoy it. Hit the damn ball."

"I think our boy here might be suffering from separation syndrome," Wally explained. "She's out of magnet range."

"Ah stuff it, Ferguson."

"See, what'd I tell ya! Irritability, it's a classic symptom."

"Can we please play some golf?" D.I. pleaded. "See, this is why women shouldn't be allowed on the golf course, it's a golf course, not a dating service."

"Hey, where else is ol' Barn goin' to meet women?"

"Well he won't meet them layin' on his couch in front of the TV." D.I. said. "He needs to get out and about."

"Like where?" Barney asked.

"I don't know... anywhere... you could meet someone in the produce department of Super K, pinchin' fruit for all I care. I hear women are attracted to produce men."

"Well I think you could be a little more sympathetic to the plight of our ol' friend." Wally chided.

"I'm concerned about Barney, I'd love to see him find a lady, but not here, not on the golf course," D.I. explained.

Wally sighed and shook his head, "Why should it matter where...?"

"Excuse me, excuse me," Barney interrupted. "I am truly touched by your concern for my love life but with all due respect, it's none of your damn business, now please shut the hell up and let's play some golf."

D.I. clapped his hands and bowed, "Thank you very much, Mr. Melton."

Wally looked at Barney in disbelief, "Hey, I'm on your side, you..."

"Eh, eh, eh," Barney scolded, holding his hands in a blocking manner. "D.I.'s right, we're here to play golf.'

"Amen to that!" Vince concurred.

All except Wally found the fairway with their tee shots, none of which were exceptional. Wally's fade, once again placed him in the right-hand rough. He had fallen into a moping silence and he wore an expression composed of anger and hurt. Barney could tell he was less than pleased.

"Look Wally, I do appreciate your concern but let's just see what happens, let's not push it... Okay?"

"Well I don't want you to miss an opportunity, I mean I'm pretty sure she's keen on you and she seems like a real nice lady."

"Well believe it or not, Wally, I'm quite capable of handling my own affairs...no pun intended. In fact, I've already asked her if she would like to play golf sometime and she said she would."

"I knew it! I knew you two weren't just talkin' 'bout the rules of golf back there. Why you ol' snake in the grass you, I knew you two were up to somethin'... You've never expressed that much passion for the rules of golf... This is great... This is just too... cool."

The four hit their second shots in rapid succession. All sufficiently mediocre enough to provide an opportunity for all to reach the green in regulation. As they drove off in pursuit, Barney watched Stella's cart disappear into the trees, in route to the next tee. He was again struck with the realization that he might be loosing touch with her. What if they weren't able to catch up? What if she had an unlisted number? How would he find her? He was filled with a sense of...... helplessness. He hurried his third shot, the club never actually contacting the ball but propelling it forward on a massive divot.

"Your rushing it," Wally instructed. "Slow it down, don't worry, we'll catch up to her."

The other three players found the green in regulation. Barney took his putter and pitching wedge from his bag.

"I'll meet you at the green," he said, dejectedly as he jogged the short distance to his ball. Wally thought it best not to reply and drove off to join the others. Unable to curb his impatience, Barney bladed his fourth shot over the green and into the woods.

"Damn it!" He muttered, slamming his club down in frustration. He drew another ball from his pocket and dropped it.

"You're all right," D.I. shouted from the green. "It hit a tree and bounced back."

Barney bent and snatched at his second ball in anger. A jolt of pain ran up his arm as the nail of his middle finger contacted the top of the ball sending the ball forward and nail back.

"Mother of Mary!" He howled in pain, shaking his hand in banjo strumming fashion then blowing on the wounded appendage. "Serves me right," he admonished with a pain-contorted smile. A trio chortled from the green. Barney looked up, trying to appear hurt by their lack of compassion but the sight of them caused him to lose the handle on a throat full of laughter.

"You guys are bad to the bone, you know that?" he gasped.

They nodded their mutual agreement, shoulders shuddering from unabashed glee.

"You okay?" Wally asked as Barney reached the green.

"Like you sadists really give a......"

"Now be nice Barn, were laughin' with ya not at ya," Vince tried to explain as Barney walked past on his way to his uncooperative ball.

"Yeah right!" Barney sneered dropping his putter on the fringe and scanning the area behind the green.

"It's over to your right just short of that small pine." D.I. said with a point.

"Where?"

"Keep going...a little to your right... see it?"

"Not yet, is it... never mind, I got it...... Thanks." Barney quickly surveyed his shot.

"Man this is gonna be a tricky pitch."

"Piece of cake for a player of your caliber and ability." D.I. stated in sarcastic confidence.

"Damn near a gimme after that shot back on five," Wally added.

"Yeah!... your right," Barney agreed, taking his stance. "Gentlemen, prepare to be amazed." Barney slowly drew his club back, paused, then pulled it down toward the ball. The club chunked into the ground then bounced into the ball with just enough force to get it airborne. The follow through caused the club to contact the ball in mid bloop producing the dreaded double hit. Barney looked up in disbelief.

"I'm amazed," Vince said stoically.

"Me too," D.I. added with a shrug. Wally could only clamp a hand over his mouth, which failed to conceal the laughter in his eyes.

"Well I'll be dipped," Barney scoffed weakly. "Haven't done that in a while." He walked the few paces to his ball and sent it onto the green with a casual one-handed swipe of the club, not bothering to stop or take a stance.

"What was that?" Vince asked.

"Looked like a walk by shooting to me," D.I. replied, placing his ball on the green and removing his mark.

Barney said nothing, stopping to trade his wedge for the putter that lay on the fringe.

"Whose away?" he asked impatiently, eyes glazed in shock.

"I think it's you D.I.," Vince answered, pointing his putter in D.I.'s direction.

D.I. two putted for his par as did Wally and Vince. Barney back handed his second putt into the cup and walked off the green in a daze.

"Three five's and Barn?" Vince asked as he placed his putter in his bag.

"Yep," D.I. confirmed.

"What's the damages Barn?"

"I'm not sure," Barney said, "how do you score a double hit?"

"Two plus a penalty," D.I. stated matter of factly.

"Three strokes?" Barney whined, "You sure there's a penalty, shouldn't it just be the number of times the club hit the ball?"

"Sorry ol' bean, you gotta take a penalty."

"I think there's a penalty, D.I.," Wally argued. "But the actual stroke is only scored as one, so...it's one plus a penalty."

D.I. shook his head. "No, it's like hitting a moving ball, so it's one for the first hit then two for the second and a penalty for hitting a ball in motion."

"Man that doesn't seem fair," Wally objected, "I don't see why he......"

"Hey it doesn't really matter whether I take a nine or a ten," Barney reasoned, "The hole's a carryover anyway, so I haven't lost anything.........yet."

"You're right, who cares." Wally said.

"Well I do,' D.I. said emphatically. "You should record the correct score at all times."

"Why, I have to adjust it down to post it anyway, it doesn't really make any difference."

"Well what if it did make a difference, what if it was to win or tie the hole?"

"But it isn't, so what's the big Frig........."

"Will you two stop your yammerin'," Vince said, unzipping a side pocket of his bag and producing a rulebook. "Let's consult the bible." Vince scanned the index. "Let's see...Ah here we go, Striking the ball more than once, Rule 14-4, page 40."

He fanned the pages with his thumb then turned back a couple of pages.

"Okay... 14-4 sez... "If a player's club strikes the ball more than once in the course of a stroke, the player shall count the stroke and add a penalty stroke, making two strokes in all."

"Lemme see that," D.I. demanded, reaching for the book.

"See for yourself D.I., it's right there in black and white," Vince said handing the book over to D.I.

D.I. took the open book and read silently for a few seconds. "Ah-ha...listen to this, '14-5 Playing Moving Ball, A player shall not play while his ball is moving. Exceptions: ball falling off tee, Rule 11-3, striking the ball more than once, Rule 14-4, ball moving in water, rule...''

"There you go," Vince interrupted. "Two strokes, just like it says."

D.I. looked up with a puzzled expression.

"Whada ya mean?" he protested in a raised voice. "You take two strokes under rule 14-4 and one from 14-5."

"No you don't!"

"Well yes you do!" D.I. insisted.

"Gimme that!" Barney snorted, snatching the book from DI's hand and scrutinizing it's contents.

"Exceptions D.I., can you say exception, or better yet, do you know what an exception is?"

D.I.'s face flushed as he realized the error of his logic.

"Yes I know what an exception is, smart-ass," D.I. retorted trying to save a small portion of his red-faced dignity. "But I still think it should be three strokes."

"Well, if I'm not mistaken," Barney cooed, waving the rulebook under D.I.'s nose. "The USGA

Rules of Golf just might supersede the Dale Iverson Rules of golf."

"Up yours!" D.I. snapped, swiping at the waving publication which Barney quickly pulled back leaving D.I. grasping at air.

Wally, ever the peacemaker, stepped in and placed a hand on their shoulder. "Guys, guys," he said calmly. "It's not worth arguing over, we've had an honest difference of opinion, we have the answer, let's move on."

Realizing D.I.'s aversion to being proven wrong, Wally quickly interjected.

"But D.I., your interpretation of the ball in motion is a point well taken and one that could be argued had the rule book not been so specific, a phenomenon that frankly astonishes me... I mean, this is the first time I have actually understood what the book is saying. Usually it refers you to another rule, which in turn refers you to still another and another and before you know it you're in a hopeless loop. By the time you get out you can't remember what brought you there in the first place. This was really cut and dried. I mean sure it could be argued......" Wally suddenly realized he was rambling and, his dissertation on the rulebook was not soothing D.I.'s wounded ego.

"Help!" He yelped, "I'm babbling and I won't shut up, somebody slap me."

Three hands rose in unison.

HOLE	1	2	3	4	5	6	7	8	9	OUT
PAR	4	4	5	4	3	5	4	3	4	36
YRDS	385	359	488	334	168	499	396	163	384	3146
D.I.	5	4	5	5	3	5				
Vince	4	5	6	4	4	5				
Wally	4	5	5	5	3	5				
Barney	3	3	7	5	2	9				

7

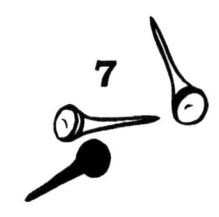

Their stint of fast play was short lived. Upon reaching the seventh tee, they could see, to Barney's delight and D.I.'s chagrin, the ladies waiting out on the fairway.

"Shouldda know'd," D.I. said dejectedly.

Barney's mood swung positive as Stella's image stood bright yet not too clear in the not too far distance.

Vince labored over the scorecard and was suddenly reminded of something he had meant to comment on.

"Hey D.I.!"

D.I. diverted his gaze from the fairway and turned toward Vince.

"Yeah?"

"That was a real nice article in the paper the other day."

D.I. stared blankly.

"Article?......"

"Yeah article... in the sport section... on Danny... Your son... You remember... that kid that used to live with you."

A ray of enlightenment flickered behind D.I.'s eyes.

"Geeze Denevi, that article appeared months ago. You a slow reader or what?"

"He moves his lips a lot," Wally volunteered.

Vince smirked.

"Has it been that long?" he asked innocently, "Sure doesn't seem like it. Anyway I've been meaning to say something to you about it, but as you have so poignantly pointed out, my short term memory is short."

"Ah, it's all coming back to me," D.I. said, closing his eyes and rubbing his temples. "It was a nice write up wasn't it?"

"Write up, what write up?" Barney wondered aloud.

"Oh the newspaper did an article on Danny and the success he's been having with the baseball team at Hamilton High," D.I. answered proudly.

"Didn't they make it to the State Championship last year?" Barney asked.

"Well they made it to the State Tournament," D.I. corrected, "but lost in the quarter finals."

"That's pretty good isn't it?"

"Well considering the circumstances," D.I. went on "it's quite remarkable. Hamilton opened just three years ago and the first year they only had freshmen and sophomores. Needless to say they only won one game that year. But the following year, they were over five hundred with only juniors and only missed the playoffs by one game."

"Wow!"

"Darn right wow," D.I. emphasized, chest expanding slightly. "Danny's done a real good job but he credits his players for all the success. I gotta tell ya, he's really been blessed with some incredible talent."

"Well it sure didn't come from your side of the family," Vince jabbed.

"No, no, not his talent, the kids he has playing for him. He's got two big kids who can really throw some heat and another kid that throws more junk than Fred Sanford. It's an awesome combination. When and if the opposing batters figure out the timing on the fast ballers, Danny sends in his junk man to clean up. It's a brutal thing to watch. I mean these poor kids are flailing away, trying to hit something that isn't there. I've never seen a high school kid that can work the ball like this guy. If he keeps his head on straight and his arm holds out, I think he'll make the majors. And if pitching isn't enough, they've got some big sticks, too. There really isn't a weak spot in the order, no one to pitch around. Got a couple of good gloves too, and good speed on the bases."

"Sounds like they have it all," Vince commented.

D.I. nodded in agreement.

"They will definitely win the state championship this year." He predicted with unabashed certainty.

There was a period of silent reservation by the other three followed by subdued nodding and noncommittal could bes.

"What I like about the article," D.I. continued. "Is that it recognized Danny's role in transforming a bunch of teenage hot dogs into a cohesive force, a team. That's hard to do without wounding their young ego or breaking their spirit."

"Well I thought it was an excellent article, you and Donna must be very proud, Danny's a great kid."

"Kid? He's a forty year old father of two."

"He's still your kid."

"Yeah... and we are proud of him, he turned out pretty good inspite of me."

"Oh man, speaking of kids," Wally said with sudden enthusiasm, "Did you guys catch that show on TV last night about the kids who have taken over the family?"

"What show was that?"

"I don't know... 20/20... Dateline... one of those news magazine shows. Anyway, it, was, pathetic. They showed three different families who's kids, somehow, gained complete control over their parents. Somewhere along the line, these parents totally lost control and were never able to regain it. One kid was even physically abusive."

"To his parents?" Vince asked.

"Yeah, he was a big, mean, nasty kid. You should of seen his parents cower when he threatened them."

"Thatta been the day his noggin woulda met Mister Louisville Slugger," Vince snorted.

"Another kid," Wally went on, "Locked himself in his room and wouldn't come out. He's lived in there for a couple of years, his parents catering to his every demand. He's set up his own little world with his own personal catering service. You should have heard him yelling orders through the door." Wally shook his head, "This kid was sick, and he wasn't going to get any better in that room."

"I'da pulled the little prick outta that room by his adolescence," D.I. huffed.

"His parents tried but the kid caused such a commotion they backed off. It was tragic. These poor people just couldn't do what had to be done and now they're just as sick as their kid. How could things get so screwed up?"

"Well, did you see that story in the paper the other day about the lady being arrested for swatting her kid on the butt?" Vince asked.

"Arrested?" Barney repeated in amazement.

"Oh yeah," Vince confirmed, "She was shopping at Kmart... or was it Walmart... doesn't matter, one of those marts. Anyway, her kid was acting up, she was havin' a real bad day and this kid just wouldn't let up, so she finally gave him a swat on the butt. Well an employee sees it and reports her to security and they have the cops waitin' for her at the checkout stand."

D.I. began nodding his head to what Vince was saying.

"You read it?" Vince asked, noticing D.I.'s apparent validation of his story.

"Yeah," D.I. acknowledged, "It's unbelievable, they cuffed her and took her away."

"Your kidding!" Barney squawked.

"If he's lyin' he's flyin'," Vince said emphatically. "Can you imagine, arrested for disciplining your own kid. And if that's not bad enough, the kid admits to the cops that he deserved it but they were not swayed...I tell ya the whole world's gone nuts."

"Speed bump mentality," D.I. stated, flatly. "They have a problem with a few child abusers and they tie the hands of all parents. The worst part is, kids aren't stupid, they're stickin' this child abuse thing right up to the hilt. They think child abuse can be anything from whippin' to not having the latest video game or designer sneakers."

"Athletic shoes," Vince corrected.

"Whatever!" D.I. snorted, annoyed by the interruption.

"I tell ya, these kids will call 911 on you in a heartbeat."

"Well I'll tell you what," Vince said adamantly, "If I was raisin' a kid today I'd probably be in jail. There are times when you've got to get their attention. I saw a lady in the store the other day, trying to reason with a toddler who was on the floor pitchin' a hissy-fit because he couldn't have whatever it was he wanted. Here she is, squatting in the middle of the aisle, tryin' to have a lucid dialogue with a two year old. Personally, I think she was at a distinct intellectual disadvantage but...... anyway, she's sayin', 'Now Billy, mommy is very disappointed in your behavior. If you can get up we can discuss it......Okay sweetheart?' Well I'll tell ya' that did a whole lotta good. My dad used to say, 'If you're so hell bent on cryin' I'll gladly give you just cause.' Then he'd blister my butt right then and there. Now I ain't sayin' that's right, but it sure seems to work. I mean I think I turned out all right...... Don't you?"

"Jury's still out," D.I. sniffed.

Barney nodded his head in agreement.

"Barbara had a little trick that worked real good in public... well, even at home for that matter. She got it from her mother who brought it over from the old country, she called it the Portagee Pinch. There's a very tender area on the back of the upper arm, right here." Barney reached over and pinched Wally on the back of his upper arm.

"Ow! That hurts," Wally protested.

"Damn straight, and if our kids started actin' up, she'd pinch 'em there, no violence, looked just like she was leading them by their arm, no fuss no muss. The kids knew to protest was useless and would without question, compound their predicament. Tears might well up and lower lips might quiver but they were perfect little angels for the rest of the day."

"Well I'm afraid you can't even do that these days," Wally said, rubbing the back of the arm. "Man that does hurt doesn't it?"

Barney smiled, "Lasts for a while, too."

"You know what really gripes me about this abuse crap?" D.I. asked, not waiting for a reply. "The hypocrisy of the government. They tell us to raise our kids, but inhibit our ability to do so. I believe, kids need limits, in fact, they actually want limits but without ability to enforce them, they're useless. As I said before, kids are not stupid and they need to know what their limits are. Will they push 'em? You bet, it's their nature but if they aren't dealt swift and consistent discipline they'll run amuck and when they run amuck who does the government point the finger at? The parents! It's a no win situation. I tell ya, there's a whole generation of spoiled brats growin' up with no conception of responsibility. What's going to happen when they hit the real world?...... Or worse yet, what's going to happen when they start running the show?"

Barney shook his head, "Raisin' kids isn't easy. It's probably the most difficult job there is. Kids should come with owner's manuals. There's no set procedure. You can raise two kids exactly the same and one grows up to be Mother Theresa, the other Attila the Hun. It's like they're preset in the factory."

"Well I don't know about that," Wally answered. "I do know it takes a lot of work to raise a kid and most of us have shirked our duty at times, myself included but no matter how hard we try, there are no guarantees expressed or implied. It's pretty much a crap shoot."

"Listen to these two doomsayers," Vince complained. "Geeze have a little faith...... I think we are more a product of our environment and parents are but one factor. Peers and neighborhoods weigh heavy in the mix. Look at me, I was raised in a tough blue-collar neighborhood. A lot of the guys I grew up with have served time, I was lucky. I have no doubt, had I stayed, I'd be in the same boat. It's really a matter of choices and the luck of the draw. I chose to leave, as did some of my buddies, but I didn't return. I was lucky, I found Tiff.'

"You sure were," D.I. confirmed.

"I was!" Vince readily admitted, "She, probably, more than anything or anyone else, has had the biggest influence on how I turned out."

"Wasn't quite enough was it Barn," Wally joked.

"Not nearly enough," Barney agreed, with a smile. "You can take the thug out of Jersey, but you can't......"

"Ahhh shad up!"

Barney noticed that Stella and the girls had disappeared around the dogleg of the difficult par four seventh hole.

"Who's up?" He asked.

"I think it's D.I." Wally answered.

"It's......D.I., Wally, me then Romeo," Vince said consulting the scorecard for the order.

"How much of this dogleg do I want to bite off?" D.I. wondered aloud as he surveyed the tee box for just the right location.

"Take it right over the trees on the corner." Vince offered.

"Yeah, right, if I was John Daly."

"Well take it under or through the trees then."

"You're a big help Denevi."

D.I. addressed his ball then sent it to the corner just right of center. Wally's tee shot took on it's usual fade, finding the extreme right-hand side of the fairway.

"Well that makes the hole play a lot longer," Wally said making a slow-motion swing trying to determine the origin of his fade.

Vince put his ball in the center just beyond the bend and in near perfect position.

Barney lined up to hit a draw that would, hopefully, work the ball around the bend and leave him only a short iron in.

"Oh man I overcooked it!" he groaned, as the ball hooked sharply toward the trees. "Keep your head up," he commanded, but the ball refused to heed instruction and disappeared defiantly into the dense foliage to the left of the fairway.

"Might want to reload Barn," D.I. suggested, "I don't think we'll find that one, looked like it went pretty deep."

"Yeah," Barney said dejectedly while fishing for the spare ball he always carried in his pocket.

"I'm playing a provisional," he informed the others.

"We know that Barn."

"Hey the rules say you must announce your intention, so that's what I'm doing. I don't want to give you sleaze balls any loopholes."

Barney's provisional started down the middle then drew perfectly around the corner and out of sight.

"Now why, in the name of Tiger Woods, couldn't I do that the first time?" he muttered walking back to the cart.

"It's one of the unwritten rules of golf, my friend," D.I. said consolingly.

The four men drove to the edge of the woods where Barney's first ball had disappeared.

"Don't go in the woods," Barney warned. "They're full of ticks. If we can't see it from here... forget about it."

The men bobbed and weaved as they peered into the shade-darkened gloom but they saw nothing.

"That's all right," Barney said, "I'll play the provisional."

Barney and Wally drove to where Wally's ball lay while Vince and D.I. advanced to their balls, which were fairly close together. The ladies were on the green. Stella pulled the pin and let it fall like a tree in a forest. Barney smiled.

"You know," Barney said, "I'm glad I don't have to raise a child in today's environment. Shoot, remember when we were growing up? We never worried about perverts, drugs and violence, we were pretty much free to roam. Not today, now, kids are passed through metal detectors, drug tested and locked down in schools that look more like maximum security prisons than institutions of learning.

"Yeah and don't forget Zero Tolerance," Wally added sarcastically, "If Zero Tolerance isn't the biggest insult to common sense since The Crusades, I don't know what is."

"I agree," Barney said, "It's because nobody wants to make a decision, take responsibility. They'd rather expel a pupil for having aspirin than saying, 'Hey, it's only aspirin what's the big friggin' whoop-de-do'."

"Makes me sick," Wally said sadly, "seems we've lost that wonderful era of innocence."

"I know........." The telltale thud of a ball landing behind them interrupting their conversation. A moment later a ball rolled from under the cart and ten yards beyond.

"What the... ...," Barney said getting out of the cart and looking back toward the tee. He saw a man stooping to retrieve his tee.

"Hey!" Barney hollered waving his arms in the air. The man who had hit the ball gave what appeared to be a get out of the way wave.

"Are they serious?" Wally asked.

"Serious jerks if you ask me," Barney snorted.

The four men on the tee stood watching but no one else hit. Barney got back in the cart, his face considerably more colorful than when he had gotten out.

"Unbelievable!" He fumed. "Like we can go anywhere."

The two men sat silently waiting, both, expecting to hear the thud of another ball behind them. They stewed in anticipation and simmered in anger but heard nothing more than their increasing pulse rate.

The ladies finally cleared the green. Wally hit his second shot, which fell fifteen yards short of the green. D.I. pulled his shot into the rough left of the green and Vince found the green but faced a long birdie putt. Barney, still a little perturbed by the group behind, flew the green with an adrenaline assisted nine iron.

"Did you see that guy hit into us," Wally asked Vince as they walked to the green.

"Which guy was it?"

"I don't know exactly, it was one of those idiots behind us," Barney interjected.

"Yeah the ball rolled right under us," Wally added.

"And when I got out and waved at 'em, they acted like we should get out of the way." Barney complained.

"Well, I give everybody one freebie," Vince said calmly, "after that, they start payin'."

"Let it go this time," D.I. advised, "but if they do it again we'll say something.

"But they could of hit us," Barney protested.

"I know, but let's give 'em the benefit of doubt," D.I. said "Maybe they didn't think they could reach us. Maybe it was an accident."

"They didn't act like it was an accident." Barney huffed.

"Keep your eye on 'em, if they do it again we'll do somethin'."

"I know they'll do it again, I just know they will," Barney muttered under his breath.

Wally hit a nice chip that gave him a tap in par. Barney chunked his pitch from behind the green and needed two more to get down for a triple bogey seven. D.I. chipped on and two putted for bogey and Vince three putted for another five.

Just as they reached their carts, a ball thumped onto the green.

"I knew it!" Barney said, "Bunch of jerks."

"They are in a hurry aren't they," Vince said quietly. "We might need to teach 'em a little golf etiquette."

HOLE	1	2	3	4	5	6	7	8	9	OUT
PAR	4	4	5	4	3	5	4	3	4	36
YRDS	385	359	488	334	168	499	396	163	384	3146
D.I.	5	4	5	5	3	5	5			
Vince	4	5	6	4	4	5	5			
Wally	4	5	5	5	3	5	4			
Barney	3	3	7	5	2	9	7			

8

The eighth hole, a one hundred and sixty-five yards up-hill par three, was backed up but not as badly as the fifth had been. The ladies had the tee and the group ahead of them was on the green, drawing ever closer to the cup. Stella glanced back when she heard the approaching carts. Barney's eyes locked on her like two heat seeking missiles tracking the warmth of a schoolboy's passion. She smiled the smile he now found familiar, a smile he was growing very fond of. He smiled back. The two carts braked to a halt beside the white tees. Barney got out and suddenly found himself walking the forty or so yards toward the ladies' tee.

"What are you doing?" His brain questioned as he plodded on. Bells and whistles sounded in his head.

"Retreat! Retreat! You are entering no-man's land! Return to base and await further instructions." his rejection defense system commanded. But Barney marched on.

"Battle stations! Battle stations!" his brain screamed in panic. "Whoop! Whoop!"

As Barney neared the ladies, he noticed all four women were looking at him.

"Mayday! Mayday!" his insecurities shrieked, "We're going down. Eject! Eject!'

Barney focused on Stella. He could now see clearly into her eyes. They were bright and full of promise. All the clamoring in his head ceased, silenced by a confidence her eyes granted him. He stopped a few yards short of where she stood, glanced at the other ladies and began to speak.

"Have you ladies settled your ruling disputes?" he asked in a surpassingly steady voice. He was actually amazed to hear the words flow forth so smoothly and impressed by their relaxed pitch and tone. No tension-choked squeak. No nervous stammering.

"Well I'm still not convinced your interpretation is correct." one of Stella's playing companions said.

"No?"

"No!" she answered, "I think your ruling was extremely biased and prejudicial."

"I have a rule book if you'd like me to look it up and show you," Barney offered.

The woman smiled.

"What I'm saying," she went on, "is, I think you're partial to our Stella.'

"Sally!" Stella protested with a blush. The other ladies twittering in the background.

"Well that may be true," Barney conceded unashamedly. "but that doesn't alter the validity of my assessment of the rules."

Barney glanced at Stella who's cheeks were bowed in a sheepish grin and tinged with embarrassment.

"Please excuse Sally," she pleaded, "she's an incorrigible tease and a brazen busybody."

"Hey! I'm not a ...."

"Stifle Sal!" Stella admonished sternly.

Sally giggled and turned toward the other two women.

"I'm afraid," Barney said, "we're both cursed with friends who derive satisfaction from our embarrassment."

"They do don't they?" she agreed, "It's like a form of cheap entertainment for them."

"Evidently screwing up their own lives isn't enough," Barney submitted, glancing over at Sally who stuck her tongue out in playful rebuttal.

"Yeah," Stella said with a sigh of resignation, "some people just have to run the show."

"GREEN'S CLEAR!" D.I. hollered impatiently from his cart back at the white tee.

"Speak of the devil," Barney groaned.

"We better get moving," Stella said turning away.

"Stella?"

"Yes," she said, turning back to face him.

"We usually go to the grill when we finish, I was wondering......"

"We do too," she interrupted enthusiastically.

"Great, maybe we could have a drink or something."

"I think I'd like that," she said warmly. "Well I'd better get moving before your friend blows a gasket."

"Yeah, he's a mess. See you later."

"Looking forward to it."

Barney turned and started back toward six eyes that tracked his every move. He couldn't believe he had actually done what he had done. Not only had he placed himself naked and vulnerable before the beast of rejection, he had slain it.

Elation bubbled up in him like a bottle of uncorked champagne. He strutted matter of factually back to the three men who stood poised to burst his bubble.

"Lord, give me strength." he prayed as he braced himself for the onslaught he knew was coming.

"Well?" D.I. asked, "What do you have to say for yourself?"

" 'Bout what?"

"Collaborating with the enemy, treason, and desertion under fire."

"How do you plead?" Vince asked sternly.

"What is this?" Barney asked, "The Inquisition?"

"No," D.I. replied, "a general court martial."

"Do I have the right of counsel?"

Wally stepped beside Barney.

"If it please the court," Wally stated in a deep voice, "I stand ready to defend this poor shmuck."

"What if it doesn't please me?" Barney inquired.

"Not a consideration," D.I. ruled, "how does your client plead?"

"Your Honor," Wally began, thrusting his thumbs beneath imaginary suspenders and glancing at Barney, "my client here, pleads innocent to all charges."

"On what grounds?" D.I. demanded.

Wally thought for a moment then blurted out, "By reasons of infatuation, temporary insanity in the presence of a pretty face and for just being a guy."

D.I. pounded his fist on the cart top. "Case dismissed!" he proclaimed with a smile.

"Your Honor," Wally protested waving his arm in the air, "I request that my client be ordered to spill his guts."

D.I.'s hand thumped the cart roof! "So be it."

"There's really nothing to......"

D.I. gaveled the top of the cart again, "Thirty lashes with a wet noodle for contempt."

"I thought you said this case was dismissed," Barney protested.

"It was but must I remind you, it was your counsel who requested full disclosure. So disclose already."

Barney looked at Wally in disgust, "You're fired!"

"You can tell me Barn," Wally whispered, "you know lawyer/client confidentiality."

"Yeah right, you're about as confidential as the National Inquirer." Barney turned to D.I. "Whip me, flog me."

"Just tell the court, in your own words, what transpired up there on the ladies tee."

"All I did," Barney began, "was ask the ladies if they had settled their rules dispute."

"That's it?" Wally moaned disappointedly.

"That's it!"

Vince walked over to Barney and put an arm around his shoulder.

"Look Barn, you've got to come up with a better approach than that if you want this relationship to go anywhere, you need to be more direct. More personal. You should ask her if she'd join you for a drink in the grill after we're finished. Somethin' that will give you a chance to get to know each other, maybe set up a date or somethin'."

"You think?" Barney quizzed.

"I know!" Vince stated positively.

Barney read the sincerity in Vince's eyes and smiled. He wouldn't say anything that might tarnish Vince's luster.

"Thanks buddy, that sounds like good advice."

The men turned their attention to the green, or more precisely, Stella.

"She does seem like a real nice lady," Wally said.

"Classy, a classy lady," Vince added.

"She's a woman on the golf course," D.I. complained but his complaint lacked it's usual bite.

"Ah, ever the romantic," Wally mused.

"Oh maaan!" A voice whined behind them.

D.I. and the others turned to see four young men pull up to the blue tees some thirty-five yards back.

"What the heck's the hold up?" one demanded gruffly.

"Don't know," D.I. offered, "but hittin' into us isn't going to make us play any faster."

None of the young men responded. The vocal one got out of his cart and walked toward them. He looked to be in his late teens, early twenties. Six foot, maybe six one with a stocky athletic build. He probably had a handsome face but it was twisted by impatience and arrogance.

"Is there a group ahead of those old hags on the green?" he asked intolerantly as he reached the tee.

"Near as I can tell there's several," D.I. answered.

"Man I've got to be in class by two, would you all mind if we played through?"

"Yeah we would," D.I. said adamantly, "those old hags, as you so rudely referred to 'em, happen to be our wives and we wouldn't like a bunch of inconsiderate flat bellies such as yourself, hittin' into 'em."

The young man glared at D.I. who retained eye contact and smiled.

"Hey Randy!" one of the other young men called from his cart, "Your cell phone's ringing."

"Well answer it," Randy shouted back abusively.

The young man returned his glare to D.I. who now simply ignored him.

"Must really be somebody special to have to have a cell phone on the golf course." D.I. mumbled aloud.

"What'd you sa........?"

"It's Kathy," Came a shout from the blue tee. "She wants to talk to you."

"Shit!" Randy spat before turning and stomping off.

"That Randy's a dandy ain't he?" D.I. snorted.

"Our wives?" Vince asked incredulously. "That's so cool. How do you come up with this stuff on the spur of the moment like that, it takes me days to come up with the perfect comeback. Did you see his face?"

"Unfortunately," Barney said, "he got angry, he should have been embarrassed."

"That's all the youth of today knows how to do," Wally added, "they get angry. God forbid they should ever feel remorse let alone offer an apology."

"They just aren't raised up right," D.I. stated, "They want everything and they want it right now."

Vince laughed lightly and shook his head, "Our wives...that is so cool."

Barney watched as Stella replaced the flag stick and walked off the green. The four men selected their clubs and strolled to the tee box. Behind them anger was mumbling.

"Who's up?" D.I. asked.

"That would be me," Wally answered, stepping forward and planting a tee deep into the turf and topping it with his ball. His swing produced a shot that started left then, what else, faded back toward the stick.

"It's all over it!" Barney announced.

"Get in the hole!" Wally urged

The ball landed softly and checked up fifteen feet below the hole.

"Great shot!" Vince applauded, "The ol' Ferguson power fade. What cha hit?"

"Three iron."

"Three?"

"Hey, its up hill and all carry," Wally said defensively, "you know I don't hit my irons as far as you all do. I always hit three here."

"Seems like a lot of club to me," Vince mumbled.

"Hey, you asked me what I hit, I told you. You see where the ball is don't CHA?"

Barney thumped the turf with his club raising a grass welt which he placed his ball on.

"What? You can't afford tees?" D.I. quipped.

Barney ignored the rib and sent his ball to the middle of the green twenty feet from the pin.

"What cha hit?" Vince inquired again.

"A sweet five."

"Five?"

"Yes, Vince a five."

Vince looked at the three clubs he held in his hands and mumbled under his breath. He dropped two clubs to the ground, dropped a ball on the grass and took his stance then backed away in indecision. He traded the club in his hand for one on the ground and took his stance again.

"Some time today would be great," D.I. scolded.

Vince hit it fat, the ball only making it three quarters of the way to the green.

"Whatcha hit?" three voices chimed in unison.

Vince didn't answer.

"I think he hit the big ball before he hit the little one," D.I. suggested.

D.I. pulled his shot left of the flag and short of the green by ten feet. There were no inquiries as to club selection and the drive to the green was unusually quiet. Vince took his wedge and putter and walked the forty yards or so back to his ball while the other three headed for the green.

"Who's got the chance for greenie?" D.I. asked walking across the green toward his ball.

"Looks like it's Wally to me," Barney answered.

"That's a tough two putt for him," D.I. teased. "Fifteen feet straight up hill and a buck fifty riding on it. He'll choke."

You shouldn't be worried about me making par," Wally said confidently, "cause I'm makin' birdie for a cool four fifty."

Vince hit a nice pitch to within four feet and D.I. chipped to within three. Barney's putt missed to the left and ran two feet past. Wally stroked his birdie putt right at the hole.

"Get in the hole!" he begged as the ball rolled for the heart of the cup.

"Keep your head up!" he pleaded as it began losing speed and leaking right.

"Drop you pig!" he hollered as it hugged the right edge and performed a one-eighty lip out.

Wally's putter fell from his hands as he turned away in disgust.

"How'd that stay out," Barney wondered sympathetically.

Wally retrieved his putter and tapped in for his par and greenie.

"Nice par," Vince soothed, but Wally was temporarily un-soothable. He snatched the ball from the cup and retreated to the carts.

"Great save!" D.I. said when Vince's four footer dropped in for par and tied the hole.

"I'll take it," Vince gushed inverting his putter and extracting his ball with the suction cup he had attached to the top of the grip.

D.I. and Barney both cleaned up their pars and the trio headed off the green in high spirits.

Before they had reached the carts, a ball landed not more than twenty feet from them and rolled between them and their carts.

"Don't even look at 'em!" Vince ordered, not altering course. He had been walking with his putter in cane like fashion, putter head in hand suction cup down. Without breaking stride, he placed the suction cup atop the offending ball and continuing on as if nothing had happened.

"Smooth as silk," D.I. whispered as the four men placed their clubs in their bags.

Four smug smiles rode the short distance to the ninth tee.

HOLE	1	2	3	4	5	6	7	8	9	OUT
PAR	4	4	5	4	3	5	4	3	4	36
YRDS	385	359	488	334	168	499	396	163	384	3146
D.I.	5	4	5	5	3	5	5	3		
Vince	4	5	6	4••	4	5	5	3		
Wally	4	5	5	5	3•	5	4••	3•		
Barney	3••	3••	7	5	2•••	9	7	3		

9

The eighth and ninth holes, to some degree, parallel each other but obviously play in opposite directions. The eighth green is easily visible from the ninth tee but the eighth tee is obscured by trees that separate the two fairways. The ladies were in the process of hitting their approach shots into the mid-length, slight dogleg right par four ninth.

Vince exited his cart, stepped around to his bag and removed his putter. He popped the impatient ball from the suction cup's grip and inspected it closely.

"Whoa Nelly!" He exclaimed jubilantly, holding the captive ball aloft in triumphant celebration. "This is one of those new Titleist balls. These puppies cost about five bucks a pop."

"Makes you wonder where them young-uns get the money to play such an expensive game with such expensive equipment," D.I. contemplated.

"Daddy probably," Barney guessed.

"Well Junior might have to call daddy for an advanced on his allowance if he keeps ploppin' five dollar balls in front of me." Vince smiled.

Barney watched Stella's cart disappear around the dogleg.

"It's clear to hit." He said walking to the tee, driver in hand. "Who's up?"

"I think it's me," Wally answered getting out of the cart, "but hit if you're ready."

Barney was ready, he sent a low screamer down the right hand edge of the fairway effectively cutting the dogleg.

"Run you little rabbit!" he encouraged, as the ball landed and seemed to accelerate.

"Nice drive!" Wally complimented walking to the tee.

"Ol' boring Barn." D.I. yawned.

Wally, allowing for the inevitable fade, lined up left, then hit a frozen rope straight as a rail down the left side. The ball ran through the fairway and settled out of sight in the left hand rough.

"Where the heck did that come from?" he protested, turning to his playmates for an explanation.

"Law of averages." D.I. shrugged.

"You finally did something right." Vince offered.

Wally searched the ground for his tee but his heart wasn't in it and he quickly abandoned the effort.

"I don't know why I bother playing this friggin' game," he protested, "I come out here and pay good money just to get all pissed off. Shoot I can stay home and my wife will gladly piss me off for nothin'."

"You just answered your own question," D.I. said, tossing Wally a tee he had found near the tee marker.

Wally made a feeble attempt to catch the tumbling tee but it bounced off his hand, hit his chest and fell at this feet.

"Great hand eye coordination Ferguson," D.I. teased, "no wonder you can't hit the ball straight."

"Pound salt!" Wally snapped, while bending to retrieve the tee.

D.I. was preparing to hit his tee shot when two carts appeared from behind the trees and stopped beside the eighth green.

"Here comes mister personality." Vince sniffed.

D.I. looked up momentarily then sent his ball in a lazy draw to the left hand side of the fairway.

The four young men were scrambling out of their carts as Vince cracked his tee ball crisply down the middle.

"It should be right in this area here." one of the young men stated, performing a sweeping point in the direction of the ball's path.

"That's where I had it too," another concurred as all four began searching for the missing ball. They didn't hear the snickering that rode in the two carts motoring down the ninth fairway.

"Man look at this." Wally complained, while looking down at the ball nestled deep in the rough.

"That's nothin' a stepper like you can't handle." Barney assured him.

"I wish I had your confidence, I'll be lucky to get it halfway there."

"Take a more lofted club, play it back in your stance, take it up sharply and hit down on it, it'll pop right out, it's a piece of cake."

"If you say so." Wally said, unconvinced.

Vince and D.I. ambled over to survey the situation while waiting for the green to clear.

Barney watched with interest as Stella skillfully blasted out of a green side bunker.

"Looks like she's gotta pretty good game." Vince said.

"Yeah it does." Barney responded automatically.

"You know," Wally said, still peering down into the deep rough, "there's something about this game I just don't understand." He paused expecting a response from one of the others. Receiving none, he made his own.

"And what is it you don't understand Wally?" he asked himself aloud, "Well, I don't understand why it's all but impossible to hit two good shots in a row.

"Newton's law." Barney stated.

"Fig Newton?" Vince asked jokingly.

"Sir Isaac Newton you dip-wad." Barney admonished.

"I thought it was Murphy's Law." D.I. contended.

"Murphy's Law only deals with the odds," Barney explained, "Sir Isaac deals with the physics of movement."

"I have a movement every morning," Wally said smugly, "sometimes two."

Vince turned to Barney.

"This doesn't have anything to do with magnets does it? Your not gonna tell us........."

Barney cut him off.

"Newton's third law of motion states: For every action, there is an equal and opposite reaction."

"So?" D.I. asked.

"So," Barney answered, "for every good shot, there's an equally bad shot. If there wasn't, the whole universe would be thrown out of balance."

"If there's anything unbalanced in the universe, it's you." Vince concluded.

"But what about the pros?" Wally questioned. "They hit lots of good shots."

Barney thought for a moment.

"Well that's where we come in."

"Huh?"

"It doesn't necessarily mean the same person who hit the good shot has to hit a bad shot. It simply means, in order to maintain universal equilibrium, someone, somewhere has to hit a bad shot."

"But why us?" Wally whined.

"Enter Murphy's law," Barney replied, "what are the odds of a pro hitting a bad shot compared to one of us hitting a bad shot?"

"So," Wally, said "you're saying our whole purpose here is to provide balance to the universe?"

"You got it." Barney confirmed.

D.I. shook his head in amazement.

"All these years I've searched for the meaning of life and it's been right here in my golf bag."

"Yep!" Barney agreed, "So the next time you hit a bad shot, take solace in knowing you just equalized Newton's law and saved the universe."

The men stood contemplating the magnitude of Barney's BS. From behind the trees they could hear the young men's confused muffled voices as they continued to hunt for the wayward ball.

"Listen to 'em." Vince said with a light laugh.

"That was a classic move Vince." D.I. said.

"You gonna give it back." Barney wondered out loud.

"Hell no!" Vince said emphatically. "That ball could have hit one of us. They didn't even yell fore, kiss my ass or anything. Obviously they have no regard for us or anyone else... so screw 'em. I can't believe they had the audacity to ask us to let 'em play through, especially after hittin' into us on seven. Like they're gonna go anywhere with the course all jammed up like this. Give me a break! Give it back? I don't think so. Bunch of inconsiderate punks if you ask me. Why I should take this ball and......"

"Okay, okay!" Barney said waving his hands in a stop already motion. "Sorry I asked."

"Well I'm sick and tired of this me first generation, you know what I'd like to see? I'd like to see 'em all first in line for the next sailing of the Titanic that's what I'd like to see. Bunch of self-centered, egotistical twerps."

D.I. walked over to Vince and patted him on the back.

"There, there, let it all out, let all those nasty ol' toxins out."

"Well it really tweaks my jaws."

"I can tell, but don't let it give you a stroke or somethin'."

"I know." Vince acknowledged, "but I just can't accept that kind of behavior."

"And you shouldn't," D.I. agreed, "but don't let it rule your life."

"I shoulda punched him right in the snot locker when he asked to play through." Vince snorted.

"He'da killed ya!"

Wally turned to Barney.

"I think your girlfriend just got a sandy." He said as the ladies cleared the green.

"She's not...... Oh what's the use." Barney grumbled under his breath.

Wally managed to advance his ball out of the rough to within twenty yards of the green. D.I.'s ball struggled but made it to the front of the putting surface. Vince came over the top and pull-hooked his shot into the same trap that Stella had just been in.

"Well that should keep the earth from wobbling off its axis." He muttered while putting his club in his bag.

"I'm afraid you're gonna have to drown that ball." D.I. said mournfully. "Once they get a taste for sand it's all over. Only thing to do, is put 'em down."

"I'm afraid your right." Vince said dejectedly.

Barney walked to his ball, Wally trailing after him in the cart.

"I think that's the longest drive you've ever had on this hole." Wally gushed.

"Just makes me wanta puke." D.I. complained in jest. "Taint fair a little dweeb like him can out drive the likes of us."

Barney just smiled, took out his nine iron and sent his ball high and straight at the stick. When it landed on the green, it hopped forward two feet and stopped dead three feet from the pin.

"That should make you puke your guts out." Barney said, tamping down his divot.

Vince looked back to an empty tee. "Looks like our boys are still looking for that Titleist. Wonder if they figured it out and got the message?"

"Even if they did, they're probably too stupid to understand it." D.I. said getting in the cart.

When they reached the green, the four men fanned out to their respective balls. A chunked pitch caused Wally's head to fall forward and his shoulders to slump. He walked the short distance to his next attempt dragging the ineffective wedge behind him. Muffled obscenities floated on the gentle morning breeze where they were eagerly plucked by inquiring ears.

"Don't dip your knees." Barney instructed, "And keep your head still, you looked up to see where the ball was going before it went."

"I know, I know. I tell myself not to do it but I don't listen."

"Concentrate!"

Wally took a couple of practice swings and positioned himself over the ball. He took the club back slowly but jerked it forward causing the blade of the club to strike the equator of the ball sending it scurrying across the green.

"Dad-burn-it!" He cursed, desperately trying to curb his tongue, which was rapidly forming words of its own. "My short game sucks!"

"Whata you mean your short game?" Vince teased unmercifully. "I'd say your whole game's in the tank."

"Vince!" Barney admonished, "Show a little compassion."

"Don't bother," Wally muttered tracking after his ball. "the man's a toad."

"Toad?" Vince yelped, placing a hand on his chest in pained distress, "I'm a toad?"

"You're a toad!" D.I. said impatiently, "Now hop in that bunker frogy and play your shot."

Vince poised on the lip of the trap, croaked, "Ribbit!" and hopped into the sand.

"Sounds like a toad, acts like a toad, shaped like a toad... ergo.. must be a toad." Barney concluded.

Vince hit a good sand shot to within four feet, smiled and said nothing.

"Don't forget to rake your flipper tracks." D.I. said as Vince exited the trap. This pulled a laugh of delight from all four men.

Wally, not wanting an instant replay of his pitching woes, chose to putt his ball from off the green and ran the ball two feet passed the hole.

"That's good, pick it up." Vince conceded graciously.

"You're sure?" Wally asked. "I've been known to miss those you know."

"I have the utmost confidence in your putting abilities. Pick it up. Besides," Vince added, "you're out of the hole anyway if it were a putt for money it'd be a different matter."

"Toad!" Wally muttered snatching his ball from the putting surface.

D.I. rolled his first putt right up to the edge of the cup. "All I had to do was hit it." He complained, nonchalantly back handing the ball into the cup for his par. "Had it trackin' right in the heart."

"Isn't that one of the Ten Commandments Arnie brought down from Mount Augusta?" Barney quipped, "Thou Shalt Not Leave A Birdie Putt Short."

"Not my first Mortal Sin and probably not my last.......I hope." D.I. added.

Vince made his four footer for a sandy par and Barney missed from three feet and dejectedly tapped in for his par.

As the four walked to the carts, Vince turned to Wally and said, "You know I'm only messin' with ya, don't cha Wally?"

"Get away from me... you'll give me warts." Wally said shying away.

"Hey Vince!" D.I. called, nodding toward the tee, "Looks like they finally gave up on that ball."

Vince looked back to the tee where the four young men were just getting out of their carts.

"Slowed 'em down a little, have to see what happens when they catch up to us." Vince replied with a crooked smile. "Don't suppose they learned anything. Hey, you gonna stop at the snack bar?"

"I need to see a man about a horse," D.I. replied.

"You guys want anything from the snack bar?" Vince shouted to Wally and Barney as they drove off.

Barney looked over his shoulder, "Probably something to drink." He yelled back. "See you over there."

Wally steered the cart towards the snack bar.

"Well, all I have to say," Wally said glumly, "somewhere, some pro is having one hell of a good round."

HOLE	1	2	3	4	5	6	7	8	9	OUT
PAR	4	4	5	4	3	5	4	3	4	36
YRDS	385	359	488	334	168	499	396	163	384	3146
D.I.	5	4	5	5	3	5	5	3	4	
Vince	4	5	6	••4	4	5	5	3	•4	
Wally	4	5	5	5	•3	5	••4	•3	6	
Barney	••3	••3	7	5	•••2	9	7	3	4	

AT THE TURN

D.I. was hot-footing it to the restroom well before Vince could bring the cart to a complete stop. Stella and the girls, drinks in hand, were just stepping away from the snack bar when D.I., in single minded purpose, brushed by. Startled by D.I.'s sudden appearance and rapid passing, the four women took evasive action which had it not been for tightly sealed lids, would have produced shrills, spills and cola stains. Expressions of surprise quickly transformed into annoyance and gasps of "What the...?" Were replaced by barks of "How rude!"

"Never place yourselves between an old man and the nearest urinal." Vince advised as he, Barney and Wally approached the ruffled ladies.

"Well I should say!" Sally said with emphasis.

"I apologize for our friend," Barney said, "I do hope you can appreciate the urgency of his situation."

"He gave us quite a start." one of the women said, "You should equip him with a siren or something."

This brought a smile from all concerned and the mood swung to easy. Barney probed his mind for conversation. Stella placed the straw between her lips and Barney watched as she drew a column of dark liquid up the plastic tube.

"Did you have a good front nine?" he asked.

She released the straw, the column of fluid collapsed back into the cup. A hasty swallow produced a carbonated hack, which left her momentarily speechless. Barney fought the urge to slap her on the back as she cleared her throat with several mini-coughs.

"A-hem! Matter of fact I did," She answered in a choked voice, "I think it's the best nine I've put together in a long time."

"That's great."

"How did it go for you Barney?" she asked in return.

Barney. He repeated to himself, suddenly discovering the name he never really cared for now sounded acceptable.

"Well if I could throw out six and seven I'd have been brilliant unfortunately, that's not an option, it's just golf. I just can't play nine without at least one disaster hole."

Vince and Wally faded toward the snack bar and the ladies dissolved into their carts leaving Barney and Stella alone.

She smiled and took another sip of her drink, her eyes not leaving his. He felt a pang of panic as words again abandon him. His eyes involuntarily diverting to the snack bar where Wally and Vince stood smiling at him. He cursed his eyes for their independence and forced his gaze back to Stella. He hoped she hadn't noticed or misread what had happened.

"Well keep it going." was all his vocal skills could muster under his self-imposed duress.

"I'll try my best." she said brightly, showing no apparent adverse affects of the nervous eyes incident.

Don't you dare complicate things. Barney scolded himself, quit trying to fabricate an incident from non-incident material. Keep it simple, simpleton, just be yourself and let things happen.

Stella looked past him and nodded, "Well I'd better go, the girls are getting antsy."

"We'll talk in the grill?" He fully intended the words to form a statement, not a question but his present insecurity was seeking affirmation.

"I'm still looking forward to it." She said with an air of certainty.

As Stella walked away, Barney stood questioning his sporadic mastery of the spoken word. How could he speak so effortlessly, if not eloquently, to her on the eighth tee and now sputter out bits of inane babble? Where had his nomadic confidence wandered off to this time?

"Barn," Wally called, "what do you want? Vince is buyin'."

"What?"

"I know, hard to believe but true."

Vince, who was leaning halfway through the snack bar window, extracted himself and turned toward Barney who quickly applied an expression of astonishment.

"This offer is subject to change without notice, so I'd advise you to accept it in the same gracious manner in which it was offered and keep your sarcastic gibberish to yourselves."

"I'll have a diet coke...... Thank you." Barney said graciously.

"That's better. You want a dog or chips or somethin'?"

"No thank you."

Vince reinserted himself into the window of the snack bar and resumed his conversation with the attractive young attendant.

"Now look at Vince," Barney thought, "he sure doesn't have any trouble conversing with the opposite sex. What sa matter for you?"

D.I. strolled by on his way back to the carts, his gait and manner much more relaxed than minutes before.

"You want anything D.I.?" Wally asked, "Vince is buyin'."

"What?......Vince?......Vince Denevi?......The Duke of frugal is buyin'?"

"Do you want something or not?" Vince bellowed, not bothering to extract himself from the window but extracting a visible flinch from the young attendant.

"Well, I really hate to pass on your annual attempt at philanthropy but, no thanks. I wouldn't want to feel behold'n to the likes of you."

"Your loss, my gain." Vince mumbled.

D.I. headed back to the carts and began totaling the scores and dots for the front nine.

"Look at this!" D.I. complained when the others returned to the carts. "I shot a thirty nine and didn't get a single dot. The Deputy shoots a forty-three and gets seven. What's wrong with this picture."

"What'd I shoot?" Vince asked blandly.

"It's always about you isn't it Denevi?" DI huffed, disappointed that no one else seemed interested in the irony of the scorecard. "You shot a......forty...... you and Wally both shot forty. You won... let's see... one... two...... two dots and Wally, you won umm......five."

"And you didn't win a dot." Vince heckled. "Geeze, that's a shame......... Just a cryin' shame."

D.I. looked at Vince. Vince could see the wheels turning as D.I. calculated his financial losses.

"There's little puffs of smoke comin' out of your left ear." Vince teased.

"I'm down seven and a half bucks!" D.I. exclaimed.

"A mere pittance to a man of your means." Barney consoled.

"But I'm on a fixed income." D.I. moaned.

"Fixed income?" Wally laughed, "If I had your income I'd be fixed too."

"You shoulda been fixed the day you were born." D.I. shot back, "A quick little snip, snip to help prune the family tree."

"Ouch!" Wally yelped crossing his legs quickly. "I don't care for that kinda talk. Makes me kinda weak in the knees."

Vince set his drink in the cup holder of the cart and placed a paper plate on the seat. D.I. eyed it suspiciously.

"You didn't get one of those thunder dogs did you?"

"Did!" Vince nodded. "Chili, onions, the works."

"Lord protect us!" D.I. prayed, "Those things produce more gas than Exxon."

"I know." Vince winked with smile. "I'm gonna light things up on the back side."

"I'm not afraid of you lighting things up on the back side," D.I. corrected, "I'm afraid that thing is gonna light up your backside. Your gonna hafta walk.........behind us."

"Way behind us!" Barney added.

"I don't know why you all are makin' such a fuss over one measly hot dog." Wally wondered, "The man can generate gas from distilled water."

"This is true." D.I. conceded, "But it's not as corrosive."

"You know," Barney stated, patting Vince on the back, "If Virginia Power could figure out a way to harness this raw natural resource, they could convert all their plants to Denevi Gas and save a bundle."

"Now isn't that a pretty picture," D.I. grunted, "A bunch of fart fired power plants up and down the East Coast."

"Could ease the energy crisis." Vince said taking a big bite of hot dog.

"Man that sure would shoot the hell out of the Clean Air Act." Barney chuckled.

"Yeah," Wally agreed, "no way they could build a stack high enough to safely vent those fumes.

"There's always a price to pay for progress." Vince commented through the side of his full mouth.

"But that's a price I can't afford." D.I. complained, "I'm already paying a heavy price by riding in the same cart with you, which in and of itself constitutes cruel and unusual punishment."

"You know," Vince said swallowing, "it has been, forever thus. Someone different, a unique individual with special gifts comes to the forefront. Is he cherished for his uniqueness? Valued for his gifts? No! He's chastised and ridiculed for being different, shunned for not fitting the mold, feared and envied for his gifts and power. Seems to me mere mortals such as you would be elated just to be in the presence of such greatness......... Yet you mock me."

"I mocketh thee, I mocketh thee." Wally said in a Daffy Duck like lisp.

The men set to trading barbs but were interrupted when a cart pulled up and a frowning Randy got out. He stomped up to D.I. who remained seated behind the steering wheel of his cart.

"Hey!" The young man huffed, "Did any of you guys see or pick up my ball back on number eight?"

"Now how could we see or pick up your ball?" D.I. asked. "You guys are playin' behind us." He explained, "The only conceivable explanation for such an unlikely circumstance would have to be, you were inconsiderate enough to hit into us...... Again."

Randy was somewhat taken aback by D.I.'s explanation.

"Was your ball round... and white... and have a bunch of those little dimply thingies on it?" Barney asked.

"You know it did!" Randy snapped.

"Didn't see it!" D.I. stated simply and directly into Randy's ever reddening face.

"You guys were off the green......"

"Evidently, so was your shot!" D.I. said calmly, "You're not suppose to hit until we are completely out of range."

While Randy and D.I. were discussing the incident, Vince was taking a good look at Randy's buddies. They all looked to be members of a football team. They all had those linebacker necks that tapered down just enough to accommodate a pinhead. It appeared they had spent considerably more time in the weight room than in the classroom. A large black man sat in the passenger side of Randy's cart and two huge white men sat in the cart behind. The two young men were so huge, it made their cart look like a Fisher-Price product. This is not good Vince told himself.

"I'll tell you what old man." Randy hissed in a hoarse voice, "I'm tired of messin' with you and your smart-mouthed little friends. I've got a two o'clock class and......"

"May I assume," D.I. interrupted, "It is not a class in etiquette and social decorum? If it is, I'm afraid you are failing miserably."

"That's it!" Randy stammered in rage.

Vince saw the large black man get out of the cart and start toward them. Vince slid from the seat, set his hot dog down and stood for what he knew was certain annihilation. But at least, he wasn't going sitting down. Barney and Wally, in nervous anticipation, got out of their cart. The big black man brushed Randy aside and stood towering over D.I. who remained composed and in his seat.

"Hey man!" he said in a deep husky voice, "I'd like to apologize for Randy here, he can be a bit of an ass-hole at times."

Randy's face transformed from rage to disbelief.

"Apologize, what th............"

"Shut up and get in the cart!" the big man commanded, turning to stare Randy down. "Don't test me Randy......get in the cart and shut up."

Randy slumped into the cart and the big man bent down and looked him in the eye. "This is the last time I play golf with you." he said to Randy who stared blankly at the floorboard of the cart. "We're suppose to be havin' fun. I'm not havin' fun, are you havin' fun?" Randy shook his head. The other two young men came over to where D.I. sat.

"Sorry man." One of them said extending his hand to D.I., who shook it graciously.

"Yeah, me too." The other said. "I thought you dudes played the whole scene pretty cool. Etiquette class, that's a good one." He laughed. "You old dudes are pretty cool."

D.I. got out of his cart and extended a hand to the large black man who took it and nearly crushed it. "Thank you young man, you have renewed my faith in the youth of today."

"Thank you sir, I'm just sorry you had to go through this."

"It was worth it." D.I. smiled.

There was momentary, awkward silence.

"Let's blow off the back nine," one of the young men said.

"Yeah," another agreed, "I've had enough golf, how 'bout you Randy?"

Randy nodded his head slowly, avoiding eye contact by continuing to contemplate the cart's floorboard.

"If you're waitin' on me," the black man said returning to his cart, "your wastin' time."

Vince fished out the Titleist from his pocket and walked over to Randy's cart. "Here's your ball back." He said holding it out in front of Randy.

"Keep it!" Randy snapped curtly.

"Don't want it, it will only remind me of you and you are one person I'd really like to forget." Vince said dropping the ball into the cart's cup holder and walking away.

The four young men drove off. The four old men heaved a collective sigh of relief as un-spent adrenaline dissipated through shuddering muscles.

"How do you stay so cool in situations like this?" Vince asked D.I. as they drove off toward the tenth tee.

"I'm a Marine, I'm The D.I." he answered confidently.

D.I. looked over at Vince and smiled sheepishly.

"What?" Vince asked.

"I also think I need to change my shorts."

HOLE	1	2	3	4	5	6	7	8	9	OUT
PAR	4	4	5	4	3	5	4	3	4	36
YRDS	385	359	488	334	168	499	396	163	384	3146
D.I.	5	4	5	5	3	5	5	3	4	39
Vince	4	5	6	4	4	5	5	3	4	40
Wally	4	5	5	5	3	5	4	3	6	40
Barney	3	3	7	5	2	9	7	3	4	43

10

The tenth hole, a moderate length par four with a wide fairway and severely elevated tee, is the type of hole that toyed with a man's self image. A long tee shot really didn't assure a low score on the hole but the wide landing area and dramatic elevation change drew a mental image that a real man just could not resist. And these real men were no exception. They could visualize their ball launching off the tee like a fighter jet catapulted from a carrier deck. They could see their ball soaring into a new dimension of time and space. A mere speck suspended in slow motion above the horizon defying gravity and alas, reality.

Collectively, they had hit more bad tee shots on this hole than all the other holes combined. Yet they persisted in testing the confines of age and the threshold of disability.

The ladies were just pulling away from the tee when the men arrived. Stella floated a nonchalant wave out the passenger side of the cart as it dropped like a roller coaster over the knoll and out of sight. After what seemed an eternity to Barney, the two carts, miniaturized by distance, appeared on the fairway below.

The four men, still reeling from their near death experience, sat in mute reflection.

"That was somethin' wasn't it?" Vince said breaking the silence.

"My whole life passed before my eyes," Wally sighed.

"That must have been boring," D.I. droned.

"Is it just me," Barney asked, "or are there more and more Randys in the world today?"

"Sure seems like it," Wally concurred.

"You know," D.I. said philosophically, "this experience illustrates just how easy it is to form an inaccurate snap judgement about people."

"What do you mean inaccurate?" Vince asked. "The guy's an imbecile."

"I'm not talking about Randy, I'm talking about the other three."

"The other three?"

"Yeah, they're with Randy, Randy's a jerk ergo they must be jerks too. Jerks by association."

"You're right," Barney said, "we automatically assumed they were like Randy."

"Well don't jerks usually travel in......gaggles......or jerkles......or somethin'?" Vince asked.

"You mean, birds of a feather?" D.I. asked.

"Exactly!"

"Well as a generality, the phrase probably has some merit but there in lies the danger. Generalizations, stereotypes, assumptions and guilt by association are poor tools for evaluating an individual. It's akin to painting a picture using only one color." D.I. explained, "No distinction, no variations, no contrast, no uniqueness."

"You think we misjudged Randy?" Wally asked.

"Could have......He probably has some good qualities......His Mommy probably loves him.......But ....I don't think so. I think Randy proved himself a genuine jerk." D.I. confirmed.

"This is pretty deep stuff comin' from an ol' redneck like you D.I.," Vince said, "you're beginning to scare me."

"See! Right there you're makin' a judgment......and you know me."

"I'm beginnin' to wish I didn't." Vince whined.

"I'll bet you think I'm the biggest bigot this side of Selma, don't you?"

"No!......Well.......Not the biggest maybe but you've said things that would lead one to believe you might be just a tad prejudice." Vince confessed. "Like women on the golf course, for example."

"I admit it, I am prejudice! We're all prejudice to some degree."

"You know, " Barney said, "I use to think I didn't have a prejudice bone in my body but I discovered I had quite a few."

"You Barn?" Wally asked in amazement. "I've never heard you say anything against anybody."

"You don't have to say it, you just have to think it." Barney went on, "The media has pretty much set my stereotypical bad guy. Young black male wearing a watch cap and or dark hooded sweatshirt. Has those large baggy pants that look like they're weighted down with enough weaponry to invade Cuba. If I see someone matching that description comin', I'm sorry, but I'm a little suspicious and a bit uneasy. I'm not apt to stop and strike up a conversation. In this day an age, I don't feel I can afford to."

"I know what you mean." Wally said, "In California we had a lot of Hispanic gangs. We'd read about them in the paper and see them on TV. These guys were mean and angry people. They had no regard for human life whatsoever. They'd just as soon cut you as look at you. We wanted nothing to do with them and I'm afraid we looked upon the entire Hispanic community with suspicion and fear.

"Well," D.I. said, "I think there's informed suspicion and there's ignorant prejudice. The problem is being there's a margin of error in both. We took an informed suspicion that Randy was a jerk and turned it into an ignorant prejudice toward the other three. And, I suspect, if the truth be told, it fell hardest on that very nice, very large and very black man."

"I'm afraid you're right," Vince admitted, "when I saw him get out of the cart I thought it was all over but the hymn singin'."

"We need to deal with people as individuals," D.I. said, "we need to know them before we begin forming opinions. Everybody deserves to start off with a clean slate, no preconceptions, no prejudice. Unfortunately, this goes against human nature."

"It's just so easy to prejudge," Barney said, "I know when I was younger I was so idealistic and, I thought, open-minded, which I was, as long as you agreed completely with my ideas. I was very intolerant and close-minded to any diversity of opinion and ideas. If you didn't agree completely with my notion of what was right, you were history. My world was, either/or, black or white and I demanded absolute alliance and allegiance from my friends. Suffice it to say, I didn't have many friends."

"Still don't!" Vince jabbed.

"I finally realized," Barney went on, ignoring Vince's stab at humor, "my being so discriminating was isolating me from a lot of good and interesting people. I was, in fact, all that I abhorred. I needed new ideas and conflicting views to keep me from stagnating ideologically. I needed to harvest the positive and plow under the negative."

"Funny how the negative weighs so heavily on our judgments." Wally said, "You'd think, we'd place more value on the positive but we don't. Just look at the evening news and the front page of the newspaper. Nothing but doom and gloom, man's inhumanity to man and greed and corruption. We need to realize that the news is not the norm and the norm is not news.

"That's true," Barney agreed, "good people living normal lives are not news because nearly everybody else is doing the same thing......... it's the deviants of society that get all the press, which makes it appear that the whole world is going to hell in a hand basket."

"Well," Vince said, "if the media is lookin' for deviants why don't we see D.I. on TV every night?"

"Vince," D.I. snapped, "does your little pea brain ever entertain a serious thought or is it too busy cranking out not so wise wisecracks?"

"Hey!" Vince protested, "You guys keep goin' off on these intellectual, philosophical tangents. We're suppose to be recreating, relaxin'. I'm tryin' to keep things loose. I swear if this round of golf was televised, it wouldn't be on ESPN it would be on PBS. I........."

"I'm surprised you were about to pronounce that." D.I. interrupted.

Vince stared blankly while rewinding what he had said.

"You mean philosophical?" he asked.

"No!" D.I. croaked, "PBS!"

The laughter erupting from three men quickly extruded laughter from the fourth, allbeit not as hardy.

"Who's up?" D.I. asked, looking past Vince to the two carts motoring toward the green.

Vince glanced at the scorecard clipped to the steering wheel. "Ummm.........It's still you." he said point at D.I. "and don't try to kill it," he coached.

D.I. didn't heed Vince's suggestion. He couldn't, the temptation was just too strong, his resistance too weak. He swung so hard it caused the club to pass under the ball sending it high into the air.

"It's a high, pop-up behind second," Vince announced like Mel Allen. "Morgan drifts back, settles under it.........and that's the ball game. How about that!" he declared as the ball dropped from view over the brink of the drop off.

D.I. wanted to say something but decided against it. He retrieved his tee and sulked to the back of the tee box. Vince added a little extra oomph to his swing, which pulled the ball into the woods on the left side.

"You stupid idiot!" he scolded himself. "All that fairway and look what you do. Stupid! Stupid! Stupid!"

"Is it me?" Barney asked, his throat unable to completely throttle a laugh.

Two gloomy nods answered his question while Wally fought valiantly to contain his amusement.

Barney teed his ball, collected himself and made one of his patented smooth swings that sent his ball on the trajectory they all had envisioned. From the tee, it looked as if the ball would carry all the way to the green but as it began to drop and drop and drop the illusion evaporated and the ball came to rest in the center of the fairway a hundred and thirty yards from the green.

"Nice ball!" Wally complimented. Vince and D.I. stood hushed by self-pity and disappointment.

Wally, goaded by Barney's success and the elevated tee, swung a little harder than usual and sent a rainbow arcing slice toward the right hand tree line. "Get down." he implored but the ball, propelled by the additional altitude, sailed on and into the trees.

"It's back!" Vince said referring to Wally's fade.

"With a vengeance!" D.I. added.

Both carts crested the drop off at top speed. It was tradition. It produced that momentary weightless sensation that floated their stomachs into their throats and their minds back to childhood. A mini-adrenaline rush lifted their spirits and all four were smiling when they reached D.I.'s ball. The ball lay at the base of the bluff in deep rough just short of the fairway.

"Well it's better than the trees," Vince said, "but not much."

D.I. got most of his five iron on the ball and it came out hot and running, rolling to just inside the hundred-yard marker. The two carts parted company, Wally and Barney fading right, Vince and D.I. hooking left. Wally found his ball resting on a cushion of pine straw and dry leaves a few yards inside the tree line. He walked into the trees to assess his options. The golf gods had been kind to him. There was an ample opening through the trees that allowed him to punch the ball out as well as advance it toward the green, which he did quite nicely, the ball winding up just short of the hundred yards marker.

Vince faced a more demanding challenge. He had a hard pan lie in the middle of a very small clearing. The clearing afforded an unobstructed swing but little in the way of unobstructed lines. The only reasonable and safe shot to the fairway, required him to punch the ball laterally if not slightly backwards. Vince, being neither reasonable nor safe, when it came to playing golf, decided to try threading the ball through a needle's eye opening in the trees. If he could execute the shot perfectly, the ball might carry all the way to the green.

"You gonna try and hit it that way?" D.I. asked in disbelief, as Vince took his stance.

"What do I have to loose?" Vince answered apathetically.

"Oh...I'd say...'bout three strokes." D.I. answered, "I'd try and punch it back through there." He continued, point at the opening back to the fairway.

"Well I'm not you!" Vince stated defiantly while taking aim at the small opening.

"I'm outa here!" D.I. muttered, beating a hasty retreat back to the cart. "It's gonna be like a pinball machine in here."

Wally and Barney drove to Barney's ball and looked back to were D.I. was emerging from the woods.

"Did he find his ball?" Wally yelled.

"Yeah!" D.I. answered taking cover behind the cart. "Heads up! There's no tellin' where it's gonna go."

Vince was obscured by trees, branches and shade, only his movements were visible to the others. They saw the swing, they saw the puff of dust from the club striking the bare dry earth but the sound was delayed momentarily by distance. Smack!...Thwack!...Crack!...Thump!...it came in rapid succession followed by a feeble "Oww!"

"You okay?" D.I. asked peeking around the cart.

After a brief silence, Vince's laughter filled the woods. "I don't believe it," he gasped hysterically, "the ball hit this tree right in front of me, ricocheted right passed my head, hit the tree behind me and then hit me right square on the butt."

"Didn't give you a concussion did it?"

"No, but thanks for your concern."

Vince, enlightened by his near miss experience, punched his third shot back to the fairway. The time spent foraging in the forest had given the ladies sufficient time to putt out and clear the green. Barney could see the red that was Stella standing on the eleventh tee.

Vince hit his fourth shot twenty yards short of the green. Barney played an easy eight that faded right and came to rest pin high but up against the right hand collar. Wally's pitching wedge landed softly and checked up fifteen feet below the hole. D.I. hit a vertically competent, horizontally challenged sand wedge to the front edge.

Vince took a number of practice swings while Barney walked over and marked D.I.'s ball. Vince's chip lacked enthusiasm coming up twenty feet short and it took him two putts to get down.

"This friggin' hole gets me every time," Vince mumbled as he plucked his ball from the hole.

"One would think, one would learn something." Wally taunted.

"One would, wouldn't one?" Vince replied, taking the flagstick from Barney and tending it while D.I.'s long par putt came up inches short.

"Nice lag Alice," he mused, knocking the ball back to D.I., "you better make that putt Ferguson, or Barney is gonna win the hole and two carryovers."

"Geeze Denevi, put a little pressure on him." D.I. groaned.

"Not to worry," Wally said confidently just before stroking his putt straight at the hole but six inches short."

"Short? You hit it short?" Vince whined.

"You know Wally," D.I. said, "ninety-nine percent of all short putts never go in the hole."

"I choked. Okay?" Wally admitted, "the pressure, the money, not to mention the lack of confidence from my "Friends." It was just too much for me to handle."

"That's all right Wall." D.I. consoled, "Barney's not a pressure player either. That's not an easy two putt from where he is."

"But I can't lose the hole," Barney said coyly. "I can only win it."

"Hey, one tie all tie has a real nice ring to it. Right guys?" Vince said brightly.

Barney struck his putt firmly. Too firmly, it ran five feet past the hole, bringing a smile to three faces.

"Got yourself a real knee knocker there Barn." Vince taunted.

"Don't leave it short," D.I. cautioned.

"I hope you make it Barn." Wally said in disgust. "Might teach these two leeches a lesson in humility and sportsmanship."

"Humility? Sportsmanship?" D.I. questioned, "Never heard of 'em."

"Me neither." Vince added.

The men fell silent while Barney stood over his putt. The putter went back smoothly, paused, then stroked the ball toward the hole. As it lost speed, the ball began to break to the left and it appeared it would miss the low side. Just before the hole, it straightened and caught just enough hole to pull it down.

"Never a doubt," Wally crowed, "never a doubt."

Vince and D.I. said nothing.

Barney removed his ball from the cup, Vince planted the flagstick back in the hole and the four men left the green in silence.

HOLE	10	11	12	13	14	15	16	17	18	IN	Total
PAR	4	4	3	5	4	4	3	4	5	36	72
YRDS	380	340	154	495	396	362	158	398	497	3178	6324
D.I.	5										
Vince	9										
Wally	5										
Barney	∴ 4										

11

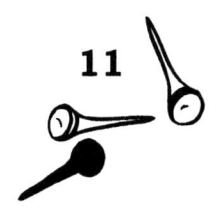

"Scores?" Vince asked as he reined the cart to a halt at the eleventh tee.

"Five." D.I. answered.

"Me too," Wally acknowledged.

"And puke face had a par ...right?" Vince said, penciling the scores onto the scorecard.

"What did you have Vince?" D.I. asked.

"Seven."

"Didn't you forget somethin?"

"What?"

"The ball hit you."

"So?"

"So you incur a penalty."

"What! It's not bad enough I got hit by the ball I have to add a penalty too?" Vince protested.

D.I. held up two fingers.

"Two strokes?" Vince howled, "Are you sure?"

"I'm afraid D.I.'s right," Barney said.

Vince turned to Wally to appeal his case but Wally simply nodded his consensus.

"Who in the hell came up with these so called rules of golf, the Marquis de Sade?" Vince wondered. "Aw what's the difference, seven, nine, who cares anyway?"

Three hands went up but Vince didn't notice. He was busy rounding a seven into a nine.

Barney looked down the fairway of the par four, slight dogleg right, eleventh hole. The hole demands a precise as well as lengthy tee shot between a fairway bunker on the left and trees at the corner on the right. But Barney was not assessing the placement of his tee ball, he was searching for a splash of red. Two ladies lulled around the bunker and an empty cart sat at the edge of the woods on the right.

"This is one tough hole." D.I. said to no one in particular.

"Handicap numero dos." Wally affirmed.

Vince, completed his accounting chores, got out of the cart and surveyed the hole.

"Man if you don't hit a good tee shot, you can't clear the water on your second." he said with an air of apprehension.

"We know that Vincent," D.I. said indulgently.

"What water?" Barney asked, "Don't look at the water, look at the green. Don't think of the water, think only of the green, Don't wo........."

"What the heck are you talking about Melton?" Vince asked in bewilderment, "You go in the water here more than anybody."

"Well just because you don't look at it or think about it doesn't mean it isn't there." Barney said, "You still have to hit a good shot. I'm just saying, you should concentrate on the positive, try to block out the negative."

Wally began signing softly, "You have to...ac-cen-tuate the positive."

"Well you're a piss poor validation of that theory." Vince complained.

"E-lim-in-ate the negative," Wally crooned on.

"I didn't say it worked for me," Barney said irritably, "I just thought you might want to try it. I mean you're the one crying about the water."

"latch on... to the a-ffirmative," Wally warbled.

"This is just great," Vince moaned, "now every time I have to hit over water, I'll think of you. I'm doomed."

"And don't mess wi......"

"Will you shut up Ferguson!" Vince shrieked.

"And don't mess with Mr. In-between," Wally blurted out defiantly. Vince gave him an eye.

"Just like a little brat," he said in disgust.

Out of the corner of his eye, Barney caught a glimpse of red. He trained his eyes on the spot and saw Stella emerging from the woods. She was like the sunrise on a brand new day Barney thought.

"Anybody wanna play Monday?" D.I. asked.

"Yeah, I do." Wally said, "how 'bout you Barn?"

Barney thought for a moment. "I guess......unless somethin' better turns up." he said with a smile.

"What could be better?" D.I. wondered aloud.

Wally pointed down the fairway to where Stella stood beside her cart. D.I.'s eyes followed the point, then without expression turned to Wally.

"Like I said, what could be better?"

"How 'bout you Denevi, you wanta play?"

"Can't, I gotta doctor's appointment."

"Anything wrong?" Barney asked.

"Oh he just can't get a handle on my blood pressure. I think he's gonna try some new medication. Just what I need, more pills. I take so many every morning there's no room for breakfast.

"And that's a bad thing?" Barney mused, patting Vince's ample belly. "Say are you?"

"Twins," Vince nodded.

"Congratulations."

"All I know," Vince went on, "is if I get any more prescriptions, I'll have to register with the DEA as a drug lord. I got pills all over the house, the kitchen counter looks like a pharmacy."

"Someone needs to come up with a senior citizen size medicine cabinet," D.I. said. "Between me and Donna, we could fill ten of those rinky-dink things that came with the house."

"Home Depot has medicine cabinets for seniors." Vince declared.

"Really?" Wally questioned.

"Yeah," Vince answered, "they call 'em storage sheds."

"Funny, Denevi, real funny." Wally tried to say seriously but couldn't.

"Welcome to the golden years." Barney said.

"Golden years? What a bunch of AARP hog wash." D.I. complained. "They're golden all right, for the pharmaceutical companies and the medical profession. And if that's not enough, we got those vultures from the funeral industry circling over head just waitin' to swoop down and pick our bones clean."

"Well aren't we the gloomy Gus today." Wally declared.

"Just a little ray of sunshine in a mean old nasty world," Barney said with a pout and a juvenile voice.

"Well it's true!" D.I. protested loudly, "There's nothin' golden 'bout growin' old."

"I don't know what you're complaining about," Barney said, "you've never had it so good. You're reasonably healthy... physically... mentally?" Barney oscillated his hand in a come-see come-saw fashion, "You've got more money than Bill Gates and a woman that, for some unexplainable reason, worships the ground you walk on. Man, it don't get no better than that."

"That's exactly what I'm complainin' about, Barn." D.I. snapped, "It's not gonna get any better. We're over the hill and on that slippery slope to eternity. We're lucky to be out here playn' golf."

"Bingo! Quit your bitchin' and enjoy it." Barney scolded.

"We are lucky." D.I. admitted, "Things could be a lot worse. It just gets my goat when everybody's paintin' such a rosy picture of growin' old."

"Hey it beats the alternative." Vince said.

"Look!" D.I. said, "It just seems that everyday I wake up to a new pain or I discover another function my body won't perform properly. My sight's dimmin', my hearin's fadin' and my bladder can't hold more than a tablespoon of pee."

"Hey you're no different than the rest of us." Barney conceded. "We just have to play the cards we're dealt. It's just nature's way of easing us into the big sand trap in the sky...... to make death a little more acceptable to us."

"Well I hope when I go it's sudden and quick." D.I. said.

"I can arrange that," Vince offered, "my cousin Big Louie in Jersey is real goo............"

"I'll let you know," D.I. interrupted, "but don't hold your breath. Check that, do hold your breath and for a long time."

"I know what you mean D.I." Wally said, "The thought of a painful lingering death really bothers me."

"It's bad enough on the person who's dyin'," D.I. added, "but it's just as hard if not harder on those around him."

"I know." Wally said, "I had an uncle who died of lung cancer. He hung on for years. The family was emotionally and financially drained. It caused a major rift among the siblings, some feeling the others hadn't contributed enough to his care and upkeep. It always seems the burden falls heaviest on one particular family member and this real or perceived inequity can tear a family apart."

"We are experiencing the same thing." D.I. confided, "Donna's mother has Alzheimer's. She's gotten real bad lately, she doesn't even recognize her own children at times, she doesn't know where she is, she's confused all the time and it scares her into these panic attacks that just rips Donna's heart out. It got to the point she needs constant care and we just couldn't provide it, we had to put her in a nursing home. This added guilt to Donna's already laden emotional load. Like you said Wally, Donna is beginning to harbor feelings of resentment towards her brother who is trying but because he lives in Colorado, he can't be here for her all the time. Every time Donna visits her mother, she comes home depressed and angry. Sometimes I sense she resents me too. I'm ashamed to admit it but I hate to visit that place. It's so depressing, so hopeless, I feel so helpless."

"All you can do is be there for her." Barney said softly.

"I know and I am but it's just not enough. I only hope I go quickly like my dad so my family doesn't have to go through this. I bought one of those extended care policies for Donna and me but I sure hope we never have to use it."

"It's scary to think we may have something like that to look forward to." Wally said glumly.

"That's why I held on to my 357 magnum." Vince said, "I only hope when the time comes, I'll have the sense to blow my brains out."

"Too small a target, you'd probably miss." D.I. scoffed.

"I'm really torn by this assisted suicide issue." Barney said, "I mean I can see the arguments on both sides, pain and suffering, financial, religious, it's a very private and emotional choice. We're talking life and death here, our life and death. We can talk and argue till the cows come home but until the grim reaper taps us on the shoulder, none of us knows for sure how we'll react. I think the will to live will prove to be stronger than we thought."

"They're finding that out in Oregon." Wally said, "After passing the right to die law only a small percentage of those people who have received their lethal prescriptions have actually taken them. Most have chosen to die naturally."

"But at least they had the choice." Vince argued.

"But whose choice is it really?" D.I. asked. "I think it's in the hands of a higher power."

"But it's my life," Vince contended.

"It's a gift," D.I. countered.

Barney looked back to the fairway just in time to see Stella get in her cart and drive off toward the green.

"I hate to put an end to all this uplifting chatter, but," he nodded toward the fairway, "I believe I have the tee."

"Fire when ready Griddley." D.I. ordered.

"Wally?" Barney asked, "How do you hit that fade?"

"If I knew, I'd stop." Wally replied curtly.

"Well this hole sets up real nice for you," Barney said, "I wish I could bend the ball when I wanted to."

"Key phrase," Wally said, "when I wanted to."

"Let's see," Barney said, "I think you align your body left of the target, then swing the club in line with the target. Sounds simple enough."

Barney lined up toward the bunker on the left then made a nice smooth pass that sent the ball, straight as an arrow, toward the bunker.

"You're suppose to fade you stupid ball!...Fade!" He hollered. The ball struck a mound just left of the bunker and kicked just far enough right and forward to clear the trap and come to rest on the fairway in perfect position.

"That's a ground fade," Vince noted, "a true fade is suppose to turn in the air."

"Just the way I planned it," Barney said with a grin.

'Now that's what I call a members, member bounce." D.I. said planting his tee to the extreme right hand side of the tee box. He stood behind the ball momentarily to pick a target. He addressed his ball and sent it soaring skyward again.

"What in blue blazes am I doin'?" he asked in frustration.

"Try teeing the ball a little lower." Wally suggested.

"You look like you're playing it too far forward," Vince submitted.

"It looks like you're hanging back." Barney offered.

"Hangin' back?" D.I. asked.

"Yeah, you know, you're swaying back on your take away and you're hanging there for the rest of the swing. I think that adds loft because the club is on it's upward path before impact."

"Sorry I asked." D.I. said dejectedly, "So all I have to do is tee it lower, play it back in my stance and don't sway on the back swing."

"That's all there is to it," Barney affirmed, "piece of cake."

Wally aimed left and faded the ball perfectly around the trees on the corner.

"That should be real good." Barney said convincingly.

Vince backed off three times to confirm his line and each time D.I.'s collar grew tighter.

"You have to actually hit the ball to make it move," he said sarcastically.

"Keep your knickers on." Vince said addressing the ball for the fourth time. When the ball finally met the clubface, it headed straight for the bunker and landed just short. Vince turned to the others. "Did that go in?" he asked.

" 'Fraid so." D.I. confirmed.

"Just trickled in." Wally verified.

Vince groaned as his shoulders slumped and his back bowed. "I've never been in so much sand," he said, not bothering to retrieve his tee.

D.I. had no choice but to lay up short of the water, a shot of about a hundred and twenty five yards. He made the nice easy swing that lay up shots produce and caught it pure.

"Get down!" he bellowed loud enough to cause the ladies on the green to turn in concern. The ball bounced twice and disappeared over the slope that fell off toward the water. One of the ladies gave the safe sign and D.I. breathed a sigh of relief.

Vince weighed the odds of his making a miraculous, long bunker shot over the water and wisely chose to lay up. Wally's ball had cut the slight dogleg beautifully and rolled just short of the water.

"It never entered my mind that the water was in play from the tee," Wally said in pleased disbelief.

"You really nailed it," Barney commended.

"I did, didn't I?"

D.I.'s ball was not visible from the fairway so all four drove to the edge of the lake to see if they could find it. The ball had obviously rolled into the taller grass inside the hazard line and the men got out of their carts and began looking in the un-mown grass.

"It's right by that hazard stake to your left." Stella called from across the lake.

The four men concentrated their search in the area around the stake.

"Man I think I'd be better off in the water," D.I. said brushing the top of the long grass with his foot trying to locate his ball. "Even if we find it I won't have a shot."

"Here's a ball," Barney announced, "what are you hitting?"

"Pinnacle," D.I. answered.

Barney bent to inspect the ball hidden in the grass.

"This is a Top Flite, you sure you weren't hitting Top Flite?"

"I told y......"

"Here it is," Vince said, pointing to an area near the stake.

D.I. walked over and stooped over the spot.

"That's it," he said glumly. He looked around to see what options were open to him. There was only one.

"I'm takin' an unplayable," he announced, plucking the ball from the hazard and walking back along the line of flight until he found a spot that pleased him, he then turned and dropped.

By the time Wally and Barney got back to Barney's ball, the ladies had left the green and were heading up the path to the twelfth.

Don't think about the water." Vince called back to Barney.

"I'm going to show you, the awesome power of positive thinking." Barney said, taking his stance. The shot was doomed at impact and the ball fluttered like a wounded duck before plunging to a watery grave forty yards short of the distant shore.

"I think you're right about the power of positive thinking," Vince hollered, "I was positive you were gonna go in the water."

Wally hit a good second shot that rolled twenty-five feet past the hole and Vince hit the green with his third shot. D.I. and Barney both found the green but were laying four.

Vince, feeling a little guilty about razzing Barney into a bad shot, walked with him to the green.

"I hope what I said didn't influence your shot." He said quietly. "That wasn't very sportsman like of me."

"No, no, that's all right, I should be able to block that stuff out," Barney said, not quite convinced of his own sincerity.

"Well I apologize," Vince said, "I was only kidding, I really wasn't trying to rattle ya.'

"Its okay. It's done. It's over. You are forgiven." Barney said with a forced smile. In truth, the more he thought about it the more it irritated him. "Anybody need the pin," he asked, automatically pulling the flag on his way past the hole.

"Evidently not!" D.I. responded.

Barney, ignoring D.I.'s jab, continued on letting the flag fall to earth with a metallic clatter.

The four men putted out in relative silence. Wally's twenty-five footer came up two feet short and his par putt just curled in the right edge to win the hole. Vince two putted for a bogey and D.I. and Barney both two putted for double bogey sixes.

HOLE	10	11	12	13	14	15	16	17	18	Out	Total
PAR	4	4	3	5	4	4	8	4	5	36	72
YRDS	380	340	154	495	396	362	156	398	497	3178	6324
D.I.	5	6									
Vince	9	5									
Wally	5	•4									
Barney	4	•••6									

12

Riding the short distance to the 12th tee, Barney mulled and simmered over Vince's lack of consideration and sportsmanship. It really hadn't bothered him until Vince had apologized. If Vince Denevi, of all people, recognized his behavior was improper.......well that pretty much validated the grievousness of his actions. But on the other hand, Barney's reconciliatory nature argued, Vince had seen the error of his ways and had asked for forgiveness. Should he not forgive? Yet again, it had cost him a ball, two strokes and possibly the hole. But on the other hand, it was he who had actually hit the ball into the water, not Vince. Barney was about to run out of other hands when the sight of Stella standing at the ball washer, flushed the entire incident from his head and buoyed his attitude.

Vince pulled the lead cart to a stop well short of where Stella stood and Wally had no choice but to pull up behind him. Barney, exited the cart and made a beeline for the ball washer.........the one named Stella.

"Oh not more animal magnetism," D.I. groaned as Barney passed by.

As he walked, Barney realized that he was once again in that rare aggressive, self-confident mode. He liked it. He had always held back waiting for things to just happen. They rarely did. He knew now, at this late stage in his life, he could ill afford to dawdle. There was a sense of urgency. He had to act and he had to act swiftly. Besides, Stella's friendly and receptive manner made being aggressive easy. He found himself operating in a comfort zone few mortal males had ever had the luxury of operating from.

"How's it going?" He asked stopping a few feet from the washer and extracting a ball from his pocket. Stella was intent on drying a ball with the towel attached to the body of the washer.

"Just took a double on the last hole," she said inspecting the ball closely.

"Yeah, me too. I drowned the second shot."

"Did you find your friend's ball?" She asked looking up and dropping the towel to swing lightly on it's tether.

"Yeah, but it might just as well gone in the lake, he had to take an unplayable."

"Well at least he didn't lose a ball," she reminded him.

"This is true."

Barney hesitated before finding his manners, "Oh, thanks for spotting it for us, we probably wouldn't have found it if you hadn't pointed us in the right direction."

"My pleasure," she said stepping away to allow Barney access to the washer.

Barney stepped forward and placed his ball in the washer.

"I always feel like an organ grinder who's lost his monkey, when I use these things." Barney said, turning the crank that spun his ball through the soapy water.

Stella giggled lightly while her eyes laughed.

"Your music box is broken, too," she said, "I think maybe you might want to consider a career change."

Barney shook his head and stopped cranking. "It's all I know," he protested, "my great grandfather was a grinder, my grandfather was a grinder, too."

"What about your father? Wasn't he a grinder?" She asked prompting Barney to continue the farce.

"Well it gets a little complicated. You see, back in forty-eight, the family monkey died of zinc poisoning. We think it was from biting too many of those World War II pennies. This was not an isolated incident, monkeys were dropping dead all over the place creating a severe monkey shortage."

"Really?" Stella asked trying to sound serious.

"Oh yeah, it was a trying time for grinders. Anyway, back to my father. With no monkeys available, my grandfather had little choice but to substitute one of the family children in place of the monkey. My cousin, Delbert, was chosen because......uh......Let's see, how should I put this...Delbert was chosen because he......Well, he wasn't the most attractive child......and, he was the only one that fit into the little monkey's vest and cap." Barney stopped and looked at Stella. She looked at Barney with a puzzled look.

"Well, what about your father?" She asked.

"Well," Barney replied, "when my cousin became the monkey, my father became a monkey's uncle."

Stella stared blankly for a few seconds.

"Oh my God!" She said, "That's the corniest thing I've every heard."

Barney blanched pale at her rejection of his humor, then quickly blushed red in embarrassment.

"I love it!" She laughed.

It was now Barney's turn to stare blankly while he tried to determine whether he was a hit or a miss.

"Did you just come up with that?" she asked in amazement.

"Not really," he admitted sheepishly, "I lay awake a lot."

"Thinking about organ grinders and monkeys?"

"No, more about sayings... phrases... like, monkey's uncle, the cat's pajamas, don't look a gift horse in the mouth, things like that. I try to figure out their meaning, their possible origin. I tend to stray a bit."

"A bit? I can't wait to hear about the cat's pajamas." She said giggling again. Barney paused to savor the giggle.

"Stella!" Came a call from the ladies tee. She turned to see the other ladies beckoning her to the tee. The group ahead was just walking off the green, she turned back to Barney.

"Gotta go," she said with a trace of regret, "talk to you later?"

"If you still want to," Barney inquired uncertainly.

"More than ever." She answered emphatically.

"S...T...E...L...L...A!" The ladies called in unison.

"Lord give me patience," she said turning toward the tee. She hesitated then turned back.

"Barney?" She said.

"Yes?"

"Have you considered medication?"

"I'm not dressed for a wedding," D.I. said when Barney returned from his ball washer encounter.

"Who said you're invited," Barney answered flatly.

Barney got into the cart with Wally to wait for the ladies to play the hole.

"Well?" Wally asked excitedly.

"Well what?" Barney replied innocently.

"How's it going? Is she interested? Are you still interested? Could she be the one? Are......?"

"Geeze Wally calm down. Your working yourself into a frenzy," Barney said, "breath into a paper bag before you hyperventilate and pass out."

"I can't help it, I just think this is so great. I mean, look at you. You look happy, you look enthused, you look alive."

"Gee-man-ne, was I that bad before I met Stella."

"Yes, you were." Wally answered quickly.

Vince and D.I. had gotten out of their cart and had come to join the roast.

"There is a marked difference between the B.S. Barney and the A.S. Barney." Vince concurred.

"Well if I was so......so dull and tedious before Stella, why on earth did you guys put up with me?"

"Comic relief mostly," Vince said with a shrug.

"I have always found," D.I. explained, "that having someone around who is worse off than oneself, tends to temper ones own shortcomings."

Barney wore a hurt expression. "With friends like..."

"Ah, ah, ah," D.I. interrupted, wiggling a finger in a metronome waggle, "no one here has used the 'F' word, so don't you go assumin' anything. Now tell us what's goin' on."

"Nothing's going on," Barney protested lamely.

"Oh come on," Vince scoffed, do we look that stupid?"

"Well now tha......"

"Put a cork in it Melton," Vince ordered, "we're not blind you know. You scurry over there," Vince pointed to the ball washer, "sidle up to her and expect us to believe you two were just washing golf balls and passin' the time of day?"

"Exactly!"

"Nice try lover boy," D.I. smirked, "I know flirtation when I see it. You two never broke eye contact and she had more sugar on that smile than a glazed doughnut."

"I can't believe this," Barney protest, "you guys are nothing but a bunch of voyeuristic nimrods. What the hell is this, one of those pathetic reality TV shows?"

"Yeah and you're about to be voted off the island." Vince threatened.

"The sooner the better." Barney hoped aloud.

Vince, D.I. and even Wally rained a flood of sarcastic accusations upon Barney to which Barney countered with equally biting denials.

A barrage of put-downs and innuendoes flew in all directions. The double negative axiom of masculine emotional reality. A guy's way of expressing his inner most feelings towards another guy. The author of the phrase, me thinks he doth protest too loudly.

And then, as quickly as it had started, it was over.

"Hey Barn, you don't like reality TV?" Vince asked.

"I think they're stupid, degrading and a sad commentary on our society." Barney answered with a tinge of bitterness.

"Is that a no?" Vince asked jokingly.

"I agree," Wally said, "those shows are about as real as Carol Dodda's hooters."

"Who?" D.I. asked.

"Carol Dodda," Wally repeated, "she had a topless joint in San Francisco, had more silicon in her boobs than Silicon Valley."

"Silicone!" Vince corrected with a chuckle.

"What?"

"It's silicone not silicon."

"Silicone Valley?"

"No you du-fus," Vince laughed, "it's silicone breasts and Silicon Valley."

"Whatever." Wally shrugged. "Silicone is made from silicon anyway so what the hell's the diff?"

"Silicone is not made from silicon!" Vince contradicted.

"Yes it is!" Wally shot back.

"It is not!"

"It most certainly is!"

"It can't be," Vince argued, "silicon is basically sand, if silicone was made from sand her boobs would be all gritty."

"You're an idiot Denevi," Wally laughed, "silicone is made from silicon and if you don't believe me, look it up."

Vince looked at D.I.

"I don't know and I don't care." D.I. answered without being asked.

Vince turned to Barney.

"I think Wally is right." Barney said.

"No he's not!" Vince insisted.

"Shut up!" D.I. ordered, "Look it up when you get home."

"Silicone is not made from silicon." Vince whispered defiantly.

The four men fell silent, forgetting what had brought them to this point.

Vince walked to the tee and began pacing off the distance between the yardage marker and the tee location.

"What's it playin'?" D.I. asked.

"I got it at one forty-six," Vince answered walking back to the cart but looking toward the green. "But it looks like the pin is in the back."

Precise distance is the key to hitting the shallow green of the par three twelfth. A short shot would be gobbled up by two cavernous bunkers in front and a long shot would find a rough infested swale behind the green.

"I'm hitting my perfect one fifty club," Wally announced confidently while walking to the tee. He teed his ball and stood back until the ladies' carts moved off toward the next hole. He hit the shot fat and the ball landed in the rough a good twenty yards short of the bunkers.

"Perfect one fifty club huh?" Vince said, walking over to Wally and inspecting the designation on the sole of Wally's club. "This is a perfect hundred club if you ask me."

"Who's askin'!" Wally snapped.

Vince didn't answer, he set about hitting his own shot.

"Get up!" He ordered as the ball began descending from its apex. Vince's ball just cleared the trap but not the fringe. "That'll work," he said in relief. "I think there's some wind up there."

"Listen to him," D.I. objected, "he's got an excuse for everything."

"That's my new motto." Vince admitted, "my new philosophy. Find a scapegoat………Find a scapegoat and milk it for all it's worth and never, I repeat, never accept responsibility for anything."

"New age thinking," D.I. commented, "that should put you in good stead in this new millennium."

Barney's shot was dead on the stick. "Oh be the club," he murmured, "you can go in the hole if you want," he added hopefully just as his ball hit the lip of the bunker and kicked back into the depths of the trap. Barney turned to his playmates with a look of shock and disbelief sparkled to his face.

"Oh no," Vince panned facetiously toward D.I., "there must be some wind up there." Vince turned to Wally, "And look what happened, Barney went right into that nasty old silicone trap."

Wally wasn't about to be suckered back into the silicon/silicone debate.

"Tough break," he told Barney.

"Game of inches." D.I. confirmed again.

"But I hit it sooo sweet." Barney objected.

D.I. shrugged, made a good swing with an eight iron that sent the ball drawing perfectly to the stick.

"Oh that's all over it," Vince whooped.

"Lookin' good," Wally added.

The ball took a short hop and stopped a few feet from the pin. At least from the tee it looked like a few feet.

"Great shot," Wally applauded.

Vince raised an arm toward D.I. who instinctively consummated the high five.

"Birdie time!" Barney exclaimed heading for the cart.

"They always look closer from here," D.I. said stoically, "it'll probably be twenty feet by the time we get up there."

"I think there are little hole gremlins that pop out and move the hole while we're travelin' to the green," Vince suggested.

"I think it's our lack of depth perception," Barney said seriously.

"True," Vince said, "you lack depth and have no perception whatsoever."

"Listen to mister one dimensional here." D.I. chastised.

"Say what you will," Vince said, "I still think it's The Hole Gremlins."

As the four neared the green it became clear that D.I.'s ball was actually within inches of the cup.

"What happened to your gremlins," D.I. crowed.

"Hey, even gremlins get a lunch break. They have a very strong union you know," Vince continued, "the....." he hesitated momentarily while his mind shuffled letters, "the... IBHG union...... puts the Teamsters to shame."

"I'm not even gonna' touch that one," D.I. said getting out of the cart.

"Nor, I," Barney agreed.

Vince looked hopefully to Wally, who shook his head adamantly. Disappointment flickered briefly on Vince's face then he shrugged and walked off to the green.

D.I. removed the pin with one hand and tapped in his birdie with the other, then placed the pin back in the hole.

Wally hit a good pitch from the rough. The ball cleared the trap and lacking backspin released toward the hole, stopping nine feet short.

Barney's sand shot caught all sand and the ball barely reached the green leaving him a long putt for par.

Vince elected to putt from the fringe and the ball stopped less than a foot short.

"That's good Vince," D.I. said, back handing the ball back in Vince's direction. "You need the pin, Barn?" He asked reaching for the flagstick.

"Tend it please, if you would be so kind." Barney answered lining up his putt.

Barney two putted for bogey and Wally made his nine footer for an all American par.

D.I. walked to the cup to replace the flagstick. He stopped, bent down and peered into the hole.

"Breaks over!" He hollered rattling the pin into the cup. "Get back to work!"

HOLE	10	11	12	13	14	15	16	17	18	Out	Total
PAR	4	4	3	5	4	4	8	4	5	36	72
YRDS	380	340	154	495	396	362	156	398	497	3178	6324
D.I.	5	6	2								
Vince	9	5	3								
Wally	5	4	3								
Barney	4	6	4								

13

D.I. leaned over and watched Vince enter the scores for the twelfth hole.

"Why are you giving me two dots on twelve?" he asked.

"One for the birdie and one for winning the hole," Vince answered.

"Shouldn't I get three?"

"Why should you get three, there wasn't a carryover."

"Don't greenies count for anything anymore?"

Vince looked dark momentarily before the light switched on. "Oh crap you're right. I'm sorry, I forgot about the greenie."

"It takes me twelve holes to finally get some marks and you try to cheat me out of one," D.I. admonished.

"I said I was sorry, I made a mistake... Okay?" Vince appealed.

"Must I watch your every move?" D.I. nagged on.

Vince's knuckles paled as his fingers drove the pencil into the scorecard with aggravated force to mark a dominate third dot beside the other two.

"There!" Vince said curtly, "Are you happy now?"

Wally walked up to the cart. "What's all the fuss about?" he asked.

"Oh the good Lord gave Denevi all ten fingers to count on but he can't get beyond two," D.I. kidded.

"If you don't want to find this pencil up your...... nose," Vince growled, waving the stubby writing implement in D.I.'s face, "you'd better shut yer yap."

Barney, not wanting to be embroiled in the scorecard fiasco, made his way to the thirteenth tee box. The long par five, plays from a moderately elevated tee, over a small ditch to a sunken fairway that gradually climbs a knoll to an elevated green.

From the tee, he could see the ladies waiting in the fairway below. Something was different. There were four ladies but no tell tale red flag to identify Stella. The mid-day sun had driven the morning chill deep into the woods and Stella had evidently shed her bright red wind shirt. It was difficult from this distance, well almost any distance now, for Barney to tell who was who. Being a typical guy, he had relied only on the red blur to distinguish Stella from the others. Being a typical guy, he had not noticed what any of the other women were wearing or for that matter, what else Stella had on.

Barney remembered how Barbara had accused him, and men in general, of not being very observant. He admitted that his power of observation was not refined enough to register the subtle nuances of feminine fashion. She said he only observed high hemlines and low necklines. She said he couldn't remember the color of a fabric unless it was formfitting spandex.

Barbara was convinced that Barney's inability to color coordinate was due to color blindness. Barney argued that a man's restricted color spectrum, only recognized three possible color combinations. White shorts and tan legs, red lingerie with creamy skin and black nylons with high heels of any shade.

Barney smiled at the places his mind could take him. He recalled how Barbara never understood how he could remember every stroke he played during a round of golf but couldn't remember what she was wearing. He felt she over exaggerated his lack of observation and attention to detail. He felt he was a bit deeper and more complex than she gave him credit for......but ......probably not much. Besides, Barney reasoned, it's really not the detailed observations, it's the over all impression that counts.

He may not notice what she was wearing or whether or not she had jewelry on but he could see her as plainly as if she were standing before him. He didn't see the clothes or the makeup or accessories, he saw her and only her.

Barney's emotional blender began churning. But this time, a new ingredient had been added, guilt. The guilt of desire for someone other than Barbara, a sense of betrayal and unfaithfulness. Stella and guilt, and oil and water mix he just could not homogenize no matter how fast his blender spun. A feeling of hopelessness fell over him.

In his mind, he knew Barbara would want him to live a complete and happy life. In fact, they had, more than once, discussed what each should do in the event they found themselves alone. But he was finding conjecture and actuality were the apples and oranges of his emotional existence. The more he tried to rationalize it, the faster his blender whirled.

Try as he may, he could not incorporate the conflicting feelings into a palatable blend. He was about to throw his hands up in despair when Barbara suddenly stepped back into the shadows of his heart and mind. She was making room for someone else to bask in his adulation spotlight. The blender ground to a halt as if she had jerked it's plug from it's socket. He experienced a new peace of mind, a lightness in his heart. Barney smiled and nodded. She may have stepped back but Barbara had not stepped out of his heart.

"Earth to Barney! Earth to Barney! Come in Barney! Over!" a voice called from beyond the realm of his inner thought.

His mental and emotional meandering crashed head-on into the reality of the moment. He stood momentarily stunned by the violence of the collision and he shook his head as if sifting reality from the chaff of daydreams.

"Where have you been Barn?" Wally asked.

"What?" Barney said still grasping from comprehension.

"You looked like you were out in the ozone layer or somethin'," Vince remarked.

"Oh, I was just thinking."

"Looked more like a fantasy to me," Vince added with an elbow nudge.

"Could we!!" D.I. said impatiently, stepping in and shooing the others to the back of the tee with his driver.

All four tee balls found the fairway with Barney's rolling just far enough past the others to cause D.I.'s head to shake in frustration.

The two carts pulled up beside one another in the fairway and the four men sat waiting to hit their second shots.

"Hey! did you notice that one guy in Randy's group had his nose pierced?" Vince asked with an intolerant tone.

"Yeah, what's with that?" Wally wondered.

"I saw a guy who had three ear rings through his eyebrow, a post in his nose and several rings in different areas of his ears." D.I. said.

"They're even piercing their tongues and navels," Wally added.

"I just don't understand it," D.I. said, "why would anybody want to pierce their tongue? That's gotta hurt like a son of a gun, gotta be real neat when they eat too."

"I guess I'm just an old fogy but I'm really not into self-mutilation." Wally said.

"Me neither," Vince added, "I mean what's the point?"

"They're just making a statement," Barney said philosophically.

"Yeah, like, look how incredibly stupid I am." D.I. said in disgust.

"You know," Wally said, "it seems the longer I live, the more I don't understand. Used to be that tattoos were restitution for a sailor's lost weekend."

"Hey! I resent the implication, Ferguson," Vince said defensively.

"Oh yeah, you were in the Navy weren't you? Do you have a tattoo?"

Vince hesitated.

"Yeah, but I wasn't drunk, I was just stupid."

"Where is it?" Wally asked, "I've never seen it."

Vince pulled his shirtsleeve up over his right shoulder revealing a small anchor and the letter USN tattooed on the upper most portion of his arm.

"I got it in San Diego before I met Tiff." He said without emotion, "Me and a couple of buddies went downtown for a couple of beers. Well back then, you couldn't go a block without passin' a tattoo parlor. It really came down to a dare, you know, I'll get one if you do. I think we all expected at least one of us to balk and render the idiotic idea null and void. But none of us had the courage to chicken out."

D.I. raised his shirt to reveal an eagle above a banner with the words 'Semper Fi' tattooed on his upper chest.

"I was drunk," he said, 'it's not something I'm proud of but I can't say I regret it."

"I thought those were standard government issue for all you Jar Heads." Vince said lowering his sleeve.

D.I. didn't respond but lowered his shirt, loosened his belt and re-tucked his shirt.

"I thought it would be a badge of courage," Vince said flatly, "but it turned out to be an indelible price tag for a moment of stupidity."

"I wouldn't go that far, Wally said, "at least it's small and ………tasteful……I mean everybody's getting them now, males, females………look at Dennis Rodman, he……"

"No! You look at him, I can't stand the sight of him," D.I. blurted out in anger. "What a disgusting spectacle of deviant behavior."

"Whoa, you sound like a real fan." Vince said somewhat shocked by D.I.'s instant anger.

"The man's a disgrace to sports and all things decent." D.I. growled.

"Some might call him a free spirit." Barney suggested.

"That's the problem, some might, but to me he's just a man with athletic ability who's found fame and fortune but doesn't know how to handle it. He wouldn't know a scruple if he sucked it up his nose. He's not a free spirit, he's a friggin' freak and a moral liability."

"Geeze D.I. what the heck did he do to you to make you hate him so much?" Barney asked.

"I don't hate the man, I hate what he stands for……or more precisely what he doesn't stand for. And it's not just him, it's this whole idea of celebrity worship. Instead of holding them to a higher standard we allow them, because of their 'celeb status', to have no standards at all. I think, because they are, so called, role models, they drag the whole of society down with 'em."

"I'm inclined to agree with you." Vince said. "The media spotlight seems to shine brightest on the morally bankrupt and lends an air of legitimacy to their behavior. It's the Jerry Springer Syndrome and what bothers me most about the whole trend is that so many people are buying into it."

"This so called reality TV and blatant voyeurism really disturbs me." Barney said. "If we have to use other people's lives as role models and entertainment......well what's that say about us. And where in the heck do they get off calling these shows like Survivor or Temptation Island reality TV. They take a bunch of exhibitionists, put them in a non-realistic situation and put them in front of a camera. You think they're going to act the same on camera as off? I don't think so. And you're right Vince, it's scary to think how popular these shows are.'

"Did you ever watch the Springer show?" Vince asked.

"I did once just to see what all the hubbub was about," D.I. answered, 'that's not a talk show it's a friggin' freak show."

"You're right," Vince said, "and what's really upsetting is the way the audience behaves. It's a sad commentary when people actually watch that stuff let alone get involved in it."

The four men fell silent and a bit melancholy.

"You know," Wally said softly, "we were talking about how the deterioration of our bodies makes the thought of physical death a little more tolerable. I think the declines of civility and morality.........well... at least as I perceive it, helps make intellectual and emotional death more acceptable.

"Quick, somebody shoot me!" Vince pleaded, "I can't go on."

"You know the sad part," Barney said, "I always thought the world would be a better place when I go."

"It will be." Vince teased.

"You know what I mean?" Barney went on, "Not that I made it any better...... but ... I just thought things would somehow get better. I thought I'd have a more optimistic outlook for the future of the human race."

"Well, now that we're thoroughly depressed," D.I. said looking up the fairway, "do you all just want to keel over right here or do you want to finish this round of golf first?"

All but Wally found the fairway on their second shots. Wally's faded into the right hand rough. Barney's second shot out distanced the others by some twenty-five yards and the muscles in D.I.'s neck tightened.

"What about you Barn, do you have any?" Wally said getting into the cart.

"Any what?"

"Tattoos."

"Noooo."

"Me neither."

Most of the balls lay near the hundred-yard marker and when the men reached them they could clearly see the ladies on the green. From this distance, Barney was able to recognize Stella by her facial features. He thought it might behoove him to observe her more closely. Barney's little inner voice narrated as he committed her attire to memory. Stella stays really cool yet looks hot in her white polo shirt and pale blue golf shorts. Her matching red visor, worn at a jaunty angle, adds a whimsical touch to the otherwise serious golfer. All in all an even par ensemble for the swinging woman.

You need help Melton, he thought to himself as he checked the other women to make sure they weren't wearing anything that might cause him confusion when viewed from afar. Maybe Stella was right, he thought, maybe medication was needed to stem his mental meandering. He watched her move about the green. She moved with purpose, very intent and very precise, there were no wasted motions. He had never seen a woman move the way she did and still maintain her femininity and humor. He was duly impressed.

"Hey Barn?" Wally asked.
"Yeah?"
"You really think there's not much hope for the future?"
"Oh I don't know, sometimes it all seems so overwhelming......so .....senseless......so inhumane."
"What do you mean?"
"Well the atrocities, the unspeakable things we do to each other, the intolerance to difference. The Albanians and the Serbs, the Israelis and the Palestinians not to mention what's going on in Africa. And right here in the good ol' US of A, a mother drowns her five children and a convenience store clerk is killed for five dollars, those aren't exactly the things that dreams are built on."
"Yeah, but those things have been going on since day one. Don't you see any improvement at all?"
"I see glimmers of hope, I see a few people trying but they're bucking the tide. The mass movement seems to be toward moral decay, the dismemberment of the family body and the prevalence of greed."
"Don't you think there are a lot of people just like us, just regular folks living the best life they can? Don't you see good people in the neighborhood helping each other out? Don't you consider yourself a good person?"
"Well I try, I mean I don't think I have purposely hurt anyone and I try to be there when people are in need."

"There you go!" Wally said with a clap of his hands. "You, me and millions just like us. You remember that phrase, The Silent Majority?" That's us. And we're not really silent, we just can't be heard above the din of a sensationalizing media. We're not news. We mustn't dwell in the negative media world, but live in the positive world in which we dwell."

Barney sat for a moment looking at Wally.

"You're a good man, Wally Ferguson." He said.

Stella winced and turned away as her putt slid past the hole. A sympathy wince contorted Barney's face at the same moment. She put on a frustration smile, gave her putter a playful spanking, then walked over and tapped in. When Sally placed the flagstick in the hole and the ladies began walking off the green, Barney noticed a club lying in the fringe.

"Club!" Barney shouted.

All four women looked at Barney who was now pointing to the area where the club lay. One woman, struck by realization, raised her hand and started back to fetch it. Stella waved and shouted a thank you that made Barney beam.

Wally was first to hit. The ball came out of the rough low and sizzling. It scampered up the green like a lizard on a hot rock and struck the pin dead on with a rattling clank. The ball bounced back stopping about four feet below the hole.

"If that hadn't hit the pin," D.I. chuckled, "it woulda wound up in West Virginia."

"It could of gone in." Wally complained.

"Quit your bitchin'," Vince said, "and count your blessings."

D.I. played a wedge to within fifteen feet. Vince's shot almost found the hole on the fly, the ball releasing and rolling just outside of D.I. Barney hit a sand wedge pin high but pulled it ten feet left.

"This game just isn't fair," D.I. complained as the four walked to the green, "the man who hit the worst shot winds up in the best shape."

"Tell me about it," Vince said leaning over to repair his ball mark that was just inches from the cup.

"Hey! That's the way I played it." Wally said, trying to convince the others.

"The Golf Gods giveth and the Golf Gods taketh away," Barney offered while marking his ball then lifting and cleaning it.

"Is this in your way?" D.I. asked pointing to his ball marker.

Vince squatted behind his ball and plumbobbed the green with his putter.

"Move it one to the left." Vince said still in a one-eyed squat.

D.I. moved his marker one putter head to the left then stood back to watch the break on Vince's putt. The putt broke hard right as it neared the hole and stopped just outside.

"Nice roll," D.I. said placing his ball and removing his mark.

"Thanks."

D.I. stood back to pick his line then approached his ball.

"Aren't you forgetting something?" Wally asked.

"Shut up, Ferguson!" Vince snapped.

"Why you sleaze-ball Denevi," D.I. barked, "I moved my mark for you, I even compliment you on strokin' a good putt and you......you were gonna stand there and let me take a penalty for not movin' my mark back?"

"Hey! Rules are rules," Vince shrugged.

"You're still mad because I called you on being hit by the ball back on number ten, aren't cha?"

"Moi," Vince said turning his index fingers toward his chest.

"You can be a real jerk sometimes, you know that Denevi?"

"Guys, guys," Barney soothed, "let's not let a quarter ruin our day."

"Well it's the principle of the......" D.I. tried to explain.

"Look!" Vince interrupted, "I wasn't going to penalize ya, I just wanted to see what you were gonna do. You know, some people don't take the rules as seriously as you do."

"Well if you're not gonna play by the rules then......" D.I. tried to protest.

"Okay already," Vince conceded, "I'm sorry. I was just trying to have a little fun. Geeze, it's not like we're on the tour here."

Wally busied himself surveying his birdie putt. He knew the whole rules flap would be forgotten before they reached the next tee. It wasn't something to get worked up about. It was the natural relationship between two hardheaded individuals who truly liked each other. Besides, Barney the omnipresent peacekeeper, would be able to broker an amicable truce.

D.I. remarked his ball and moved his marker back to its original position then placed his ball and removed the mark. He looked at Vince for his approval. Vince walked over and closely inspected the placement.

"Wasn't it......?"

"You have a real death wish don't you?" D.I. laughed as he raised his putter in a threatening manner.

"Looks good to me," Vince said stepping back. "hit away!"

D.I.'s putt was a carbon copy of the one Vince had hit.

"Didn't you go to school on my putt?" Vince asked.

I did, but unfortunately it was Ol' Miss." D.I. said backhanding the ball into the cup for his par.

The two former antagonists quickly formed an alliance encouraging Barney to make his birdie putt. They had all but conceded Wally's straight up the hill four footer and needed Barney to tie the hole and force a carryover.

"Nice putt, Alice," D.I. groaned as Barney's birdie putt came up a full foot short. "Did the wind blow your skirt up or somethin'?"

"Did you leave the putter cover on?" Vince asked, "Or was it a full ten finger choke?"

Barney gagged as he banged the ball into the back of the cup.

"I hope you make it, Wally," he said while retrieving his ball from the cup.

"We do too, Wally," Vince said. "Hit it real hard, you don't wanta be a woose like someone I know."

"Yeah, make sure you get it to the hole," D.I. said in a treasonous tone. "Hit it hard, don't be short."

"Straight up and in." Wally muttered to himself before stroking it, "straight up and in."

"Nice putt," Barney applauded.

"Yeah, real nice," D.I. mumbled as he placed the flag in the cup.

"I think we ought to rename The Deputy, Artie." Vince said while walking off the green.

"Artie?" D.I. wondered.

"Yeah," Vince confirmed, "Artie Choke."

HOLE	10	11	12	13	14	15	16	17	18	Out	Total
PAR	4	4	3	5	4	4	8	4	5	36	72
YRDS	380	340	154	495	396	362	156	398	497	3178	6324
D.I.	5	6	2	5							
Vince	9	5	3	5							
Wally	5	4	3	4							
Barney	4	6	4	5							

14

After D.I.'s traditional pause for the cause, at the porta-potty adjacent to the thirteenth green, the two carts coasted down the hill to the fourteenth tee. The ladies were congregated around the drink cart in the middle of the fairway and Barney almost pulled an eye muscles trying to wrest Stella from the human collage.

"I wonder who's workin' the cart today." Vince said squinting into the distance.

D.I. and Wally gazed down the fairway.

"It looks like Melissa," D.I. said shading his eyes with one hand.

"Ahh the sweet Melitha," Vince murmured with a moist Sylvester the Cat like lisp.

"It looks like Jennifer to me," Wally said blinking to refresh the image on his aging retina.

"Mmm, the lovely Jennifer," Vince cooed.

The strain of focal distance caused Barney's eyes to water and the scene smudged like a watercolor awash in an artist's tears. His eyes were in danger of permanently locking in the crossed position, a condition his mother had often cautioned him about. Barney quickly averted his gaze, closed his eyes and pinched the bridge of his nose to stem the flowing ache from behind his eyes.

Whoever was operating the drink cart, concluded her transactions, returned the cart to the cart path and headed in the direction of the three men laboring to recognize her.

"It's Jennifer," Wally said.

"No it's not," D.I. argued, "it's Melissa."

"No, it is Jennifer," Vince said with certainty.

"It's Meliss......no, it's Jennifer," D.I. finally admitted as the cart drew nearer.

The drink cart pulled off the cart path and stopped along side the three grinning men who had walked a few steps to meet it. Jennifer, a striking blonde, blue-eyed young lady, sat demurely behind the wheel. She wore a pink polo shirt, snug white shorts and a golden tan. She also wore a smile capable of melting the entire Scandinavian snow pack.

"Hi guys," she chirped in a melodic tone.

"Where have you been?" D.I. demanded in false agitation. "A man could die of thirst out here."

"Not an old camel like you, D.I.," Jennifer shot back, "what can I get for you?"

"An old camel? She calls me an old camel, then she wants to sell me somethin'."

"I love camels," Jennifer purred with a wink, "I think they're cute."

"Nice try sweetie but I ain't buyin' it," D.I. grumbled, "I'll have a diet Coke and a cup of ice......please."

"How 'bout you Vince?" she asked swinging her long tan legs out of the cart and standing up.

Vince stood momentarily speechless.

"What's your pleasure, Vince?" She asked again while walking to the back of the cart and opening a compartment filled with ice.

Wally walked over to Jennifer, placed the back of hand to the side of his mouth and whispered, "You should never ask a dirty old man a question like that. It produces a massive conflict between perceived ability and physical reality. This, in turn causes severe brain cramps which render the victim stupid."

"Run away with me," Vince gushed suddenly.

"See what I mean," Wally said waving an arm in Vince's direction.

"Let me take you away from all this." Vince went on.

Jennifer, familiar with the symptoms of male multiple childhood disorder knew that the shock of brutal honesty was the most effective therapy.

"Maybe," she said, "if I were fifty years older, nearly blind, had no other prospects and in dire desperation...... I might consider it."

"So I've gotta a shot!" Vince whooped with a grin.

"You guys crack me up," Jennifer giggled, "now what would you like...to drink Vince?"

"Well let me think...Geeze you've made me sooo happy...umm...give me a Power Ade...or a Gator Ade...one of those lemon lime......Ade things."

"Better give him First Aid," D.I. laughed, "I think we're loosing him."

Jennifer fished through the bin of ice and extracted a diet Coke and set it to the side. She closed the bin and moved to the other side of the cart and opened another. The three men maneuvered themselves so as to afford the best possible vantage point. Jennifer swirled the ice and pulled an orange Gator Ade from the frigid ice, water mixture.

"You said lemon lime right?" she asked peering into the bin.

"Yeah but orange is fine if....

"No I know there's one in here somewhere." She gave the ice another grinding swirl. "Ah, there you are you little devil." She said triumphantly raising the elusive drink in a cascade of cold crystalline water. She took two plastic cups and scooped ice from yet another bin and set them beside the drinks.

"Wally?" She asked.

"You have another one of those?" He inquired pointing to the Gator Ade.

She pursed her lips into a frown of mild irritation.

"I'll have a Lemonade," he recanted quickly.

Her smile returned and she withdrew a can of lemonade from the icy depths. She set the can aside and shook the water and chill from her hand.

"You want anything to drink, Mr. Melton?" She called to the solitary figure on the tee.

"What?"

"Would......you......like......something......to...... drink?" She repeated in a halting, monotone voice.

"Uh......Um......An......Ice......Tea......Please." He answered in kind.

"Hey!" D.I. protested, "How come you call him mister?"

"I respect him!"

"Ouch!" Vince cried clutching his chest, "Somebody pull this dagger from my heart."

Jennifer handed Wally his lemonade. "You want ice?" She asked.

"No thank you."

"Do you want ice... Mister Melton?" She cooed to Barney as he made his way toward the cart.

"Ow!" Vince groaned weakly.

"Please." Barney nodded while pulling a rumpled twenty from his front pocket.

"I'll get these," he said.

"It's already taken care of." Jennifer said.

"What? Who?" Barney asked.

"One of the ladies ahead of you." She replied pointing down the fairway. "I just have to take her change back."

"Well let me get something for you," Barney said turning toward his cart.

"Taken care of." Jennifer said.

Barney turned and stared blankly for a moment.

"Which one was it?" He asked.

"I don't know her name," Jennifer conceded, "I've seen her out here before......she's the one with the real pretty hazel eyes. Real sweet lady."

"Stella!" Barney said in a hushed voice.

"You know her?"

"We just met today."

"You must have made quite an impression." Jennifer smiled.

Barney blushed slightly in an "aw shucks" fashion.

"The man's a hound." Vince said.

Jennifer giggled, "I think it's sweet," she said, "want me to take her a message?"

Barney froze.

"Well?" Jennifer asked.

"Just tell her... Thank you."

"That's it? You don't want to tell her something a little more personal?" She asked.

"Thank you......very much." Barney offered feebly.

"We need to hone his wooin' skills." Vince said apologetically.

"You think?" Jennifer asked in astonishment.

"You're a woman," Wally said, "make something up. Something you women like to hear."

"You guys are pathetic," Jennifer said in disgust, "you would think after all these years, you would know what women want."

"You'd think," Wally said, "but?"

All four men stood with blissful ignorance shining from their faces.

"We haven't got a clue."

Jennifer got in her cart and looked at them and shrugged. "I'll think of something," she said, "something with a little more passion than thank you... very much." She turned the cart around and started back down the cart path.

"Just tell her thank you," Barney called after her sensing his destiny was once again in the hands of others. "Just tell her thank you."

"You realize," D.I. said to Barney, "that you are now obligated to that woman."

"Jennifer?"

"No you idiot! What's her name...St...Stella."

"You're a kept man, Barney Melton." Vince said.

Barney looked down the fairway. The ladies had disappeared around the dogleg. He watched helplessly as the drink cart with its messenger and unknown message tracked after them.

The fourteenth hole, a dogleg right par four, requires a long and accurate tee shot down the right hand side if a player has any hope of reaching the green in two. This means flirting with a stand of tall trees at the corner. A long tee shot left of center is in danger of running through the fairway and into the water that runs along the left side of the fairway from the dogleg to the green.

Wally's tee shot started down the center, faded right and disappeared behind the trees at the corner. Several tattletale leaves fluttered a warning as they floated down from the area where the ball had disappeared. Wally turned to the others who stood with expressions of total non-commitment.

"I think you'll be okay." Barney said trying to sound convincing.

"It just barely nicked a branch but I think it was long enough to get around the corner." Vince agreed.

"You never know." D.I. said bending to tee his ball, "It's a game of inches."

"If it made it," Wally said hopefully, "it should be real good."

"Twas a magnificent shot." Barney commended.

D.I. pushed his tee ball toward the trees.

"Get through!" he begged hoping the ball would somehow pick its way through the maze of branches and find the fairway on the other side.

"I didn't hear it hit anything." Vince offered.

"Me neither," Barney added.

"Game of inches." Wally said with a smirk.

"Touche'," D.I. said while fetching his tee.

Vince moved forward to hit next.

"I hate this hole," he said with meaning, "I'll bet I can count the times I've reached in regulation on one hand."

"If it's no more than two," D.I. teased.

"Don't you start that crap again," Vince warned, "or I'll......"

"You'll what?" D.I. challenged.

"I'll......I'll give you two of these." Vince held up a tightly clinched fist, narrowed his eyes and pursed his lips.

"What are you gonna do, smother me with those pillows?" D.I. quipped.

"Float like a butterfly, sting like a bee." Vince said shaking his fist at D.I.

"A shot of Raid will cure that," D.I. jabbed, "hit the ball already."

Vince went into his most deliberate, make D.I. fume, pre-shot routine. He wiggled, he waggled. He stood motionless over the ball for an extended period then backed off. He looked at D.I. to assess the effectiveness of his tactics.

D.I. felt a tightening in his chest. "You were obviously a sloth in a previous life." He said unable to bridle his impatience.

Vince smiled with satisfaction then sent his drive drawing dangerously close to the water.

"Get down!" He implored

"Get back up again!" D.I. urged.

The ball bounced and disappeared over a mound just short of the water.

"I don't know," Barney said, "it might be wet."

Vince shrugged, "Whatever." He said trying not to feed D.I.'s gloat, "I hit it good."

Barney's tee shot split the middle and was long enough to flirt with the lake at the outside of the dogleg. A long sigh of relief oozed from him when his ball remained visible at the end of it's roll.

"That was close," D.I. said turning for the carts, "hope you don't have to stand in the lake to hit your next shot."

"Hey, as long as it's dry!" Barney answered with a smile of contentment.

As the two carts chased after the four tee balls, the drink cart with Jennifer at the helm, rounded the corner and proceeded up the path on a near collision course. Barney hoped Wally would pull the cart onto the fairway and proceed to his ball thus avoiding any further discussion of Stella's generosity and the subsequent *thank you* debacle. He was appreciative of Stella's generosity and he hoped that he was the reason for her thoughtfulness. He also wished she hadn't painted him into this obligated corner.

"Let's go see if we can find Vince's ball." Barney prodded, hoping Wally would veer left and across the fairway to where Vince's ball had disappeared.

"Don't you want to hear what Jennifer told Stella?"

Barney's stomach performed a twisting two and a half somersault.

Barney's pucker string drew taut. He did want to hear what Stella said, but not from Jennifer. Not in front of three guys hungry for badger fodder. Barney watched helplessly as Jennifer pulled along side. He forced a weak smile through his fear and embarrassment.

Jennifer didn't bring the cart to a complete stop. She skillfully feathered the throttle to keep the rough idling engine alive.

"Everything's cool." She said with a thumbs up motion. She mashed the accelerator to the floor, the engine hesitated, belched a cloud of dark smoke into the air then propelled the cart up the hill.

Wally looked like a child whose first lick had toppled his double dip, ice cream into the hot sand.

"That's it?......everything's cool?" Wally called after the accelerating cart, but his words were beaten down by the rumbling exhaust.

Jennifer had delivered Barney from the lion's den and he prayed a blessing upon her for her discretion and tact. She had effectively defused a bomb in the hands of three Amour Terrorists. His mood lightened and his body relaxed like a spent rubber band.

"I can't believe it," Wally objected, "she hung you out to dry."

"Looks like you're the one left hanging." Barney answered.

"How can you say that? Don't you understand? Things were said on your behalf and you have no idea what it was or the response there to. This is a potential booby trap... a landmine waiting to blow your foot right into your mouth."

Barney sat for a moment thinking about what Wally had said. He began to see the logic in Wally's reasoning. That in itself frightened him. His head began to throb. All this posturing, all this maneuvering to gain some perceived romantic advantage was beginning to wear on him.

D.I. and Vince veered right to search for D.I.'s ball. Wally and Barney continued down the cart path.

"There's a ball right in the middle," Barney said as they rounded the dogleg.

Wally pulled the cart along side the ball and peered down, "Yep, that's my little darlin'."

"That sure came out good didn't it?" Barney said.

"Yes it did!"

Wally turned the cart back towards the woods.

"Did you find it?" He called.

"We got it," Vince called, "but he doesn't like it."

Wally swung the cart toward the mound that Vince's ball had gone over and the two men started searching the deep rough between the fairway and the lake. Barney got out of the cart and began probing the shoreline while Wally continued searching the backside of the mound.

"Got it!" Wally announced using his hat to mark the balls' location.

They heard the sound of a club striking ball and turned to see D.I.'s ball scooting through the right hand rough and into the fairway a few yards past Wally's ball.

"Nice out!" Wally called into the woods, but there was no response.

"He's not a happy camper." Barney assumed as D.I. stomped his way back to the cart.

All the time spent looking for balls and punching out had given the ladies ample time to hole out. Barney watched their carts cross the lake and climb the hill to the fifteenth tee. His emotional state confused him.

Vince let out a grunt of displeasure when he saw how deeply his ball had settled into the rough.

He walked to the cart and selected what appeared to be a long iron and returned to where the ball lay hidden. He tossed Wally the hat he had used to mark the ball's location and took his stance.

Wally and Barney looked at each other in puzzlement over the club selection but said nothing. Barney glanced at D.I. who just gave a "whatever" shrug.

Vince took a mighty swing. The long grass wrapped around the hozzle causing the clubface to close abruptly, which in turn, plopped the ball dead left and into the water.

"I hate this hole!" Vince bellowed as he pounded his club back into the rough to remove the residual grass.

"You should have used a more lofted club and played back to the fairway," Barney instructed.

"Why didn't you tell me that before?" Vince asked in irritation.

"Would you have listened?"

"Probably not." Vince conceded.

"Well, there you go then," Barney concluded.

"Now what?" Vince asked.

"Well...you have three choices," Barney said, "you can drop another ball where you are, drop anywhere along the line of flight, which wasn't much, or two club lengths from where the ball crossed the hazard, no closer to the hole."

Vince looked for an area that offered him the most relief within the confines of his options. He finally settled on a spot two club lengths from the hazard. He dropped a ball and his shoulders dropped when the ball buried itself in the rough. Exasperation set his jaw and he thrashed at the ball with the same club he had used on his last shot, with like results.

"This blankety-blank-blanking hole," Vince hollered using all of his New Jersey blue adjectives for descriptive color.

"Vince," Wally said, "you need to get your head in the game and your ego out."

"Aw what do you know, Ferguson?" Vince snapped, "I'm done with this hole give me an eight or whatever, I don't care."

"There's a difference between an open mind and an empty one." Wally muttered, "But thanks for listening."

Barney, despite being in the rough, had a pretty good lie, an actuality that didn't escape Vince who sat slouched behind the steering wheel, arms folded tightly across his chest. Only a white lily could make him look more pitiful.

Barney played a beautiful five wood to the front of the green and Wally's four iron faded right ending up pin high and twenty feet right of the flag. D.I.'s third shot found the bunker short right. He said nothing, returned his club to his bag and slumped into the cart beside the slouching Vince. The cart slowly moved off dragging an aura of gloom along with it. Vince's arms remained folded and the cart steered itself in a sweeping arc toward the lake. The two sullen golfers appeared content to end their despair in healing waters. Vince's right arm raised and jerked the wheel to the right and the cart swerved back to the fairway. Vince's arm flopped lifelessly back to his chest and the cart began another lazy loop back to the lake.

"Looks like the pity wagon needs an alignment," Wally observed with a chuckle.

"Yeah," Barney answered, "they're both heading for the bummer tent and when Vince gets like that there's no reasoning with him."

"I know, I shouldn't say anything but I can't help myself."

"Not to worry," Barney consoled, "one good thing about Vince is, he forgets very quickly."

"Hey, we all do."

As if on cue, Vince straightened in his seat, grabbed the wheel with both hands and steered a direct course to the cart path. He dropped D.I. off near the bunker and drove the cart around to the parking area behind the green. He bounded from the cart and fetched a rake from behind the bunker. D.I. hit a good sand shot to within three feet. Vince dutifully raked the trap then hurried to tend the pin for Barney's long lag putt, which came up five feet short.

"You can pull it for me." Wally requested while executing a quick plumb-bob.

"It didn't break one iota," Wally whined as his putt stopped six inches right of the hole, "I hit it right where I wanted to, too. Stupid ball didn't break." Wally walked over and one handed the ball into the cup for his par.

"Nice par," Vince said with meaning.

"Thanks."

Barney grimaced when his five-foot par putt refused to drop and he had to settle for a three putt five.

Vince talked D.I.'s three-foot bogey putt into the cup.

"That's one good bogey," he said waiting for D.I. to retrieve his ball so he could place the flag stick in the hole.

"It was, wasn't it?" D.I. agreed with a smile.

The two men walked off the green in gleeful conversation.

"Man!" Barney whispered to Wally, "That's was one humongous mood swing."

"Times two." Wally added.

HOLE	10	11	12	13	14	15	16	17	18	Out	Total
PAR	4	4	3	5	4	4	8	4	5	36	72
YRDS	380	340	154	495	396	362	156	398	497	3178	6324
D.I.	5	6	2	5	5						
Vince	9	5	3	5	8						
Wally	5	4	3	4	4						
Barney	4	6	4	5	5						

15

Vince sat hunched over the scorecard while entering the scores from the fourteenth hole.

"Let's see...D.I. had a very impressive five, the pencil recording the five in the appropriate space, "I had the dreaded and depressing... snowman," the pencil slowly traced two perfect circles one on top of the other then added an inverted smiley face, "Wally you had a..."

"Par!" Wally answered quickly and proudly.

"Nice four, Ferguson," Vince praised while the lead deposited a neat numeral four on the scorecard, "and the Deputy had a five, right?"

"Yeah, a three putt five," Barney sulked.

"Just the score," Vince admonished, "no commentary, there's no place on the scorecard for excuses or explanations, just the facts man."

"Five, five, five," Barney blurted out in rapid succession.

"Got it," Vince said impatiently, pulling back from the scorecard to admire his handy work.

"Oh, and Ferguson gets another skin," he said bending forward again to record the fifty cent dot next to Wally's score.

Vince sat back in the seat and looked over at D.I. who sat mutely staring off into the distance.

"Man that Jennifer is quite a looker isn't she?" Vince said expecting an immediate and enthusiastic response.

D.I. looked over but said nothing.

"And Melissa...... she's no slouch either," Vince continued, "I mean when you think about it, all the cart girls are really good looking...... don't ya think?"

"Tom's no dummy," D.I. stated flatly, "he knows the quickest way to extract a dollar from a man's wallet is with a pretty smile and a nice pooper."

"You got that right," Vince agreed.

"I wonder why that is?" Wally asked.

"Geeze Ferguson, if you don't know, I ain't gonna tell ya." Vince groaned.

"No I mean it," Wally persisted, "why should four old farts like us, with one foot in the grave and the other on a banana peel, go all ga-ga over these attractive young ladies?"

"Because we ain't dead yet?" Vince cracked.

Wally looked at Vince. "Do you really think a girl like Jennifer would actually go for an old goat like you?"

"Of course not!" Vince said, "Besides, they start it by flirting with us. They know we're harmless old coots, and we know nothing will come of it so it's just an innocent flirtation. Although, I can understand how a young and impressionable, innocent girl like Jennifer might be enamored by the old Denevi charm."

"Enamored?" D.I. snickered, "Nauseated would be more like it." D.I. paused then quickly added, "Is there such a thing as an innocent young girl these days."

"One can only hope." Vince said.

"Well what if a girl like Jennifer did become enamored with you, Vince?" Wally asked, "What would you do? Would you pursue it?"

Before Vince could answer, D.I. interjected, "It would be a death sentence."

"What do you mean?" Vince asked.

"Trying to keep up with a young thing like Jennifer would more than likely kill you, and if she didn't, Tiffany most certainly would."

Vince thought for a second, "Yeah you're right, I'd be a dead man," he fought back the urge to recite the old man's cliché, "yeah but it would take a week for the undertaker to pry the smile off my face."

"Then why do we act like we want something like that to happen?" Wally questioned, "I mean we're happily married, we're older than dirt, and we couldn't handle it if, by some strange abomination, a girl like Jennifer did fall for the old Denevi charm."

"It would be the end of civilization as we know it," D.I. said sadly, "up would be down, right would be wrong and hippopotami would fly. All the centuries of reason and rational thought would be rendered senseless, chaos would reign."

"I don't think we have to worry," Wally said, "there's no form of dementia or level of depravity that could cause a young woman to stoop so low."

"Hey!" Vince complained, "I'm beginning to feel a little offended here."

Barney put an arm on Vince's shoulder.

It's not your fault," he consoled, "it's just one of those guy things. It's like being a gelding with a stallion's libido. An old coot with an adolescent's ego. It's the Dirty Old Man Syndrome."

"Oh no you don't Melton!" Vince cried, "We're not going through another one of your hair brained theories.

"Not a theory," Barney persisted, "It's a fact!"

"So you know all about the Dirty Old Man Syndrome?" D.I. asked.

"Oh please don't feed the animals," Vince pleaded.

"Well," Wally said, "I'm curious to find out why we have this compulsion to captivate every woman we meet, when in reality, we have no need, nor are we in a position to pursue a relationship."

"Somebody shoot me now." Vince moaned, "or better yet, somebody shoot the Deputy."

"It will please me to enlighten those who seek knowledge," Barney said holding his hands in guru fashion and bowing slightly. He looked up and noticed that the ladies had hit their second shots and had cleared the fairway.

"But first," he said, "we must purge our minds of all thought, a redundancy in Denevi's case, by striking a small orb with a large stick. I believe you have the honors, Mr. Ferguson."

Hole number fifteen, a straight away par four, plays from an elevated tee, across a small creek, to a fairway that rises abruptly to about the same elevation as the tee. A tee shot of two hundred yards or more would reach the plateau near the one fifty marker. Anything short of that, would die into the up slope and leave a long and blind second shot.

"Get up!" Wally coaxed, as his ball landed just short of the crest and clung to the bank like a grape on a vine.

D.I. hit next and his ball cleared the slope, kicked hard left and ran into the left-hand rough.

"What the heck did that hit?" He wondered aloud.

"Must of hit a sprinkler head or something," Barney suggested as he prepared to play his tee shot.

"What the...?" Barney questioned when his ball popped high into the air. "Carry! Carry!" he implored as the ball began descending toward the creek not more than a hundred yards off the tee. Barney turned to the others.

"Did that go in?" He asked.

"I never saw it bounce," Wally said, "I think it might of plugged on the other side."

"I think it went in the creek." D.I. surmised.

"I'm pretty sure it cleared the creek," Vince said, "but not by much."

"Think I should hit another?"

"Might be a good idea. If it did go in the creek it's a goner and the chances of finding it in that mush on the other side are slim to none."

Barney backed off the tee to allow Vince to hit. Vince's ball bounded onto the right hand side of the plateau and rolled another twenty yards.

"Nice ball," Barney said stepping forward to hit his provisional.

"Thanks."

Barney's ball rocketed off the club and cleared Vince's ball on the fly.

"Don't take it out on me," Vince protested.

"Geeze Melton, you crushed that one." D.I. said, "was there a little anger in that swing?"

"Just a tad." Barney admitted with wry smile.

"When I grow up, I wanna be just like you." Wally quipped.

"Don't set your goals so high." Barney cautioned. "It will only lead to disappointment."

The two carts crossed the small bridge to the other side of the creek and turned onto the fairway and proceeded to a point along the line of Barney's first ball. The area between the creek and fairway was a low-lying marsh. The four men walked along the edge looking for any sign of Barney's ball.

"Forget it" Barney said after a short time, "Even if we find it, it will be un-playable."

They turned to their carts and climbed the steep hill to Wally's ball, which was close enough to the crest to afford a view of the green. The ladies were milling around and in no apparent hurry to putt out.

"Okay, O learned Swami," D.I. said to Barney, "enlighten us."

A whimper escaped Vince's throat.

"I sense skepticism and impatience here, Grasshopper," Barney said solemnly, "truth can not penetrate the wall of doubt and ignorance."

"Speak already!" D.I. commanded.

Barney propped his feet up on the dash of the cart, clasped his hand behind his head and leaned back into the seat.

"Dirty Old Man Syndrome," Barney began, "or DOMS, is an affliction that strikes a whopping ninety three percent of all males over the age of sixty. Symptoms may vary greatly from individual to individual, but generally speaking, the severity of symptoms is directly proportional to age. Indeed, some victims may exhibit no outward symptoms at all, while others may be completely consumed by the disease.

On the mild side, symptoms could be as insignificant as a heightened appreciation of the feminine form, speech containing moderate sexual innuendo or a mild lusting within the heart. More severe symptoms are sexually explicit and crude language, wanton ogling, and lewd and lecherous behavior."

Barney stopped and looked at Vince.

"What are you looking at me for?" Vince asked defensively.

Barney shook his head then posed this question, "What causes DOMS?"

Not getting nor expecting a reply, Barney went on.

"Well there are two trains of thought on this. One over simplification adheres to the sentiments expressed in an old country and western song, 'All women look beautiful at closing time."

Barney scanned his playing partners.

"Gentlemen, we're nearing closing time and it's our last call."

He paused for effect but got none.

"I tend to believe," he proceeded, "that DOMS is much more complex than that. Although, the closing time analogy could very well be a contributing factor."

A recent study, published in the American Journal of Medicine, concluded that DOMS is the direct results of three major factors: *exposure, attitude and longevity*. Let's define each and then, we can discuss their relationship to Dirty Old Men. Let's start with *exposure*. Now what do we mean by *exposure*?"

"Oh, inform us old wise and ancient one." Vince panned.

"Well," Barney said, "the average American male is exposed to hundreds of visual sexual stimuli each day. TV, movies, magazine, all vie for our attention by parading a virtual cornucopia of sultry, lip licking vixens with unkempt locks cascading into cavernous canyons of cleavage. Human Barbi Dolls jiggle about in flimsy outfits of translucent fabrics measured not in yards but millimeters and they speak to our basest instincts."

Barney stopped momentarily to wipe small beads of perspiration from his brow. Vince reached for his cup of ice while D.I. and Wally sat transfixed in their seats. Barney took a quick drink of his ice tea.

"Young women today," he resumed, not wanting to lose his audience, "walk around attired in the most provocative of fashion. I mean these days, any self-respecting hooker dresses more conservatively than your average teenager. So you know what I mean about exposure. Now, what about *attitude*?"

"What about *attitude*?" Vince echoed.

"Well I'll tell you."

"As I knew you would."

"The study concludes," Barney continued, "that Hollywood's influence on society's sexual attitude has been much greater than the industry would have us believe. In fact, the study names the entertainment industry as the single most significant force in molding and mutating our moral code. The study found, that the industry's emphasis on sexual content and their glamorization of promiscuity and other deviant lifestyles, without the counter weight of moral responsibility, has surreptitiously inflated the importance of sex in the collective mind of American society."

Barney took a quick breath.

"And what, you may ask, does *longevity* have to do with the price of tea in China?"

Vince simply waved a hand in resigned acquiescence and Barney continued on with out missing a beat.

"*Longevity* is a double edged sword affecting both the mental and physical aspects of male sexual orientation. Mental sexuality in the male of the species, is pretty much set during puberty and changes little during the remainder of his life. Physically however, the male peaks early and begins a gradual, sometimes imperceptible, decline. This ever widening gap between the mental and physical sides of male sexuality causes an imbalance within the sexual-being thus creating conflict, confusion and dementia. Generally speaking, the longer a man lives the greater the imbalance, consequently, the more agitated, confused and demented he becomes. In layman terms, our sexual mind simply outlives our sexual bodies. Because we have been programmed to be the sexual aggressor and because of our natural instinct to propagate, and because procreating is so darn enjoyable, we just don't know when to quit.

A peripheral but important side affect of *longevity* is the clashing of moral values. Moral values and sexual attitudes are formed early in life and as we age we witness a loosening of the moral code. These changes clash with what we were brought up to believe as right and proper, this in turn, further compounds our sense of frustration and confusion.

Now when we throw in a sense of urgency such as the closing time scenario, we have a recipe for debauchery. In our confusion, we may feel we have been cheated. We may have an unrealistic notion as to what is right and acceptable. We might feel we need to make up for lost time before our last call has evaporated.

As you can see, the combined forces of *exposure, attitude, longevity* and urgency can destroy and old geezer's perversion immune system thus rendering him a Dirty Old Man.........Questions?"

"Have you been smoking some of that wacky tabacky, again?" Vince asked.

"Does your therapist know you think like this?" D.I. wanted to know.

"Where can I get a copy of that study?" Wally requested seriously.

"Ferguson!" D.I. croaked in laughter, "Wake up and smell the Maalox. There's no study, it's all a figment of Melton's acute dementia."

Wally looked at Barney with a puzzled expression.

"No study?"

Barney shook his head.

"Really?"

Barney nodded.

"Geeze, you could of fooled me." Wally admitted.

"Apparently, he did," Vince said with a chuckle.

"It all made sense to me," Wally mused.

"That should have been your first clue." Vince said.

"No, I mean it. Mentally I feel the same as I did when I was twenty and the physical decline does cause an imbalance and I do tend to think of sex more often and......"

"Hit the ball!" someone shouted from the tee behind them.

The four men had been so engrossed in conversation, they had failed to notice that the ladies had cleared the green and the group behind was growing impatient.

"Yeah, yeah, keep you knickers on." D.I. mumbled as he drove the cart to the right and towards Vince's ball.

"How far do you think it is?" Wally asked, hand posed above his bag waiting to determine which club to pull.

"You've got about one eighty," Barney gauged by eye, "but with that up hill lie, it's going to come up on you so you'd better use one more club."

Wally pulled the club and hastily hit a shot that flew high and straight but landed just short of the putting surface.

"You were right," Wally said, "I should have hit an extra club."

"Have I ever lied to you?" Barney asked.

Wally shot Barney a wrathful glare.

"A recent study in the American Journal of Medicine......" he muttered in a mocking manner.

"Oh yeah, well besides that?" Barney said sheepishly. "But I'd never intentionally lie to you about distance and club selection."

"That's very comforting."

"Ohhh Yeah!" Vince whooped when his crisp iron shot stopped pin high and fifteen feet left of the hole.

"Nice shot!" Barney called as the two carts crossed paths in the middle of the fairway. Vince performed an abbreviated fist pump out the side of the cart as it sped towards D.I.'s ball.

D.I. caught a flier from the rough and his ball scooted off the back of the green like a cat with a turpentined butt.

Barney lifted his fourth shot high in the air and it landed as softly as a butterfly with sore feet, just a foot below the hole.

"Pretty." Wally said as Barney tamped down his divot with the sole of his club.

"Thanks." Barney responded automatically and without enthusiasm. He wished the short putt remaining was for birdie instead of bogey.

The four men, not wanting to be a factor in the slow pace of play, hurried to the green. Wasting little time with golf etiquette, they quickly embraced the virtues of ready golf. D.I. pitched from behind the green and before his ball had come to rest, Wally's chip shot rolled past it in the opposite direction, struck the pin, bounced six inches straight up and fell into the hole. All motion stopped.

"That's a birdie?" Wally shrieked in surprise.

"Now that's, an ugly." Vince said.

"You'd better make your putt," D.I. warned, "or Wally gets three dots."

"Well thanks for the added pressure, numb-nuts." Vince snapped.

"Hey, I'm rootin' for ya." D.I. explained.

"You'd root for Hitler if it would save you fifty-cents!"

When Barney pulled the pin a hush fell over the green. Vince lined up the birdie putt then stroked it toward the hole. The ball skirted the left side and wound up six inches directly behind the hole.

"Nice read, Magoo." D.I. scolded.

"Nice par." Barney said playing a perfect foot wedge back to Vince who casually scooped the ball into the air with the back of his putter and caught it with his free hand.

"Whoa," Barney commended, "very impressive motor skills for a………Dirty Old Man."

"Thank you on both counts." Vince said with a vain smile.

"Bad word! Bad word!" D.I. grumbled when his par putt stopped just short of the hole.

Barney tapped D.I.'s ball back to him then tapped his short putt in for his bogey. The four men walked quickly off the green.

"That was an all American bogey, Melton." D.I. said when they reached the carts.

"Would have been a better birdie." Barney complained, "But you're right, I'm lucky to be getting out of here with a five."

"What happened to those guys who were in such an all fired hurry to hit?" Vince asked looking back down the fairway, "I don't see them anywhere."

"They're probably back by the creek looking for balls." Wally guessed.

"I don't think they're very good players." D.I. supposed, "Look how long it took them to catch up with us. I mean we've been held up all day so how fast can they be? If they can't wait a little on the last few holes, screw 'em!"

"You're not going to create another scene are you?" Barney asked.

"Me?" D.I. answered in false surprise, "I don't create scenes, I end 'em and quickly exit stage right."

"Yeah, and hurry to your dressing room for a quick change of shorts." Vince added.

HOLE	10	11	12	13	14	15	16	17	18	Out	Total
PAR	4	4	3	5	4	4	8	4	5	36	72
YRDS	380	340	154	495	396	362	156	398	497	3178	6324
D.I.	5	6	2	5	5	5					
Vince	9	5	3	5	8	4					
Wally	5	4	3	4	4	3					
Barney	4	6	4	5	5	5					

16

The four men encountered the typical par three backup when they arrived at the sixteenth tee. Stella had once again positioned herself at the ball washer. Barney once again seized the moment.

"Thank you for the drinks, that was very generous of you." He said as he approached her.

"My pleasure," she answered with a smile. She looked into his eyes. "The cart girl relayed your most thoughtful and endearing message."

A jolt of panic momentarily incapacitated Barney as Wally's words of warning echoed in his mind. What had Jennifer told her? How should he respond?

As the seconds stumbled by, Stella's, warm expression began to cool. Barney realized he would have to try and bluff his way through this uncertainty.

"Well you know," he said nonchalantly, "what can I say.........I mean it's the least I could say."

Confusion clouded her face. "Damn," he thought, Wally was right, what had Jennifer told her? How can I respond to the unknown. He tried to read her expression but came up blank. He quickly changed direction.

"So......how's your game holding up?" He asked brightly, hoping to veer away from the verbal potholes, which lay before him.

She frowned and stared at him through suspecting eyes.

Barney could feel the noose of deceit tighten around his neck.

"Barney?" She asked, "You did mean what you said didn't you?"

"Just now?" He asked in a futile evasion maneuver.

"No, to Jennifer?" She said, her suspicion growing.

"Every word!" he rationalized, knowing that he had indeed meant every word when he told Jennifer to ... thank her... thank her very much. The noose cinched ever tighter.

Barney smiled weakly. Stella looked away.

"What's wrong?" He asked.

"Nothing!" She answered tersely. She turned towards the tee, "I'd better go." She said dejectedly and she walked away.

The floor dropped out from under him leaving him dangling from the gallows of failed deception. Any attempt at explanation strangled by the weight of his embarrassment. His blender instantly whipped guilt, hurt, confusion and anger into a pill that was just too bitter for him to swallow. He reacted in true masculine fashion.

"I don't need this!" He said to himself, trying to convince himself that it was he who had been wronged. He was the innocent victim of a woman's overreaction to words he knew nothing about. "Damn it." What was it that Jennifer had said to her? And what did he say that caused the whole thing to blow up in his face?

"I'm too old for this kind of aggravation." He told himself, "To hell with her!"

Barney stomped back towards the carts.

"Trouble in paradise?" D.I. inquired as Barney passed by.

"Stuff it Iverson!" Barney snapped.

D.I. looked at Vince with a wide-eyed "Whoa" look on his face. Vince got out of his cart and walked back to where Barney was throwing himself into the seat next to Wally.

"Man you really called it, Wally," Barney huffed, "I'm toast!"

"What happened?" Vince asked.

"Damned if I know," Barney said shaking his head, "She asked me if I meant what I told Jennifer, and when I told her every word, she went all moody on me and walked away."

Vince looked at Wally then back to Barney.

"What we have here is a simple failure to communicate." He said lightly, "We can have all this all cleared up in no time flat."

"Don't bother!" Barney grumbled.

"Now don't let one little misunderstanding limit your possibilities. You can't afford to ignore opportunity when it comes a knockin'. Besides, it's way too early in the relationship to just let it go. You really don't know each other. You could be throwin' away a new life, a shot at true happiness."

"My life is just fine...thank you very much." Barney fumed.

"Oh really, like layin' around dreamin' about magnets and dirty old men is an existence we all strive for. You have a shot at companionship and all that comes with it." Vince placed a hand on Barney's shoulder. Barney looked up. "And all that comes with it." Vince repeated it with a wink.

"Yeah right!" Barney mumbled.

"You know what I'm hearin' here?" Vince asked, "I'm hearin' wounded pride. I'm hearin' the pathetic cry of a bruised ego, that's what I'm hearin'. Are you really gonna let this little misunderstanding jeopardize your future? Come on Melton, shed the pity boots and get your feet wet. Swallow your bitter pride and taste the sweet fruits of life. Do something even if it's wrong! Let the possibilities fly."

"I don't know......" Barney began but D.I.'s authoritarian voice interrupted.

"Look Barney," D.I. said, "you did a typical guy thing. You tried to fake your way around something rather than admit you didn't know what was going on. We'll tell a lie even when the truth sounds better.

"That's because if we tell 'em the truth, they'll hurt us." Vince said.

"No it's not!" D.I. scolded, "We like to appear as if we know everything so, rather than tell 'em the truth and appear a little ignorant, we get caught in a red faced lie and look totally stupid. I don't know why we do it, but we must derive some form of perverted satisfaction 'cause we keep doin' it over and over and over again. We have this gross misconception that women are gullible and they'll believe anything we tell 'em. Women have this intuition thing that picks up lies faster than Denevi can down a cannoli. Women place a high premium on honesty and they'll nip the buds off your blooming relationship before it has a chance to bear fruit."

Vince looked over at D.I. "Who said that? Who are you and what have you done with D.I.?" He asked.

"Can it Denevi, I'm on your side."

"I repeat, who are y........."

D.I. interrupted before Vince could finish.

"Look, as much as I hate to admit it, I'd hate to see ol' Barney miss out on a chance at ......at......you know..."

"Love!" Vince injected impatiently, "Amour, Zip-iddy-do-dah."

Barney looked over at Wally who remained mute.

"Well?" Barney asked him, "how do you think I should run my life?"

"Well that's entirely up to you," Wally answered, "but since you asked.........I'm with them."

"Then it's unanimous," Barney said looking to the ladies tee.

The ladies seemed to be holding a confab of their own. They stood huddled on the tee, Stella looking like a quarterback receiving instructions for the last play of the Super Bowl. She shot a pleading glance in Barney's direction.

"Step aside!" Barney said as he stood and brushed Vince back with a firm wave of his arm. He stood gathering his thoughts and courage. He set his jaw.

"I'm going in! Cover me!"

"Go get 'em tiger!" Vince cheered.

"Go for it!" Wally encouraged.

"Poor bastard," D.I. whispered as Barney marched off to his destiny.

When Stella saw Barney coming, she broke ranks and marched to meet him.

"I'm sorr.........," they said in unison as they approached one another.

"Look," Barney said taking charge of the conversation, "I don't know what Jennifer told you," Stella began to speak but Barney continued unabated.

"I don't know and I don't want to know. The words didn't come from me and they weren't mine. I simply wanted Jennifer to thank you but," Barney threw a thumb over his shoulder in the direction of the three men watching intently from the white tee, "the public relations firm of Busybody, Meddlesome & Buttinski, didn't think that was sufficient so they hired Jennifer to lobby on my behalf. I'm sorry. I should hav......"

"No!" Stella interrupted, "You needn't apologize, I, unfortunately, employ a similar firm." She thrust a thumb over her shoulder towards the three curious ladies watching from the red tee.

Barney laughed a hardy laugh and Stella joined him. Barney turned to look at his friends who were smiling and offering thumbs up applause. He turned back to Stella and they both looked at the ladies in waiting who were performing subdued low fives and nodding mutual agreement.

"Well," Stella said, "looks like we have made everybody happy."

"Appears so." Barney agreed, "Are you happy?" He asked scanning her face.

"Ecstatic!" she replied with sparkling eyes, "And you?"

"D-e-e-e-lighted!" he answered with emphasis.

They stood silent for a moment, then Barney's expression took on a more somber tone.

"If I had told Jennifer more, she would only have relayed the words, not their meaning not my feelings."

Stella's hand found Barney's, he squeezed it gently and blushed slightly. He couldn't believe how easy it was to talk to her. He couldn't believe the things he was saying and he suddenly wondered if he was saying too much too soon. They had just met, for crying out loud, and here he was spilling his guts and pouring out his heart. For all he knew, she could be a Gold-Digger, a Jezebel, a Black Widow or all of the above. But right now, he didn't care, he would take his chances. Time was of the essence, his life was not just fine thank you very much, there was a huge hole in it, a hole begging to be filled.

"I haven't been this open with anyone in a long time." he said quietly, "I mean we hardly know each other, yet......I know you."

His face contorted into a question.

"Do you know what I mean?" he asked hopefully.

She nodded. Emotion constricting her throat and glistening in the corners of her eyes.

"I'm sorry." he said "I didn't mean to......"

She shook her head, squeezed his hand and smiled a quivering smile.

"Yoo-hoo!" called a voice from the ladies tee.

Stella quickly brushed a moisture trail from her cheek and glanced over her shoulder. Sally pointed in the direction of the vacant green and shrugged apologetically. Stella turned back to Barney.

"I better go," she said dejectedly.

Barney nodded and reluctantly released her hand.

"We still on for the grill?" he asked.

"Well duh!" she responded in disbelief.

"I just don't want to assume anything," Barney explained, "and I don't want any more misunderstandings."

"Good thinking," she said with a flirtatious wink.

"A-hem!" came Sally's reminder.

"Duty calls." Stella said with a smile, "See you in the grill if not before." She turned and walked to join her friends. Barney watched her for a moment, then turned and floated back to the tee area where he was welcomed as a conquering hero.

"Are we to assume, from that smile on your face, that things went well?" Vince inquired.

Barney nodded.

"All is forgiven?" Wally asked.

Barney nodded then turned to D.I. who stood in stoic silence.

"Do you have anything to ask?" Barney questioned.

"Me?" D.I. answered with a noncommittal expression, "Why would I care one way or another.

"Oh listen to him," Barney said stepping toward D.I.

"Now don't do anything stupid." D.I. said with a rapid back pedal.

"Come 'ere you," Barney ordered, "why you're nothin' but a big ol' care bear in grizzly clothing."

"Melton, if you touch me I swear I'll......"

D.I.'s left heel struck the tee marker causing him to stagger backwards. As D.I. struggled to remain standing, Barney lunged to help him but couldn't reach the teetering D.I.

"Timberrr!" Vince called out as D.I.'s lanky frame began to topple backwards. D.I., realizing all hope of remaining upright was lost, buckled at the knees and twisted so as to cushion his fall with outstretched hands. The inertia of Barney's lunge caused him to lose his balance and he stumbled forward and collapsed in a heap on D.I.'s back. The force of the fall produced a guttural grunt from D.I. and a mournful groan from the Deputy.

Vince's face drained of all frivolity and Wally gasped as the mass of legs and elbows came to rest on the ground. A long anxious moment passed before Vince and Wally could move to the aid of their fallen comrades.

"Are you all right?" Vince asked, kneeling beside D.I. who lay face down beneath Barney.

"Get this moron off my back!" D.I. bellowed through a laugh.

Wally stooped to help Barney, but Barney rolled off D.I. and lay on his back laughing at the sky. Vince helped D.I. to his feet.

"Melton," D.I. said while brushing grass clipping from his clothing, "we're too old to be performing tricks like this. We could have fractured a hip or split a spleen or somethin'."

"I know." Barney agreed, "I'm sorry. You okay?"

"I'm fine. You okay?"

"What happened?" a concerned female voice asked.

Barney turned his head and shaded his eyes from the glaring sun. An angelic image stood over him, the sun highlighting her hair into a radiant halo, her face softened in shadow.

"Are you all right?" Stella asked.

Barney raised himself onto his elbows and shunted the sun's glare with a squint.

"Yeah I'm fine," he answered.

"What happened?" she asked again.

"Oh," Vince began, "ol' Barn and D.I. were involved in a tumbling accident. I'd score 'em pretty high on technical merit but their artistic interpretation needs a lot of work."

Barney scrambled to his feet and quickly brushed himself off. He could feel the heat of embarrassment flush his face.

"Just a little male horse play run amuck." Barney explained weakly. "I'm fine."

"You sure?"

Yeah."

The sixteenth plays 156 yards from an elevated tee, across a small meandering creek to a deep but narrow green that follows the contours of a slope running left to right and back to front. Bunkers await balls hit to the left or right. The front is open but the slope inhibits any roll on shots hit short. The creek only comes into play on exceptionally horrible shots.

"Keep your head up!" Wally implored as his ball faded toward the bunker on the right-hand side of the green. The ball landed on the fringe, took the slope and rolled toward the edge of the bunker. "Whoa! Stop right there!" He commanded but the ball rolled on defiantly. "Oh don't go in th...... Damn It!" He shouted spinning around in frustration while his ball trickled off the edge and ran to the bottom of the severely sloped trap.

"Tough break." D.I. said in a voice lacking sincerity.

Wally didn't appreciate D.I.'s lack of tact and told him so with a piercing glower.

Whether it was providence, fate or poetic justice, D.I. hit an exceptionally horrible shot, which indeed brought the creek into play.

"Look at this," he snapped, "I hit a good foot behind the ball, look at this divot."

"I thought you needed a grading permit to move that much earth." Vince mused.

"Tough break." Wally said in a voice tinged with just a hint of vengeance.

"Is it me?" Barney asked pointing a finger to his navel.

"Tis indeed!" Vince nodded.

Barney set his tee and sent a high seven iron drawing to the center of the green.

"Oh that's pretty," Vince applauded.

"Good looking shot." Wally praised.

The ball landed, took one hop and stopped dead about ten feet short of the pin.

"That was really a smooth swing," Wally cooed.

"Thanks." Barney said humbly but knowing it was the truth.

"Now I've got somethin' to shoot at," Vince said, "let's just see if I can get inside ya and steal that greenie away."

"Be my guest," Barney invited confidently.

"Well I'll be dipped," Barney cackled in amazement when Vince's ball appeared to stop just inside and right of his.

"By George, I think he's got it." Wally opined.

"Hard to tell from here," Vince said, "but it's gonna be close."

"If those hole gremlins don't mess with it." Barney said.

"That's right," Vince said, "I'd better run up there and stuff a twenty down the hole."

D.I. had returned to the carts, taken a selection of clubs and was power walking towards the creek before the others had even left the tee.

"Looks like D.I. is trying to walk off a little steam." Wally told Barney as they started down the cart path.

"Yeah, why don't you let me out down by the creek and I'll see if I can help him locate his ball. He was more concerned about his divot than he was about where the ball went. "I think I've got a good line on it."

"Be careful, he's like a wounded bear, give him a few minutes to cool down before you say anything."

Barney walked over to where D.I. stood peering into the depths of the steep banked creek. D.I. had an, I'd rather be sailing expression, on his face.

The creek was really more of an upscale drainage ditch not more than eight to ten feet across from edge to edge. It had steep grass covered banks that fell nearly five feet to a nearly flat creek bed.

"I had it right in line with that bare spot on the other side there." D.I, responding with a muffled grunt.

Barney began scanning as he slowly walked along the bank. He pulled up short and pointed down.

"There's a ball down there."

D.I. awoke from his trance and walked over to where Barney stood. He looked down and saw a ball laying on a small sand bar in the middle of the creek. Just a trickle of clear water wound it's way along the bottom barely wetting the bottom of the golf ball.

"You know?" D.I. stated, "I think I can get that out of there without taking a drop."

Barney looked over at D.I. whose eyes were now ablaze in hope.

"You sure?" He questioned.

"Yeah," D.I. answered confidently, "look, I've got a good stance, it's sittin' up nicely and it's far enough from the bank to get it up and out."

"I don't kn......"

"Piece of cake!" D.I. said sorting through the clubs in his hands. He selected his sand wedge, handed Barney the extra clubs, then eased himself down onto the creek bed. He stood beside the ball and surveyed his situation from ground zero.

"Looks a little different from down here," he said, slowly swinging his club to get a feel for the shot, "but I still think I can pull it off."

"Good luck." Barney said, while at the same time thinking, "Your gonna need it!"

D.I. settled over the ball. He raised up to eye the flag position then settled back. He drew the club back, slowly following it's arc, with his eyes, to ensure it cleared the bank behind him. He slowly swung the club over the ball and checked the path of the follow through. Satisfied all was in order, D.I. took his final stance. Barney drew in a deep breath and prepared himself for the tirade that was sure to follow the failed execution of such an abstruse shot.

A mist of agitated water escorted the ball above the creek bank then fell back like the first stage booster of an Atlas Rocket. The ball accelerated up and away. D.I. clambered up the opposite bank to witness his miracle. The ball reached terminal velocity, coasted to its peak, then fell softly to the green within a foot of the pin.

"Yes!" D.I. exclaimed with an enthusiastic fist pump. He climbed the last few steps to the top of the bank and stood tall. He turned and looked back across the creek. Barney paid silent homage with an arms extended bow to his most immediate idol. An idol splattered with creek bottom.

Vince had only seen D.I.'s ball land on the green. His attention had been focused on who was closest to the hole and who had won the opportunity for making greenie, birdie and winning the hole. The coveted triple dot, the duffer's hat trick. It was very close, but Vince was sure he was the closest. Wally had been occupied by his situation in the sand trap and had missed the miraculous shot all together.

"Nice shot!" Vince said automatically, not knowing the true nature of the event. Wally, still a resident of bunker oblivion, said nothing.

"Nice shot?" D.I. barked, "Geeze, I hit the shot of a lifetime and all I get is, nice shot?"

Vince looked confused.

"Shot of a lifetime? You pitched it close, it's a nice shot, what do ya want me to do.........hire a band.........declare a holiday?"

Wally looked up from the bunker to see what all the commotion was about.

"Is that your ball next to the pin D.I.?" He asked.

"Yep!" D.I. said proudly.

"Nice shot!"

"Again with the nice shot." D.I. mumbled to himself.

D.I. stomped the muck from his shoes and began gently brushing the splatter from his clothes with the back of his hand.

"Bring me a towel will ya Barn?" D.I. called back across the creek to where Barney was making his way along the bank towards the carts, "And my putter... unless you all want to concede the putt?"

"I concede nothing." Vince said belligerently, a little put out by D.I.'s narcissistic attitude.

"Looks good to me after a shot like that." Barney said.

"Yeah me to," Wally agreed, "even Vince could make a putt that close."

"Did I miss somethin'?" Vince asked Barney in bewilderment, "Why is D.I. making such a brew-ha-ha over a relatively simple pitch shot?"

"You missed something alright," Barney confirmed, "you had to see it to believe it. I would have given a million to one odds that he wouldn't even get the ball out of the creek let alone on the green."

Vince's expression changed from bafflement to astonishment. He turned to D.I.

"You hit it out of the creek?"

D.I. nodded and a smile bowed his mud freckled cheeks.

"I thought you took a drop and simply hit a nice pitch shot."

"I know," D.I. said, "I've heard nice, twice."

"Well let me amend that to fabulous, simply fabulous." Vince chirped with a prance and a limp wrist wave, "Pick it up, it's good by me, you simply exquisite savage you."

"D.I. strolled onto the green and plucked the ball from the putting surface.

Barney tossed D.I. a towel and D.I. ran the towel over his speckled face then began cleaning his ball.

"Oh crap!" He spat out dejectedly.

"What's the matter now?" Vince wondered.

"This isn't my ball," D.I. said in a tone barely audible to the others.

"Not your ball?" Vince cackled, "You mean all this hullabaloo has been over a two shot penalty?"

D.I. looked at Barney.

"You said that was my ball."

"No I didn't." Barney protested, "All I said was, there's a ball. It's up to you to identify it."

"Oh man, I don't believe this." D.I. moaned.

"Well you did play the shot out of a hazard, there's no penalty if you want to go back and play your ball, if we can find it that is."

D.I. looked back to the tee where two groups waited impatiently.

"Naugh," he sighed, "I'll just take a five."

"Hey," Barney said consolingly, "It was still a ni.....great shot."

"Yeah, and that's like puttin' whipped cream on horse poop." D.I. mumbled.

Wally blasted from the green side bunker and it took him two more to get down for his bogey. It was determined that Vince was, indeed, just inside of Barney and therefore had a chance for the one hole triple dot. Barney's birdie putt missed and he tapped in for par. Vince's three dot dream slid by on the low side and he awoke to a cruel single dot reality when his par putt could only secure the greenie and tie the hole for a carryover.

Oh, what could have been, haunted Dale Iverson and Vince Denevi as they walked off the sixteenth green.

HOLE	10	11	12	13	14	15	16	17	18	Out	Total
PAR	4	4	3	5	4	4	3	4	5	36	72
YRDS	380	340	154	495	396	362	158	398	497	3178	6324
D.I.	5	6	2	5	5	5	5				
Vince	9	5	3	5	8	4	3				
Wally	5	4	3	4	4	3	4				
Barney	4	6	4	5	5	5	3				

242

17

When the four men arrived at the tee of the difficult par four seventeenth, they could see the ladies waiting in the fairway at the bottom of the hill. Barney stared at the two distant carts and wondered if one of the occupants was going to become an important factor in his life. The possibility titillated as well as scared him. The uncertainty caused him to fluctuate between fantasy and reality. His anarchistic mind producing a wide range of lawless thoughts. His mind and emotions were in a state of chaos. He desperately searched for a certainty that would restore a sense of order.

D.I. got out of his cart, stood beside it and began rotating his shoulder in a gingerly manner. His face wore a modulated wince.

"Something wrong with your shoulder?" Barney asked.

"Yeah it doesn't feel right, like a pinched nerve or somethin'. Might have been when I fell back on sixteen."

"Geeze I'm sorry D.I. I shouldn't have......"

"Don't worry about it, it'll be fine. I get these things all the time, besides, it was an accident."

"Accident!" Vince said in a huff, "It was o-n-l-y an accident. A phrase of instant redemption, the Golden Goose of the National Bar Association, the swan song of defense attorneys everywhere. Accident my foot, if you ask me there's no such thing as an accident."

"What do you mean no such thing as an accident?" Wally questioned, "They happen all the time."

"Well things happened all the time but rarely are they true accidents." Vince answered crisply, "We only call them accidents to shirk responsibility and elude blame. Lawyers try to temper the severity of their client's actions by calling them accidents."

"Aw your full of it, Denevi." D.I. scoffed.

"Am I?" Vince countered, "How many times have you heard the phrase, the gun accidentally discharged?"

"We've all heard that," D.I. said, "So what's your point?"

"My point is," Vince mocked in agitation, "some idiot picked it up and pulled the trigger. The gun didn't discharge accidentally, it functioned just as it was designed to. Now, if a gun was layin' in a shoe box on a closet shelf and it went off, well that would be closer to an accident but more accurately, I'd call it a malfunction."

"The only malfunction around here is your brain." D.I. gibed.

"I think," Barney said, "the definition of accident is, an unexpected and unintentional event, so accidents do happen."

"Exactly!" Vince agreed, "That validates my contention."

"It does?" Barney asked, "How do you figure?"

Vince sighed heavily.

"Someone intentionally picks up a loaded gun, pulls the trigger and the expected results would be?" Vince paused and waited for Barney to finish the statement.

"The gun goes off." Barney conceded reluctantly, "But........."

"No buts about it," Vince said sternly, "this scenario doesn't satisfy either requirement of your definition. In fact, it would have been more of an accident had the gun not gone off, because that would have been unexpected. But again, we wouldn't call it an accident, we'd call it a malfunction. An unexpected malfunction not an accident."

"I see what you're trying to say but I don't accept your blanket statement of no accidents. I mean what about traffic accidents?" Barney asked.

"Ahh, traffic accidents, one of my all time favorites." Vince said, "We label them accidents yet we go to great lengths to affix blame and determine a cause. By your own definition, a true accident would have neither."

"What do you mean?" Wally piped in, "People don't drive around and intentionally run into each other."

"True," Vince agreed, "but people do intentionally speed, run lights, tailgate and more often than not, drive like idiots. When a person intentionally does these things, the expectations of crashing goes up. We now have an intentional and expected event waiting to happen."

"Well," D.I. said, "I don't know why your getting all upset. I mean, it's only a case of semantics."

"Exactly," Vince stated emphatically, "the word has been bastardized. It should be reserved for true accidents." Vince smiled at D.I., "Like the circumstances surrounding your birth."

"Why you......I oughtta," D.I. drew back as if he was going to pop Vince on the nose but the motion caused him to wince and he began rotating his shoulder again.

"That really is bothering you isn't it?" Barney said in a voice laced with concern and guilt.

"It's fine, just a little uncomfortable in certain positions. Don't worry about it."

"Geeze I feel awful about this," Barney said. "maybe you sho......"

"Maybe I should pop you in the nose right after I do Denevi, then we'll all feel better."

"You know that's true," Wally said.

"Huh?" D.I. said, surprised that the pacifistic Mr. Ferguson would condone violence. "You think I should bust 'em one?"

"No no, not that," Wally corrected, "I was referring to what Vince had said about accidental birth." Wally held out his hands in a defensive manner, "Not that I'm saying yours was accidental, but just the other day our daughter in-law confided to Doris that little Billy was an accident. Now how can they claim he was an accident when they must have done the exact same thing they did to have little Luis? What were they expecting, a rain check?"

"My point exactly!" Vince agreed, "Cause and effect. It's not that the results are unexpected, it's more that the results really aren't what we wanted."

"I get it!" Wally exclaimed, "If you pull the trigger, expect the gun to go off. If you drive recklessly, expect an acci.......... I mean expect to crash. And if you have intercourse expect to be expecting."

"Can you really call any of them unexpected, unintentional?" Vince asked smugly.

"Accidents smaccidents its all a bunch of gibberish if you ask me," Barney said turning away. "who cares?"

"I swear," D.I. sighed, "playin' golf with you three Bozos is like a trip through the looking glass and falling down a rabbit hole."

"Who's up?" Barney asked as he watched Stella and the girls head up the fairway and out of range.

"It's you or Vince," Wally said, "but it was so long ago I don't remember."

"A mind is a terrible thing to waste." Vince said, walking to the driver's side of his cart and peering down at the scorecard.

"Hmmm......well I'll be...... it's little ol' me...," he said in a voice devoid of humility.

"Geeze, talk about a true accident," D.I. mused.

Vince looked up from the card and gave D.I. a forced smile.

"Then," he continued, returning his attention to the scorecard, "it's......Barney......followed by......Wally and last, and most certainly least, D.I."

From the tee, the seventeenth hole plays downhill for roughly two hundred and fifty yards then up hill another hundred and fifty to the green. If a player's drive doesn't reach the bottom of the hill, he is left with a downhill lie and an uphill shot. To make matters worse, the uphill portion of the fairway slants from left to right. This wreaks havoc on players who move the ball left to right, i.e.... Wally Ferguson. One of the many physical laws governing the movement of a golf ball declares: A ball moving left to right striking a left to right slope, will accelerate by a factor of ten and equals a walk in the woods.

Vince pulled his driver from his bag and made his way to the tee. Wally walked beside him.

"By the way," Wally said, "I haven't wasted my mind, I've simply misplaced it."

"If that makes you feel better," Vince responded, "go with it."

Vince's tee shot found the fairway as well as the bottom of the hill. In fact all four players did the same. D.I.'s hugged the one fifty marker on the left, Wally's flirted with the right hand rough and Barney lay-in-between.

"Wow!" Vince exclaimed, "All four balls in the fairway."

"A true rarity for this group." D.I. added, as the four pleased seniors headed down the fairway in high spirits.

The spirit of mutual accomplishment reigned supreme as the men waited for the ladies to clear the green. Barney busied himself by observing the play and movements of a particular member of that group. The other three men sat silently contemplating notions of great social and spiritual significance.

Somewhere, off in the distance, came the Boom... Boom... Boom of amplified bass. Somewhere, an auto stereo system was pumping out more watts than Con Edison. As the unseen car thudded its way along an unknown route, the four men looked at each other in disbelief.

"There goes another future deaf and dumber." D.I. said.

"He's already dumb." Vince corrected.

"Yeah and he'll be deaf before he's thirty." D.I. concluded.

"Why do they have to play it so loud?" Wally questioned.

"Because they can." Barney answered, "I took my CD player into the shop the other day to have it looked at and I couldn't believe the sound systems they had."

"Noise systems," D.I. corrected.

"Whatever," Barney continued, "all I know is that the power supply looked like something out of the space shuttle and the speakers took up the whole trunk. I'll bet they lose fifty-horse power when they crank those puppies up.

"But what's the point?" Wally wondered.

"It's a status thing," D.I. said, "you know, the biggest, the best, the loudest."

"The dumbest." Vince tacked on.

"But the human ear can only handle so many decibels." Wally argued.

"Not when it's connected to a brain the size of a pea." Vince explained in jest.

"Besides," D.I. offered, "having blood clots in the inner ear creates a dampening affect."

"Well I think the whole thing is stupid," Wally huffed, "it ought to be illegal."

"It is in most states but whose gonna enforce it?" Vince reasoned.

"Geeze if it's this loud here, can you imagine what it's like to be inside that car?" Wally asked, "I mean how would you hear a siren or anything? I just don't get it."

"I think, they think, they're cool." Barney said, "And they think everybody will be impressed with their choice in music so they crank it up so everybody will know just how cool they really are."

"That's what pisses me off," Vince said, "what makes them think I want to listen to their crap anyway? I'd like to have the option of selecting my own music inside my own car but when one of those Yahoos pulls up I have no choice. I think they do it just to piss me off!"

"And they're obviously succeeding." Barney jabbed.

Vince nodded and stretched a thinned lip frown across his face.

"It doesn't happen often enough to upset me," D.I. said in an indifferent manner, "in fact, I think it's kinda funny."

"Funny?" Vince asked, "What the heck's so funny about it?"

"Oh I don't know," D.I. said, "just seein' some moron tryin' so hard to be so cool jivin' to music three times above the distortion level......it kinda strikes me as funny."

"Well they still piss me off." Vince gripped, "Self-centered little dweebs."

The last thumps of bass faded into the distance.

"Well," Barney said with a clap of his hand, "we got all that out of our systems. Now what?"

"What's with this rap music?" Wally blurted out, "Is there like only one......ah... what would you call it... it's not a song, there's no melody, is it just called a rap or what?......Anyway, they all sound the same to me. And what makes a rap star? Seems like any no talent can get up and spew out a bunch of obscenities to a primitive drum beat while someone scratching the tone arm across a record, I mean, what's with that? And why do they call it rap anyway? Sounds more like babble, should be called babble babble, if you ask me. And where do they get off calling themselves artists? Shoot, if that's art, I'm Michelangelo. And how come.........?"

"Wally, calm down, take a deep breath, you're hyperventilating." D.I. interrupted.

"Ah, I just don't get it." Wally fumed.

"I think you have to be a convicted felon to be a rap star." Vince suggested.

"And if you shoot someone," Barney offered, "you shoot yourself right to the top of the charts."

"I just don't get it," Wally complained again, "what the heck has happened to music?"

"It's just a natural progression." Barney said, "It's all relative to your generation and culture."

"Well I definitely don't relate to it!" Wally snapped, "and I wouldn't call it a progression, I'd call it a degradation."

"And that's how it should be." Barney said, "Look I don't care for it either, but hey, it's not our music."

"You got that right!" Vince concurred. "My music died with Buddy Holly and the Big Bopper."

"Exactly," Barney said, "its' the music we grew up with, it was the music we related to and if you remember correctly, it was also the music our elders called, devil music."

"But we've moved on." D.I. stated, "I mean I still like to hear some of that Ol' Time Rock and Roll, but I also like some pop, classical and even a little country now and then, but I just can't stand rap."

"And you shouldn't because it's not meant for comfortable, upper-middle class honkies like us." Barney explained.

"Well they certainly succeeded in that regard." Vince cracked, "Cause this ol' Honky Wop can't stand that crap."

"To tell you the truth," Wally added, "I find it intimidating and a little scary. I don't see much difference between rap and inciting a riot."

"That's right!" D.I. agreed, "When you have a bunch of young impressionable kids listening to a steady stream of hate and violence, you can't really be surprised when they become hateful and violent."

"Well I have to admit," Barney conceded, "the transition from Be-Bop-A-Loo-La to Gangsta Rap leaves a lot to be desired. I remember arguing with my own kids over the degradation of Heavy Metal. To me it was just amplified noise with no redeeming value whatsoever."

"I'm with you on that score," Wally said, "it just seems that popular music......or whatever they call it, is sucking us right into a sewer of depravity. Have you seen some of those music videos?"

"Music porn is more like it," D.I. said, "MTV makes the Playboy Channel look prudish. I saw Madonna on MTV defending her musical fornication as artistic expression protected under the first amendment."

"That's what I mean," Wally said, "where the hell is it going to end? Each generation has to take it further and further. What's next, snuff videos on the kill for Thrill Channel?"

"It's not just the music of today," D.I. said, "it's entertainment in general. Entertainment is going to hell in a hand basket and it's taking us all along for the ride. Any self respecting........."

Vince held out his hand in a stopping motion. "Whoa!" He said sternly, "I believe we've already had this conversation."

"We have." Barney agreed.

"We have?" D.I. questioned.

"We have!" Vince stated with conviction. "Several holes back!"

The four men looked at each other.

"So is there a law or somethin'?" D.I. asked, a little perplexed.

"Yup!" Vince affirmed.

"And what law would that be?" D.I. wondered.

"I think the law against whippin' a dead horse covers it," Barney interjected.

"That'll cover it." Vince agreed with a nod and an appreciative point at Barney for his support.

"So that's it?" D.I. asked.

"That's it! Case closed! End of conversation." Vince fired in rapid succession.

D.I. shrugged and sat back in his seat. "Geeze," he muttered, "I thought this was America. I thought I could talk about anything I wanted to. Silly me."

The men fell silent. Barney's attention returned to Stella while D.I. tried to remember the wording of the first amendment. Vince was mentally preparing arguments to rebut D.I.'s case on freedom of speech and Wally watched a squirrel scamper across the fairway.

"Am I away?" Wally asked as he walked the short distance from the cart to his ball. Vince looked to the left where D.I. stood beside his ball then back to the right to Wally. He eyed them both again, looked at D.I. and said, "Mr. Iverson.........the short knocker, is away."

D.I. ignored the tease and proceeded to hit his second shot just short of the green.

"Nice shot Ma'am." Vince heckled.

D.I. said nothing.

Wally, hoping to avoid a walk in the right-hand woods, aimed well left to compensate for his inevitable fade and the slanting fairway. It worked. His ball started left, stayed left and disappeared into the left hand woods.

"Damn it!" He cried, "Every frigging time I play my fade, it never fades?"

"You know?" D.I. said, "You ought to talk to Kenny about taking a lesson to correct that slice."

"It's not a slice, it's a fade." Wally protested.

"Whatever!" D.I. shrugged.

"Besides, Kenny charges seventy-five bucks for a half hour." Wally complained.

"Might be money well spent." Vince suggested.

Wally thought for a moment then shook his head.

"I can't see spending seventy-............"

"Then live with it!" D.I. snapped. "And stop complainin' about it. Geeze, accept it or fix it."

Wally sulked his way back to the cart.

"You were a little harsh on him weren't you?" Vince asked with unexpected compassion.

"Well he needs to do something about it, and you know as well as I do that Wally won't do anything unless you give him a swift kick in the gumption. Look at him, he looks so pathetic sittin' there but I guarantee you he's thinkin' about takin' a lesson."

Because the green was relatively flat compared to the slope of the fairway, the actual putting surface could not be seen from where the men were standing.

Barney's second shot appeared to hit the green but its exact location was unknown.

"Did that make the green?" Barney asked.

"I think so," Vince answered, "I saw it bounce once then disappear."

"Should be fine," D.I. confirmed, "It was a good lookin' shot."

Vince hit a semi-blade that never got more than six feet off the ground. The ball had enough velocity and topspin to counteract the slope and it ran up to and onto the green.

"Pretty shot!" D.I. scoffed sarcastically.

"It's on the green, puke face, where's yours?" Vince taunted back.

Wally and Barney drove along the line of flight of Wally's ball, and stopped where the ball had entered the woods.

"I got it," Wally said flatly as he got out of the cart and took several paces into the trees. He stooped to clear some twigs and leaves from around his ball then stood back to assess his situation. It was not good. He had to hit, a shot low enough to clear the overhanging branches yet high enough to carry the bunker guarding the left front portion of the green, a narrow green that sloped right into a bunker on the other side. The best he could hope for was a good lie in either bunker and then getting up and down in two. Wally returned to the cart, selected a seven iron and trudged back into the woods. Realizing the futility of the shot, Wally wasted little time in pre-shot routine and quickly punched the ball toward the green. The ball ticked a branch just enough to redirect it downward where it struck the cart path at the precise angle to pop it up and over the trap. The ball then glanced off the handle of a bunker rake effectively slowing as well as directing it toward the hole. The ball rolled true and directly at the cup and a quartet of "Ohhs" erupted as it passed over the left edge of the cup and stopped five feet beyond. Wally could only laugh at his good fortune. He didn't even try to convince his playmates that the shot came off just as he had planned.

"Off the limb, off the cart path, over the trap, off the rake, nothin' but green." Vince intoned.

Wally, still shuddering in joyous disbelief, threw his hands up and proclaimed, "Well, you know, what can I say?"

Barney had been a little puzzled and a bit concerned. He could see D.I.'s ball short of the green, Vince's ball on the front of the green and now Wally's was close to the hole but he couldn't see his ball anywhere. He was certain it had hit the green but he could not see it. Wally returned to the cart and the two drove to join Vince and D.I. who had parked and were walking to the green.

"Anybody see my ball?" Barney asked as he stepped from the cart and surveyed the area.

"I thought you were on the green," D.I. said scanning right to left.

"Must have rolled off the back." Vince suggested.

"Did you check the hole?" Wally asked.

"Yeah right," Barney scoffed as he strolled to the back of the green and began looking in the long grass.

Wally paused by the hole on the way to his ball and peered down.

"There is a round white object down there." He said pointing at the hole.

Barney ignored Wally's attempt at levity and continued to search the area behind the green.

Vince walked to the hole and looked in.

"There is a ball in there, Barn." He said.

"Ha, ha, it is to laugh," Barney sniffed not wanting to be the brunt of his friend's warped and often cruel sense of humor. But, he conceded to himself, the thought of his ball finding the cup did indeed appeal to him. It certainly would explain why he couldn't find it.

"Well if this isn't your ball," D.I. said stooping to extract a ball from the cup, "Whose is it?"

Barney turned and looked at the three men gathered around the hole. If this was an act, he thought, they were giving an Oscar winning performance.

D.I. held a ball out towards him.

"Your kidding!" Barney exclaimed still not willing to swallow the hook.

The men stood motionless in a truth or consequences stand off.

"Titleist marked with a red B," D.I. said inspecting the ball in his hand.

"That would be an eagle!" Barney exclaimed excitedly.

"Yes indeed!" D.I. confirmed with a broad smile.

Barney sprinted to the hole where he completed three forceful high fives in one continuous swipe.

"I don't believe it," he said taking the ball from D.I. and inspecting it. "It is my ball." He proclaimed proudly, "Just shows to go you, miracles really do happen."

After a chorus of praise and congratulatory pats on the back, Barney pocketed the ball and tended the pin while the others holed out. Wally completed his miraculous par save, D.I. took three to get up and down and Vince three putted for bogey.

"That was quite a hole wasn't it?" Wally whispered to Barney as they neared the cart. Barney's broadening smile ran out of face and had to wrap around his ears.

HOLE	10	11	12	13	14	15	16	17	18	Out	Total
PAR	4	4	3	5	4	4	3	4	5	36	72
YRDS	380	340	154	495	396	362	158	398	497	3178	6324
D.I.	5	6	2 •••	5	5	5	5	5			
Vince	9	5	3	5	8	4	3 •	5			
Wally	5	4 •	3	4 •••	4 •	3 •••	4	4			
Barney	4 •••	6	4	5	5	5	3	2 •••			

18

The tee of the straight away par five eighteenth, afforded a view of the entire hole. The men could see, off in the distance, a group on the green. They could see, a group waiting for the green to clear. They could see, the ladies waiting on the group waiting for the green to clear. They could see, they would have to wait.

"This has got to be the slowest round of golf we have ever played." D.I. complained.

Vince glanced at his watch then did a double take.

"Holy Moly," he said in amazement, "It's going on two thirty, that's a………," as Vince's mind computed the numbers, his fingers automatically tallied the results by extending one at a time until his entire left hand was wide open. "That's a……"

"Five and a half hour round." D.I. groaned.

Vince looked at his hand, which closed into a loose fist. The mental wheels turned once more and the fingers again opened in sequence each accompanied by a slight head bob.

"Right!" He said, "Five and a half hours."

That's too slow." Wally said, "There's no excuse for………"

While the others hemmed and hawed over the length of play, Barney gazed down the fairway and heaped thanks and praise upon whoever had contributed to the monumental holdup, for they had provided him the time and the opportunity to meet Stella. His gaze had settled on her as she waited in the fairway, her image softened by distance and smudged through ripened eyes. A wispy wistful image producing both calm and chaos, comfort and agony. A soothing ache invaded his very essence. Barney stood in convoluted silence until a voice pulled him from his emotional conundrum.

"I see your buddy is trying to buy your Redskins a championship." He heard Vince intone to D.I. in a baiting manner.

Vince was fishing for D.I.'s composure. He knew speaking ill of D.I.'s beloved Redskins was an act of sacrilege. He had seen D.I.'s jaw muscles tighten at the mere mention of the team's owner. Vince cast another rhetorical lure into D.I.'s pool of contentment.

"If the Skins don't go to the Super Bowl, it sure won't be for the lack of money." Vince teased, waiting patently for D.I. to bite.

"The man's an idiot!" D.I. chomped, "He's taken a great organization and flushed it right down the salary cap commode.

Vince yanked hard on his imaginary fishing pole setting the hook deep into D.I.'s passion.

"But look who he's buyin'," Vince said, playing with D.I.'s loyalties, "nothin' but superstars. They can't lose."

"He's buyin' a bunch of head trips," D.I. snapped, "he's not buyin' Superstars, he's buyin' superegos, egos almost as big as his. Shoot, if this keeps up, he's gonna hafta buy bigger helmets. Might just as well rename the team, The Prima Donnas while he's at it."

"Fish on!" Vince told himself as D.I. raged on. "I'll tell ya somethin' else, there's gonna be a heavy price to pay down the road, just you wait and see. That poor coach really has his work cut out tryin' to make a team out of a bunch of selfabsorbed showboats.

Vince gave the thrashing D.I. a little slack. "I tell ya somethin' else," D.I. ranted on in a voice oozing contempt, "Free agency has ruined pro football. It's created a bunch of greedy egotistical traitors. Heck, I don't think they should even call it a sport anymore, there's no sportsmanship, no loyalty."

"Well," Vince said, "you had Prime Time, he was a player."

"Dion!" D.I. snarled, "He was the biggest showboat in the league. I kept hopin' someone would clean his clock and knock a little humility into him."

"No one did." Vince said, reeling in slowly.

"How could they?" D.I. responded, "......I hafta admit, he was a good cover man but don't even ask him to make a tackle."

"Sounds smart to me." Vince said, reeling a little faster.

"That doesn't surprise me," D.I. shot back, "you've never given a hundred percent in your life."

"Whooooa," Wally and Barney gasped.

Vince, unscathed by the verbal barb, reeled on.

"Well I think Dion was a great acquisition."

"He was a multi-million dollar liability." D.I. growled. "A multi-million dollar has-been."

"Exactly!" Vince stated firmly.

D.I. looked quizzically at Vince, surprised by his apparent agreement.

"That's why he fit in so nicely with the rest of the Redskins and that's also why the Cowboys dumped him!" Vince said with a mischievous laugh.

The mention of the loathsome and much despised Cowboys caused D.I. to flounder momentarily. Vince mentally gaffed and boated the stunned D.I. who flopped about the deck like a nervous tuna."

"You son of a........."

"Now D.I., don't get your hemorrhoids in an uproar," Vince cautioned. "I'm just playin' with ya.

Besides, Dion can still dance, maybe he can become a Hoggett or somethin'."

"That's what I'm talkin' about!" D.I. boomed, "I can't stand to watch all the dancin' and gyratin' that's going on. Hey, if they wanna dance, they should join the ballet, if they wanna play football, then play football and play it with a little class. Vince Lombardi used to tell his players, "When you get into the end zone, act like you've been there before."

"Exactly!" Vince concurred, "Use to be, when a player made a good play, he got a small pat on the ass from his teammates and that was it. Now it's a friggin' choreographed Broadway Show."

"Yeah, as if fame and fortune ain't enough for 'em, they have ta rub it in everybody's face." D.I. said.

"Sour grapes." Wally commented suddenly.

"Huh?" Vince questioned, "What do you mean sour grapes?"

"Sounds like you're envious." Wally stated with a shrug.

"I'm not envious," Vince protested, "well......maybe of being a professional athlete......I mean who wouldn't but that's not what we're talking about. We're talking about bein' egotistical twits."

"Yeah!" D.I. added, "We're talkin' about someone doin' the job he's paid to do then makin' a big to-do about how great he is when he does it. I mean you don't see a surgeon remove a gallbladder, spike it on the operating room floor and go into a little shuck and jive, do ya?"

"I don't know," Vince said, "I was asleep at the time."

"You know what I mean," D.I. snapped.

"All I know," Vince griped, "is it's gotten way out of hand. It makes the NFL look as pathetic as the WWF.

"Hey!" Barney objected, "Don't you go bad mouthing a fine organization like the WWF."

D.I., Vince and Wally looked at Barney for a second then quickly dismissed his statement as a feeble attempt at humor.

Vince flung the words from his ears with a rapid shake of his head and continued on. "I think the league should do something about it."

D.I. slowly turned his berating eyes away from a reddening Barney.

"The league says it doesn't want to inhibit the spontaneity." He said slowly.

"Spontaneity, my Aunt Bertha's girdle!" Vince scoffed, "They're about as spontaneous as my daily movement. Shoot, I bet they rehearse their little performances more than the Radio City Rockettes."

Barney nodded his agreement.

"It's gotten to the point where I watch very little in the way of sports anymore." He said, "Shoot, I used to watch anything that was on and tape others to watch later. Now it's pretty much golf and Nascar."

"Nascar's not a sport!" Vince sniffed indignantly.

"I'm not going to argue with you over what constitutes a sport," Barney stated, "I'm merely stating my own viewing preferences."

"Bunch of Red Necks drivin' around in circles," Vince jeered under his breath.

"Well I really don't care what you……"

"Anybody beat an eagle?" D.I. interrupted as the ladie's carts began moving up the fairway. "If not, you're up Melton."

The men walked to their carts for their clubs of choice. Barney picking up the conversation.

"I don't care what you say Denevi, Nascar is the number one spectator SPORT in America and I enjoy watching it. If you have any qualms about whether it's a sport or not, take it up with ESPN or any other network that calls it a sport. Frankly, I don't give a damn what they call it, I like it."

"You only watch for the wrecks!" Vince said, changing tactics.

"That's part of it," Barney admitted, "but that's not all of it. I like the color, the sound, the excitement of it. There's a drama, a finality to it. Forty-two drivers on the ragged edge."

"Speaking of drivers, how 'bout hittin' the one in your hand so we can finish this marathon round." D.I. commanded. "You all can finish your discussion in the clubhouse."

Barney was about to hit his drive when Vince's voice caused him to back off.

"We can't finish it in the clubhouse," he heckled in a childish whine, "Barney's got a date."

"It's not a......"

Vince interrupted Barney's protest with a childhood rhyme. "Barney and Stella sittin' in a tree k-i-s-s-i-n-g."

Wally giggled.

Barney blushed.

And D.I. thundered, "COULD WE?"

All banter ceased but Wally continued to giggle, albeit a little nervously. Barney proceeded to blush to a deeper crimson and Vince beamed in naughty satisfaction.

"I guess it's true what they say about aging back into childhood," D.I. chided, trying hard to keep a straight face. He finally had to turn away from the collective immaturity before him. He was ashamed that it delighted him so.

Barney, unable to regain complete composure, hit an anemic tee shot that, although straight, did not make it to the fairway. Wally, whose giggle had morphed into a silly grin, sent his ball, true to form, looping right. Vince, feeling gratified by his ability to cause havoc, laced one down the middle. D.I., trying to act annoyed, but failing miserably, smacked his best drive of the day, possibly of his life.

"You're cute when your angry." Vince said with a wink.

"Yeah and your ugly all the time!" D.I. retorted.

The four men left the tee in good humor. D.I. and Vince drove down the cart path while Wally and Barney drove along the line of flight of Barney's tee shot.

"Should be right in here," Barney said as Wally slowed the cart. The two men scanned the area until they reached the fairway where they turned around and began backtracking.

"How far do you think it got?" Wally asked.

"Should be right in here," Barney replied, pointing and making a circular motion indicating an area just to the right of the cart.

Barney got out of the cart and began walking the area.

"I'm going to drive back a little further," Wally said steering the cart in a serpentine manner back toward the tee.

Barney's face took on a puzzled expression with a hint of aggravation.

"I don't understand it," he mumbled to himself, "It should be right here."

The more he searched, the more agitated he became. He stomped and kicked his way around the area. Few things irritated Barney Melton more than loosing a ball that he should be able to find. It was one of those pet peeves that ran contrary to his naturally easy going demeanor. It was as if, all his pent-up aggravations and frustrations could be vented under the guise of a lost ball.

"Damn!" he hissed so hard it made his knees buckle, "I hate this I really ha........."

"Barney!" he heard Wally call.

He looked up to see Wally point down at a spot twenty-five yards further back.

"You got it?"

Wally nodded.

"Got your mark on it." he confirmed.

Barney trotted back to where Wally stood. He stooped and inspected the ball laying deep in the grass.

"That's it!" Barney beamed in true relief, "Thanks."

The deepness of the grass dictated that a lofted club be used to extricate the ball and advance it to the fairway. Barney utilized a nine iron to successfully accomplish both goals. Even though he lay two and still away, he felt wonderful. And why not he thought. He had met a woman he was interested in, he had just recorded an eagle on the previous hole and all those emotional toxins had just been purged from his system like steam through a boilers' safety valve.

Vince and D.I., who had continued their discussion on the American Sport's scene, drove out to meet Barney and Wally where Barney's ball now lay.

"As long as there's a Redskin team," D.I. was telling Vince, as the cart came to a stop, "I'll be a Redskin fan."

Vince nodded his agreement.

"You know," he said, "It's a shame how ticket prices have pretty much priced the average fan right out of the ol' ball park."

"Ain't that the truth," D.I. agreed, "you know what really gets my goat?"

"What?"

"If a team makes it to the Super Bowl, most of those fans who paid the price and supported the team all season won't get to go. They have to win a lottery to get tickets. I think each participating team only gets like......ten thousand tickets for their fans."

Vince nodded.

"It's somethin' like that," he agreed.

"The rest," D.I. continued on, "go to a bunch of VIPs and their mucky-muck wives who don't even like football."

"Boo-Hoo-Hoo, life just isn't fair," Wally cried in a phony wail, then adding firmly, "Get over it!"

"Who in the heck yanked your chain." D.I. asked belligerently.

"Yeah," Vince growled holding a fist in front of his clenched teeth, "If we wanted anything outta you we'da kicked it outta you."

"Oh please," Wally scoffed.

As the others, bantered in feigned hostility, Barney got out of the cart, selected a club and prepared to hit his third shot. The others continued their oral sparring.

"Do you mind?" He admonished, "I'm trying to concentrate on this shot."

They fell silent and Barney walloped one right down the center and long.

"Did you hit the driver off the deck?" D.I. asked.

"I did." Barney said smugly as he slipped the head cover on the club and dropped it in his bag with a resounding thud.

"Show off!"

Wally was next to play. Because the fairway narrowed up ahead, and because his ball was positioned on the extreme right-hand side, Wally needed to hit a fade if he hoped to reach the green in three. Normally this was not a problem, unless of course he actually thought about and wanted to hit a fade. A fact he had illustrated oh so vividly back on seventeen. A fact still floating freely on the surface of his memory and diluting his confidence.

Barney saw Wally adjust his grip and stance. He sensed Wally was thinking. This was not good.

"Wally," Barney said, "what are you doing?"

Wally backed off the ball and looked at Barney, the glaze of concentration clouding his eyes.

"I'm going to try to hit a fade around those trees." He answered pointing his club down the narrowing fairway.

Barney walked over and stood beside him.

"Look, Wally," he said calmly, "just pretend you're on the tee. Take your normal grip, your normal stance."

"But..."

"Listen to me," Barney instructed, "take your normal stance, your normal grip, pick a target that's left of the trees...say that crooked little tree up there on the other side of the fairway..."

"But..."

"Wally, aim at that little crooked tree up there, use your normal stance, your normal grip and pretend you're hitting your driver off the tee. Clear your mind of all thought and hit the ball."

Wally just stood there.

"Go on," Barney urged gently, "hit the ball to that little crooked tree."

Wally did as Barney had instructed. The ball started for the little crooked tree, it began to turn but turned left instead of right.

"Noooo!" Wally cried, "Right you stupid ball go right."

The ball did not go right, it continued to curve to the left until it struck a tree on the far side of the fairway. It ricocheted to the right and rolled to the center of the fairway.

"Well done." Barney said with a chuckle, "Not quite how I had envisioned but you can't argue with the results."

Wally slowly turned to face Barney.

"Don't you ever tell me how to hit a ball again." He hissed through clenched teeth.

Barney raised his shoulders in perplexity and turned his palms up quizzically.

"What do you mean?" He asked, "Look where your ball is."

"A hook!" Wally stammered, "I hit a friggin' hook. All my life I hit a friggin' fade and you make me hit a friggin' hook."

"Just shows you what you can do when you set your mind to it." Barney said with a widening grin.

"Just don't give me any more tips, okay?"

"Okay!"

Vince and D.I. arrived at Vince's ball.

"How far out do ya think I am?" Vince asked staring down the fairway.

"Prob'ly two fifty, two sixty." D.I. answered.

"Think it's that far?" Vince questioned.

"It's what I said ain't it?"

"Doesn't look that far......I think I'll go for it. You think I should go for it?"

"Sure, you go for it............you won't make it."

"No?.........You don't think I can make it?...... I think I can make it."

"Then go for it and stop asking for my opinion."

Vince gazed down the fairway again, then back at D.I.

"You know," he said, "there's no real trouble in front of the green so even if I don't make it it's not gonna hurt me."

"True."

"Then your sayin' I should go for it?"

D.I.'s chin fell to his chest in resignation.

Wally and Barney pulled up beside Vince's cart.

"What's the matter?" Wally asked.

"Whatcha mean?" Vince asked back.

"What's the hold up? Why haven't you hit yet?"

"He's going for it." D.I. stated with a roll of his eyes.

"Ha, that's a good one," Barney laughed.

Vince glared at him.

"You're a good two sixty out," Barney challenged, "there's no way in hell you can get there."

Vince looked down the fairway again.

"Doesn't look that far," he said, "I think I can get there."

D.I.'s head dropped again, one hand rising to massage his forehead.

A few quiet moments passed.

"I think I can hit," Vince said, "I probably can't make it...if I do, it won't be on the fly."

"If you do, I'll buy you a pitcher," Barney said.

"Me too," Wally added.

Vince looked at D.I. who was still massaging his forehead.

"What about you D.I.?" Vince asked, "You gonna buy me a pitcher if I make it?" D.I. did not look up.

"I'll buy you a pitcher if you'll just shut up and hit the friggin' ball." He groaned.

"Geeze, I can't lose," Vince cried, "I get a pitcher whether I make it or not."

"Not any more," D.I. said flatly, "The deal was, you'd shut up and hit the ball......your still yakin'."

"I'm shuttin' up," Vince said pulling an imaginary zipper across his lips.

D.I. massaged more vigorously.

"It's too late!" He said.

"Why don't you do what Barney does and hit your driver off the deck." Wally suggested.

"I've never tried that," Vince answered, "I've thought about it but never tried it."

"Just pretend you're hitting a three wood." Barney volunteered, "That's what I do."

"He can't hit a three wood." D.I. quipped. "he can't hit anything he's too busy flappin' his lips."

Vince flashed a mocking, real funny, smile.

"You've got a good lie," Barney goaded.

"Hey what the hey, it's worth a shot," Vince said, pulling his driver from his bag, "nothin' ventured nothin' gained I always say."

"So venture already!" D.I. complained intolerantly.

Vince looked up the fairway to confirm all the ladies had reached the green.

"Get ready to yell fore," he instructed Barney, "I wouldn't want to hit your new girlfriend on the noggin."

Barney frowned but nodded.

Vince fidgeted through his pre-shot routine not quite convinced of the driver/fairway combo. Finally, to D.I.'s relief, he actually hit the ball. And man did he hit it.

"FORE!" Barney roared. He could see the ladies take evasive action by covering their heads and ducking away. The ball landed short of the green and rolled. Just how far it rolled he couldn't tell.

"Did it make it?" Vince asked in shock.

"I can't tell," Barney answered, "but it's close."

The ladies slowly recoiled from their defensive crouches and looked back towards the four men who stood in dumbfounded silence. Barney offered a feeble wave and the ladies reciprocated and went about their business.

"That," Wally said in admiration, "was a golf shot."

Vince looked at his club.

"I gotta try this more often." He said with a gratified grin. He raised the club to his lips and gently kissed it, "You, my little darlin'," he cooed, "are sleepin' with me tonight."

"That's supposed to be a reward?" D.I. questioned.

D.I.'s tee ball lay well beyond where Vince had hit his second shot. A fact that shown brightly on D.I.'s face.

"Let's see," D.I. said, getting out of the cart and pointing back to the spot where Vince's ball had been, "It was two sixty from waaay back there," he said with special emphasis on, 'way back', "What do ya think Vince, about forty or fifty yard difference?"

Vince understood it was pay back time for his Redskins fishing trip so he accepted his fate with dignity.

"I'd say twenty, maybe twenty-five tops." He said.

D.I. smiled, "Two sixty minus...FIFTY, equal...two ten to the pin."

Barney and Wally elected to sit back and watch whenever D.I. and Vince staged one of their vanity fairs. They were not above aiding and abetting aggravation if it presented itself but this situation was self-propelled.

"What's the yardage from the white tees?" D.I. asked Vince who had remained seated in the cart.

Vince looked down at the scorecard.

"Four ninety seven."

"Four ninety seven minus...two ten equal...two eight seven. Wow! That's a two hundred eighty-seven yard drive." D.I. gloated unabashedly, "Two hund........."

"All right already," Vince croaked, "It was a nice drive."

"Nice?"

"Great!" Vince corrected, "A great drive."

D.I. frowned.

Vince threw up his hands.

"Okay," he cried, "It was a truly magnanimous, magnificent and, I may add, bombastic drive."

This seemed to please D.I. and he got in the cart to wait for the green to clear.

Vince looked over at Barney.

"So what's your plan, Romeo?" He asked.

"Plan?"

"Yeah you know, what's your strategy, what are you gonna talk about, where do you want this to lead?"

"I just thought I'd play it by ear, let things just kinda happen."

"Barney, Barney, Barney," Vince tisked, "you're so naïve, so innocent. Things just don't happen, you have to make them happen. Women like a 'take charge' kinda guy, you gotta play to your strong suit, so to speak."

"That being?" Barney asked glumly.

"Oh I don't know, it could be anything, the important thing is you need direction, a script if you will. You need to control the situation."

"That sounds a little conniving to me," Barney protested.

"Exactly!" Vince affirmed.

"Shouldn't I just be myself?"

"Absolutely not!"

"I don't know," Barney balked, "it's just not my style."

"Style, you have no style, that's what I'm trying to tell ya."

"Oh, thank you very much, that makes me feel soooo much better."

"Look," Vince said, "here's what you do......"

"Forget it!" Barney snapped, "I'm sixty-three years old for crying out loud, I think I'm capable of handling this."

"Well do you have an ice breaker?" Vince asked in a sense of urgency, "At the very least, you gotta have an ice breaker."

"I'll think of something."

"How 'bout......?"

"I said, I'll think of something! Okay?"

"Okay fine," Vince moped, "do it your way. I was only trying to help but if you don't......"

"Oh for the love of God, Vince," D.I. groaned, "give it up!"

As the ladie's carts disappeared down the path to the parking lot Barney felt a wave of anxiety rock him. What if she doesn't go to the grill? Was that the last he would see of her? What was he going to say to her if she was in the grill? His mind frantically searched for answers. They were not forthcoming.

"You hittin' five wood?" Vince asked as D.I. pulled the distinctive head cover from his club.

"I can hit a five 210," D.I. said confidently.

"Reality check!" Vince exclaimed, "First of all, no matter how long you think your drive was you're more than two ten out. Two eighty-seven...give me a break, you couldn't hit a ball two eighty-seven off a three hundred yard cliff. And secondly, even if you are (cough) two ten out, you can only get one eighty out of a five wood and that's on a good day."

Well, this was no longer a difference of opinions, it was a challenge. D.I. could no more change clubs now than admit he voted democratic back in 1960.

When D.I. addressed the ball, tension contorted his face. The muscles of his forearms bulged as they drew his hands into a white-knuckle grip that choked the life right out the club. His body so taut he could barely flex enough to get the club behind the ball. It was not a pretty swing. It was not a pretty shot. The club struck the top of the ball driving it into the firm earth, which in turn bounced it into the air. The total results of bounce and roll netted maybe seventy yards.

"Now you can hit the five wood." Vince jabbed mercilessly.

D.I. spun around and raised his club as if to send Vince's head two ten. Wally and Barney gasped,

Vince flinched and brought his arms up for protection.

"Do you know what an arrogant jerk you are?" D.I. boomed.

Vince nodded from behind his up held arms and flashed a crooked smile.

"Do you know, nobody gets my goat quicker than you do?"

Vince nodded again, his smile broadening, his arms dropping a bit.

D.I. faked a swing, Vince ducked instinctively nearly ramming his head into the windshield of the cart. Barney and Wally gasped again.

"Why I put up with you is a mystery to me," D.I. said lowering the club.

"Me too." Vince admitted, "I just can't help myself, I never know when to leave well enough alone. I just have to take it one step beyond."

"Tell me about it." D.I. said, "how does Tiff put up with you?"

"The woman's a saint," Vince said, "she......"

"She'd kick the stuffing out of you if you tried that crap at home," Wally interjected.

Vince nodded.

"She does." He lied.

Wally was next to hit. He had a true one eighty to the green, a distance that lay just outside his comfort zone. He thought about laying up but chose valor as the better part of discretion and faded a lovely four wood to the front of the green. He accepted the accolades of his peers with humility and relief.

Barney hit his fourth shot left of the green and D.I.'s third shot, for some reason, felt obligated to follow.

"What are you going to talk to Stella about?" Wally asked Barney on the way to the green.

"I don't have a clue," Barney confided, "I wasn't concerned about it 'til Vince piped up, now I'm all apprehensive and worked up over it. Man, he sure has a knack for pushing people's buttons, doesn't he?"

"Especially in D.I.'s case." Barney amended.

"He does make a concentrated effort when it comes to D.I. doesn't he?"

"That he does, but you've got to admit there's never a dull moment with those two around."

"I swear," Wally said, "one of these days those two are going to go to blows. I really thought D.I. was going to wrap that five wood around Vinny's neck."

"I don't think so," Barney contradicted, "I think they love it. And it's not only Vince, D.I. gets in his fair share of shots, too, don't cha know? They're like a couple of heavy weights circling around just throwing jabs, no knockout punches. I'd call it a draw."

As Barney walked to the green he looked toward the parking lot to see if he could see Stella and the ladies but most of the area was screened by trees. Anxiety was running rampant.

"Don't worry," Wally consoled softly, "everything will work out fine, if there's anything I......"

"I know and I appreciate it," Barney quickly interjected.

"Well, anyway, I'm really excited about this. I've been concerned about you."

"Me? Really?"

"Yeah, other than playing golf a couple of times a week what do you do? Sometimes when Doris and I sit down to dinner, I picture you sitting alone in the flickering glow of the evening news eating a microwaved TV dinner. I've prayed you'd find someone to keep you company, someone to talk to, to go out with. I know, you think things are fine but they could be so much better if you had someone special to share your life with."

Barney stopped and turned to face Wally. He saw genuine delight in Wally's eyes.

"You know," Barney said, "I thought I was comfortable in my life, and I guess I was but I gotta tell you, the feelings I have experienced today really make me feel alive."

Wally gave Barney a firm pat on the back.

"Go for it Barn!" Wally exclaimed, "I wish you all the best."

The two men smiled. Barney felt that little tell tale pain in the back of his throat that usually announced tears of joy. He fought back the tears and choked off a sob even though he knew he'd feel better releasing them. He turned quickly and walked off to find his ball and hid his tears.

D.I. had already found his ball and was searching the area for Barney's as Barney approached.

"You should be right here in the same area," he said looking up. Barney could not conceal the redness in his eyes and D.I. quickly averted his eyes back to the long grass surrounding the green. The two searched in silence, one with blurred vision the other clouded, neither man wanting to embarrass the other.

"I got it!" Barney croaked, as he nearly stepped on his ball, which lay partially hidden beneath a leaf.

D.I. looked up and confirmed what he thought he had seen.

"You alright?" He asked.

"Yeah." Barney nodded, the pain in his throat worsening. He looked over to where Vince and Wally were busy preparing for their next shots then back at D.I. who was looking at him with questioning concern.

"I am truly blessed," he said in a hoarse voice. Two sparkling tears, too joyous to be denied, streaked

Barney's cheeks and kissed the corners of his smile. He saw D.I.'s expression of concern soften into compassion. He wasn't sure, but for a brief moment, he thought he saw the sparkle of moisture in D.I.'s gaze. He wasn't sure, but had the truth been known, there was that little pain in the back of D.I.'s throat.

Barney pitched on and two putted for a double bogey. It was the most satisfying double bogey he had ever had.

D.I. pitched on and two putted for a bogey. He wasn't satisfied with it but he felt good.

Wally two putted for his par and remained ecstatic.

Vince's driver, off the deck, second shot, had come up a mere ten feet short of the green. He played a nice chip shot, made the putt for birdie winning the hole and a fifty-cent birdie. All in all he was a happy man. Hand shaking and backslapping ushered a contented foursome off the green.

All was right in their world.

HOLE	10	11	12	13	14	15	16	17	18	Out	Total
PAR	4	4	3	5	4	4	3	4	5	36	72
YRDS	380	340	154	495	396	362	158	398	497	3178	6324
D.I.	5	6	2	5	5	5	5	5	6		
Vince	9	5	3	5	8	4	3	5	4		
Wally	5	4	3	4	4	3	4	4	5		
Barney	4	6	4	5	5	5	3	2	7		

THE 19TH HOLE

The two carts drove to Wally's Cadillac where they deposited Wally, Vince and all their gear. D.I. then drove off to his car and Barney to his. While he transferred his clubs from cart to car, Barney scanned the parking lot for signs of Stella. Finding none, he rationalized that the ladies were probably already in the clubhouse or perhaps, they parked in the lot located on the other side. He did not want to think about the third possibility but it lingered in his mind like the scent of her perfume.

He changed out of his golf shoes, scanned the lot again, slammed the trunk lid closed and drove the cart back to where Wally and Vince were waiting beside the vintage caddie. Barney surveyed the lot from his new vantage point. Nothing. D.I. wheeled around the end of the row of parked cars and came to a screeching halt beside the other cart.

"If you all are waitin' on me, you're wastin' time." He announced. Vince jumped in beside him and away they went. Wally clambered into the other cart, which took off in hot pursuit.

Barney had been fretting ever since Vince had questioned him about his lack of a strategy. Maybe he should have a plan, an approach, but he found, much to his dismay, that he was unable to fabricate one. Indeed, he found himself unable to conjure up the most rudimentary or utilitarian form of an icebreaker, a contrivance Vince had stressed as the main catalyst in the crystallization of human relationships. Barney now felt an urgent need to have something......anything.

By the time the four men entered the clubhouse, the crescendo of Barney's anxiety was at it's peak. His heart was beating like a Buddy Rich drum solo, Gene Krupa, wailed away on the cymbals in his head and the Hines Brothers vigorously tapped their way across the pit of his stomach. He feared if one more neuron fired within his brain, he would pass out.

A quick glance around the grill confirmed what he had dreaded most. Not a sign of Stella or her friends. The drumming in his chest slowed, his head went numb and the Hines Brothers went into a melancholy soft shoe. The sense of disappointment over not seeing her was somewhat offset by a sense of relief in not seeing her. Disappoinment overruled however.

D.I. beat his usual path to the little boy's room while the others headed for the grill.

Vince pointed to an empty table by the windows and the three men made their way to it and sat down.

Barney could not conceal his disappointment.

Vince looked around the room.

"Looks like you've been stood up." He said without expression.

"Oh real nice Denevi," Wally hissed, "why don't you just kick him in the groin."

"I didn't mean anything by it," Vince protested, "I was just making an observation."

"I'm sure Barney is well aware of the situation," Wally admonished, "I don't think he needs you to slap him in the face with it."

"I wasn't sl........."

"It's okay." Barney interrupted glumly, "It's no big deal." He lied, knowing full well, it was.

"Maybe they're in the pro shop," Wally suggested, "or in the restroom."

"Yeah," Vince agreed brightly, attempting to do a little fence mending.

"Doesn't matter," Barney said pushing back his chair and standing up.

"I gotta go to the head," he said blandly.

As he walked away he heard Wally jump on Vince's case again.

"You're a real piece of work, you know that Denevi?"

Vince mumbled something in his defense but Barney didn't hear nor cared what it was.

On the way to the restroom, Barney did peer into the pro shop on the hope Wally might have been right. Nothing! His eyes glazed in emotional shock. The one word question, 'Why?' fogged his mind like a hot breath on cold glasses. He wore an expression of the living dead as he plodded on towards the restroom.

D.I., exiting the men's room, jerked open the door just as Barney was preparing to push. The resistance free push sent Barney stumbling into the startled D.I., causing both men to grope and grapple for stability. Although neither had been at fault, both offered instant apologies followed closely by offers of sincere and complete absolution. Embarrassment colored their faces and nervously chuckled in their throats while composure struggled for a foothold.

"We've gotta stop meeting like this." D.I. said, straightening his shirt.

Before Barney could collect himself, D.I. slid past him and disappeared as suddenly as he had appeared.

"What next?" Barney asked himself. The men's room door, gently nudged him aside as it returned to the closed position.

Barney's body instinctively performed the duties required of it. His psyche however, remained dazed by the day's events. While washing his hands, he noticed an image in the mirror before him. A ghostly image void of animation or spirit.

"You friggin' idiot," he scolded, "why can't you just leave well enough alone? You had to get yourself all worked up over this.........woman......and now look at you. You're so friggin' pathetic, you sorry excuse for a man."

The momentum of his violent mood swing quickly carried him through self-pity and head long into anger.

"What kind of person would do this kind of thing?" He thought, "Is this how she gets her kicks? Batting those long lashes over those hazel eyes, smiling ever so sweetly with those sugary lips while at the same time lying through her perfect pearly whites. Oh I'd love to play around with you she says! I'll see you in the grill she says. Yeah right! Lying little hussy played you like a Stradivarius...... and you, you big dummy," he thought scowling into the mirror, "you just sucked it all up like an industrial strength Hoover."

Barney splashed some cold water on his face to cool him down and ease a burning in his eyes. He reached for a paper towel but found the dispenser empty. "Perfect!" He whispered, "Just friggin' perfect!"

Returning from the men's room, Barney still entertained hopes of finding Stella seated in the grill. But once again, his hopes were dashed. He noticed four glasses of water had been placed on the table.

"Have you ordered?" He asked drawing his chair under him.

"We were waiting for you." Wally answered.

"You're all too kind," Barney said lightly, endeavoring to restore normalcy to his life.

Heather, a petite young thing of voluptuous proportions, placed one hand on the back of D.I.'s chair and the other on her hip.

"Ready to order now?" She asked impatiently.

"Ice tea, BLT on toasted wheat." D.I. blurted out.

Heather blinked, committing the order to memory.

"Don't you want a beer?" Barney asked.

D.I. shook his head, Barney shrugged.

"How 'bout you Wally?"

"Sounds good to me," Wally agreed, "how 'bout you Vince, you want a beer?"

"Is the Pope Catholic?" Vince grinned.

Heather frowned and shifted her weight to her other foot.

Barney looked up at her.

"A pitcher of your coldest brew and three frosty mugs." He said.

"Bud or Bass Ale?" She asked curtly.

Barney looked at the other two for a sign of preference. Finding none, he ordered Bud.

She blinked.

"And to eat?" She asked, staring at Barney without so much as a whisper of humor.

"Um...I'll have a turkey club on wheat...please."

"Chips or potato salad?"

"Chips."

She blinked.

Her cold stare fell on Vince who, over the objections of his keepers, ordered a cheeseburger with fries.

Blink.

"I'll have the chicken salad on rye." Wally volunteered quickly, hoping to avoid the icy glare.

"That it?" She asked.

The four men looked at each other and nodded.

Heather blinked, turned on her heels and scurried off.

"Great memory, killer bod, personality of a wombat." D.I. commented.

"Glaring proof that looks aren't everything." Vince added.

"Why does Tom keep her around?" Wally asked.

D.I. flashed a "Well Duh" look at him.

The question mark on Wally's face slowly straightened into an exclamation mark.

"Noo!" He breathed in disbelief, "Tom and Heather are..."

"Yep!"

"Heather's..."

"Yep!"

"Who sez?" Wally demanded.

"Ferguson, you're about as observant as a stump." Vince commented.

"So you really don't know, do you?" Wally argued, "You just think......"

"We know!" D.I. interrupted, "Everybody knows, 'cept you."

Wally looked at Barney who simply nodded.

Mouth agape, Wally gazed around the table at the other three men.

"Better shut that yap before a bee flies in" Vince suggested.

Wally's mouth closed slowly then opened to utter a hushed, "Wow."

Heather brought the pitcher, three mugs and D.I.'s tea. Wally looked at her then at Tom who was working behind the counter.'

"You need something?" She asked tersely.

"Who?... Me?" Wally stammered, "No... I don't need anything."

She left to charm another table.

Barney poured a beer and slid it over to Wally.

"Here, drink this, it'll calm you down."

He filled another mug for Vince then the third.

"You sure you don't want a beer?" He asked holding the mug out towards D.I., "I can get another mug."

D.I. shook his head.

Vince pulled the scorecard from his back pocket and a pencil from behind his ear.

"Okay," he said dabbing the pencil point with the tip of his tongue, "now for the bad news." He ran the pencil along a column of numbers. "D.I. you had a grand total of... two dots."

D.I. shook his head and frowned into his glass of tea. Vince drew the pencil along another column of figures the point dipping each time it encountered a dot.

"I managed a total of...six."

The pencil traced and dipped again.

"Wally Mart, you had...eleven dots and Bernard, you had..." the pencil dipped thirteen times, "thirteen?"

The number produced an audible groan from D.I.

"So." Vince continued, "D.I., you owe Barney... five fifty, Wally... four fifty and you owe me... two bucks."

D.I. leaned forward and pulled his wallet from his back pocket.

"Looks like macaroni and cheese for the rest of the month," he said woefully as he began flinging bills onto the table.

"I," Vince said, "owe Wally... two fifty and Barney ... three fifty. And Wally, you owe Barney a buck.

Two more wallets fell open and more bills fell upon the table. Money changed position faster than on a Vegas crap table. Two quarters that originated in D.I.'s pocket, accompanied a five-dollar bill across the table to pay off Barney. The two quarters plus a dollar bill were then slid from Barney to Vince in exchange for another five. Vince promptly placed the quarters on two dollar bills and slid them over to settle his account with Wally. Wally passed a dollar bill to Barney, for payment in full and slid the two quarters back to D.I. as change for the five D.I. had passed to him. D.I. threw two dollars at Vince and returned the two quarters to the pocket from which they had come. The pigeons had been plucked. The winners had been paid.

Barney reached for the pitcher and topped off the three beers.

"Thank you gentlemen." He said folding his winnings and stuffing them into the small breast pocket of his shirt, "Your generosity is greatly appreciated." He forced a smile and took a long swig of beer. It was a hollow victory.

"Steals the bread right out of my poor grandchildren's mouths." D.I. complained just as realization struck.

"Damn it Denevi," he croaked, "I had three dots on twelve? Not two!"

Vince looked at the scorecard and blanched.

"You're right," he admitted, "one of the dots looks like part of the two. I missed it."

"Not two," D.I. objected, "three dots."

"Yeah three dots," Vince agreed.

"You said two."

"No, I said one of the dots looked like part of the two." Vince said, becoming a little aggravated.

D.I. stared at him blankly.

"One dot looked like part of the two," Vince repeated, "the number two."

D.I. nodded but there was no comprehension registered in his stare.

"You had a birdie two on the hole and the third dot looks like it's part of the number two... I missed.. I'm so-o-o-o sorry. Here see for yourself," Vince said taking the scorecard and holding it up in front of D.I.'s face.

D.I. snatched the card, shot Vince a look and then scrutinized the card.

"Hey," he said lightly, "this one dot looks like it's part of the two."

Vince threw his hands up in triumphant relief.

D.I. flipped the card back across the table like a Frisbee.

Barney tossed two quarters across the table to D.I.

"I don't have fifty cents," Vince said coldly, "I owe ya."

"I got change." D.I. responded, "Pay up!"

Vince grudgingly slid one of the dollars in front of him back over to D.I. D.I. in return, promptly slid two quarters back to Vince.

"I don't have any quarters either." Wally said sheepishly. Vince slid the two quarters over to Wally who slid them over to D.I.

"I owe you." Wally said.

"I trust ya." Vince said glancing at D.I.

"Hey, what did I shoot?" Wally asked, "I think I had a pretty good round."

"I haven't totaled the scores yet." Vince said reaching for the card.

Vince manipulated the numbers in one column.

"Let's see...D.I., you shot...44 on the back and you had a," he flipped the card to the front side, "39 on the front for a grand total of... 84."

"Eighty-three." D.I. corrected, shaking his head at Vince's dubious math skills.

"Whatever!" Vince said working on the next column.

"I had an... 86."

He worked the third column from left to right then looked up puzzled. He looked back down and worked the column right to left.

"Something's wrong!" he said checking his figures again, "I'm coming up with a 76 for Ferguson."

"Really?" Wally chirped, "I knew I was doing well but not that well."

Vince tossed the card to D.I. who scanned it once and tossed it back.

"Seventy-six." He confirmed.

"Lemme see," Wally said excitedly, reaching across the table.

Vince pulled the card back.

"Lemme add up the Deputy's score then it'll be suitable for framing." Vince said adding the final column.

"Eighty-four, Barn." Vince said handing the card to a beaming Wally who eagerly perused it.

"Great round Ferguson." D.I. complimented.

"Super round." Barney added.

"That's my best round ever." Wally gushed, still staring at the scorecard.

"Kudos," Vince said raising his glass.

"Here, here." The others toasted.

The four men set to casual conversation and rehashed the shots that had made the day so special.

Barney drained the pitcher equally into the three mugs then held it high as a signal for Heather to fetch another. This did not please her but she obliged.

When Heather delivered the food, it was swift, accurate and taciturn. When Vince requested ketchup for his fries and Barney mayo for his club, Heather suffered a silent conniption fit.

"I sure hopes she's worth it," D.I. mumbled as she stomped off.

The condiments were not forthcoming, a circumstance that grates heavily on the already thin patience of senior men. Vince took matters into his own hands. He got up, went to the counter and procured the requested items from Tom. This did not escape the scornful eyes of Heather. She hurriedly tossed several packets of mayo and ketchup on the table just as Vince returned from the counter. She produced a malicious, in your face smile, turned and walked off in a huff.

"What a sweetheart!" D.I. said reaching for the second half of his BLT.

"She's a bitch!" Vince said trying unsuccessfully to open a packet of ketchup with his fingers. "I hate these things!" He said in frustration, resorting to the use of his teeth to open the stubborn packet. He squeezed the contents onto his fingers as well as his fries. "You can't open these things without getting it all over." He complained, licking ketchup from his thumb and forefinger. "And what am I supposed to do with this... this body bag?" He wondered, holding out the not quite empty but totally messy container. No one offered a solution so he flung it onto one of the tables where it deposited a red skid mark. He set to opening another pesky packet. "Why can't they just put a bottle of ketchup on every table?" He asked through clenched teeth.

"Too expensive, labor intensive and wasteful." D.I. answered.

Vince was too busy fighting another packet to rebut D.I.'s statement.

Wally, whose eyes had followed Heather as she left the table, washed down a bite of chicken salad with a gulp of beer.

"Hey!" He said in annoyance, "I don't give a flyin' fig if Tom's tapping her or not, he should fire her sorry ass."

Stunned by the sudden display of wrath from the normally forgiving Ferguson, the others sat back and gawked at him.

"Well," he blushed, "why should we have to pay the price for his pleasure? It's bad business."

"Don't sugar coat it Wally," Vince said, "tell us what you really think."

"You don't want to know what I really think about you right now." Wally growled at Vince.

"You're right on both counts," D.I. said, "nothin' sours a customer faster than poor service."

"It's not that it's poor service," Barney amended, "It's rude service and to me that's worse because as you said, it sours your mood and ruins your day."

They all nodded and returned their attention to their lunch. Barney picked up the third portion of his club and extracted the long toothpick that held the layers together. He skillfully separated the sections and slathered them with mayo. Using the fingers of both hands, he nimbly reassembled the three-tiered section of sandwich and raised it to his mouth. Realizing his mouth could not accommodate the height of the morsel, he attempted to compress it. Lubricated by the generous application of mayo, the stack bowed in the middle then began to disintegrate. A cascade of turkey, cheese, lettuce, tomato, bread and mayo tumbled down the front of Barney's shirt. His natural reaction to scoot back, allowed a portion to continue on into his lap. He looked across the table to where D.I. clasped a hand across his mouth to contain the last remnants of his BLT. Barney could only smile.

"Could this day get any better?" He croaked.

Barney noticed D.I.'s grin fade and his attention divert to something behind him.

Barney felt a hand fall on his shoulder.

"Hey sailor, buy me a drink?"

He turned to look past the long lashes and into those hazel eyes. The luscious lips parted in a broad smile, revealing her dazzling white, perfect teeth. Barney began to stand but the hand on his shoulder resisted.

"Please," she said, "don't get up."

Vince scooted his chair towards Wally, grabbed a chair from the table behind him and placed it next to Barney.

"Won't you join us?" he invited motioning to the empty chair.

"May I?"

"Of course!" Vince affirmed.

"Please!" Barney urged.

Stella looked at Wally who smiled and nodded. D.I. motioned to the chair.

"Take a load off," he said without feeling.

"Thanks," she said sliding between Barney and the chair and sitting down. She smiled at Barney then noticed the sandwich debris on his shirt, on the table, and in his lap. Her eyes widened.

"What happened to you?" she asked with a giggle.

Barney blushed and began picking turkey bits off his pants.

"Aw my club kind of... exploded on me." he explained brushing cheese fragments off his chest.

"I'll say it did, here, let me help you,' she said dipping a napkin into a water glass and dabbing the front of his shirt.

Barney concentrated on the mess on his lap while Stella worked on his shirt. Barney asked for the napkin, stood up and wiped the seat of his chair catching most of the crumbs with his free hand. He dumped the refuse on his plate and cleaned the table in the same manner.

"That will have to do." He said dropping the napkin on his plate and sitting down. He looked at Stella. "This has been some kind of day," he said in mild exasperation. He continued to look at her while trying to decide if he should be angry at her or glad to see her. He had little control over the verdict; he was elated.

"I'm sorry it took so long to get in here," she apologized, "but Sally's daughter called and said she wouldn't be able to get to the school in time to pick up her son, so she asked Sally if she could do it. Well you know grandmas can't say no so it threw us into a bit of a tizzy. The other two ladies decided they had better get home because it was getting late. I had come with Sally so I had to get Ruth to drive me home to get my car. Luckily, it's not too far and I made it back before you left."

"No need to apologize," Barney said, savoring every word of explanation.

"Well I just felt awful after telling you I'd meet you here, you must have......"

"It's okay," Barney said, "I'm just glad you made it."

"I may have set some unofficial land speed record in the process." She grinned.

This made Barney feel good. They looked at each other for a while.

"Where are my manners?" Barney blurted out suddenly, "What would you like?"

She stared.

"To drink?" He explained, "Or eat?"

"Oh," she said scanning the table, "beer's fine."

Heather, who had been cleaning the next table, responded to Barney's request for another mug in her usual air of annoyance.

Barney filled Stella's mug then started to top off the others.

"No more for me," Vince said holding a hand over his mug, "Wally and I have to get going." Wally looked surprised.

"We do?"

"Yes, we do!" Vince said jerking his head in the direction of the door.

Wally looked at his watch. Then was visibly struck by what Vince was implying.

"Oh geeze......I nearly forgot," he said, quickly whitewashing an olive drab fib, "I've got to... stop on the way home and ... pick up some things." He stood self-consciously and smiled weakly at Stella and Barney who clearly saw through his well-intentioned charade.

"We really do have to run... don't we Vince?" Wally asked, begging for Vince's confirmation.

"We do." Vince confirmed, standing and looking at D.I.

D.I. rose to his feet, "I gotta go make a tee time for Monday." He said with true conviction. "It was nice meeting you Stella," he said with a warm smile, "and Barney, if you don't have anything better to do," he winked, "I'll see you Monday."

"Nice meeting all of you," Stella said giving each an individual glance and nod.

"Nice meeting you," Wally answered suddenly feeling guilt free.

"It was indeed a pleasure," Vince purred, reaching for Stella's hand, which she offered willingly. Vince bent and brushed his lips over the back of Stella's hand. He remained stooped, looked her in the eye and said, "You be nice to our Barney."

She nodded.

The three men turned and headed for the counter to settle up with Tom.

"I'm paying for the beer!" Barney called after them.

"That's understood!" Vince answered over his shoulder.

Barney turned back to Stella.

"Friends," he shrugged, "God bless 'em."

Barney raised his mug.

"To friends." He said.

Stella raised her mug.

"To friends!" She echoed, "And more!"

Their full mugs clanked a dull salute. They both took a long swig and sat back in shared contentment. Barney could feel the alcohol beginning to mellow his mind and loosen his inhibitions.

"Did you want something to eat?" He asked.

She thought for a moment then looked at her watch.

"Well if I eat now," she said, "I can skip dinner... or ..."

"How about," Barney said, "if you'd like," he amended, "we go somewhere nice for dinner? You like Italian, or seafood or what?"

"You know," she said, "I really don't feel like going out." Barney's heart sunk, "Why don't you come over to my place for some of my world famous seafood pasta?" His heart bubbled. Stella fumbled in her purse for a pen and paper. She began scrawling on a small pad of stick-ems.

"Here's my phone number and address," she said as she wrote, "do you know where Maple Drive is?" He wanted to but didn't.

"No." He answered.

"You know where Wal-Mart is on Jefferson Avenue?"

He did.

"Three lights south of Wal-Mart is Elm, there's an Exxon station on the right, turn left on Elm, two blocks to Maple, turn right it's the third house on the left." She peeled the top stick-em off and handed it to Barney. He looked at the neat flowing script, his mind trying to digest the directions.

"Oh dear," she said, "you haven't had a chance to say yes or no. You'll have to excuse me, I sometimes get ahead of myself. Would you like to come over for dinner?"

"You are excused, and I'd love to. I have a nice bottle of Chardonnay that's been cooling it's heels in my fridge just waiting for an excuse to be opened."

"Perfect." She smiled.

"What else can I bring?"

"Just yourself."

"Then it's settled." he said raising his mug again.

"Settled!" She validated, clanking her mug to his.

294

They both took another long drink and fell silent. He noticed Stella's upper lip wore the remnants of a foam mustache. He had to fight an overpowering urge to kiss it off her face. She noticed his stare was missing her eyes.

"What?" She asked.

"You have a little foam on your upper lip." He said reaching over and squeegeeing her lip with his thumb. She took his hand in both of hers, he added his other hand to the clasp and they froze in a moment of rekindled sensuality. He had all but forgotten the effervescent joy of another's touch, the pure pleasure of another's company. He now realized he was not the same person who had forced himself out of bed that morning. He now realized what a wonderful difference a day can truly make.

He thought of Barbara and how one person could redefine his life.

He looked deep into Stella's eyes.

Could it happen again? He wondered. Would it happen again? He asked himself.

It could, the hazel eyes answered him.

HOLE	10	11	12	13	14	15	16	17	18	IN	Total
PAR	4	4	3	5	4	4	3	4	5	36	72
YRDS	380	340	154	495	396	362	158	398	497	3178	6324
D.I.	5	6	2	5	5	5	5	5	6	44	83
Vince	9	5	3	5	8	4	3	5	4	46	86
Wally	5	4	3	4	4	3	4	4	5	36	76
Barney	4	6	4	5	5	5	3	2	7	41	84 ♡

Glossary of Golf Terms and Phrases

ALBATROSS. A double eagle. Don't worry about it, it never happens. If you must know, see eagle and subtract 1.

ACE. A score of one on any hole. Also see hole in one.

AWAY. The ball that is farthest from the hole is said to be away. Normally, the away player is next to hit.

BACK or THE BACK or THE BACK SIDE. The last nine holes (10-18) also referred to as the inward nine (back to the clubhouse).

BALL MARK. 1) A marker, usually a coin or other small flat implement, used to mark a ball's location on the green so the ball may be lifted, cleaned, etc. and placed back in the same position.
2) The indentation caused when a ball lands on the green. (Proper golf etiquette requires players to repair their ball marks.)

BIRDIE. One stroke under par. Example: A player plays a par 5-hole in only 4 strokes. This is a glorious event for most golfers. Remember, in golf, it's the lowest score that wins.

BLADE. 1) The lower edge of the clubface.
2) Shot played where the blade, not the face, of the club strikes the ball. This causes an undesirable low trajectory and high velocity. Not generally considered a good shot but in golf, one never knows.

BOGEY. One stroke over par. Example: A player plays a par 3-hole in 4 strokes. Not a good thing but not the end of the world either. Double Bogey. Two strokes over par. Example: A 6 on a par 4 (may cause muttering). Triple Bogey. Three strokes over par (expletive could fly). Quadruple Bogey. Four over par (expletives and clubs often take flight). Quintuple bogey, 5 over par and so on and so on.

BREAK. 1) The influence gravity has on the path of a rolling golf ball.
2) The favorable or unfavorable influence a tree or other outside source has on the flight of a golf ball. This is commonly known as good breaks and bad breaks, which are subjective and dependent upon who actually hit the ball. A recent study by the Bad Bounce Institute, clinically proved that bad breaks occur at a ratio of 23,675.89 to 1 over good breaks. I do not question the results.

BUNKER. A depression or hole filled with sand or tall grass.

CARRYOVER. If a hole is played and no player wins the hole outright (has the lowest score) the hole is said to be carried over, i.e. the value (wager) of the hole is added to the next and so on until a player wins. Also see, one tie all tie.

CART or GOLF CART. A specially designed vehicle for transporting two golfers and all their equipment around the golf course. Carts are powered by either gas or electric batteries. A good cart has four drink holders and an ice chest.

CHILI DIP. 1) When a player, playing a chip shot to the green, dips his knees causing the club to stub the ground before striking the ball. This causes a poor shot that usually comes up far short of the intended shot. A common and infuriating event.

2) A condiment served at the nineteenth hole. Also see chip.

CHIP. 1) A chip is a shot played from just off the green using a lower lofted club than a pitching wedge. The difference between a chip shot and a pitch shot is, the chip shot is low and runs farther along the ground whereas the pitch shot flies higher and stops quicker when it hits the ground. The circumstance dictates what shot should be played for the best possible results.
2) An accompaniment for chili dip.

CHUNK. The club strikes the big ball (the earth) before striking the little one (the golf ball). The chunk is the chili dip's big brother.

CLUBHOUSE. The main building on the golf course. The clubhouse usually contains the pro shop, grill and or restaurant, bar, offices, and locker rooms.

COURSE. The layout over which a round of golf is played. The standard golf course consists of two sets of nine holes, which are designated as the front nine and the back nine. A complete round of golf is played over both sets of nine holes for a total of 18 holes. Each hole is unique in its design and character and has a par value ranging from three to five. A hole's par value is generally proportional to its length, i.e. The longest holes being par 5 and the shortest being par 3 and those in between, par 4. A regulation course consists of four par 5 holes, four par 3 holes and ten par 4 holes. The holes may be arranged in any sequence. The total par for such a course is 72. Trust me or do the math yourself. Because a score of 72 is so unattainable to the majority of golfers, most courses have an additional hole. (Please see nineteenth hole.)

CUP. A plastic device that is inserted into the hole to support the flag stick as well as shore up the walls of the hole. The term cup is synonymous with hole.

DIVOT. 1) The grass and earth displaced during a shot.
2) The scar left in the turf following a shot.
3) A player who doesn't repair 1 or 2.

DOT. A dot is placed on the scorecard to indicate which player has won the hole or recorded any number of optional awards such a birdies, greenies, sandies etc. To insure domestic tranquility, it is highly recommended that all options and their reward (dollar amount) be agreed upon prior to the beginning of play.

DRAW. A ball flight that gently curves right to left. rhp*

DRIVER. 1) The longest club commonly known as the 1-wood, usually played from the teeing area. Also see wood.
2) The operator of the golf cart.

DUFFER. Please see hacker.

EAGLE. Two strokes under par. Example: A player takes only 3 strokes to play a par 5-hole. Players scoring an eagle have been known to kiss their playing partners flush on the lips.

FADE. A ball flight that gently curves left to right. rhp*

FAIRWAY. A closely mown path from tee to green. The preferred and easiest route to making par. (No guarantees expressed or implied) The fairway usually has rough and hazards running along both sides so, hitting the fairway, (landing and keeping your ball in the fairway) is desirable but difficult.

FLAG STICK. Well duh! A stick that has a flag on it. The flag stick is placed in the hole so the hole's location can be seen from a distance.

FOOT WEDGE. A player improves his lie by covertly kicking his ball back in bounds, or out of the rough. This is a definite no-no unless you get away with it.

FORE. A word shouted to "FORE" warn others of an incoming golf ball.

FRONT, THE FRONT or FRONT SIDE. The first nine holes (1-9) also referred to as the outward nine (away from the clubhouse).

GOLF. The ultimate four letter word.

GREEN. A closely mown smooth grass surface containing the hole. Also known as the putting green or putting surface because this is where players putt (roll their ball using a putter). Green is also a color but you should already know that.

GREENIE. (Optional please see dot) On a par three hole, a player is awarded a greenie if 1) his or her tee shot (first shot on the hole) ends up on the green and 2) is the closest ball to the hole. Usually the player must also make par or better to secure a greenie. Greenies and their monetary value should be agreed upon by all players involved prior to the beginning of play.

HACKER. A mediocre to poor golfer. (Roughly 97.5% of all golfers are classified as a hacker but only 2.6% actually admitting to it.)

HANDICAP. A scoring system that allows players, of all abilities, to compete with one another on a reasonably level playing field. The fairness of the system is unfortunately directly proportional to the honesty of the players.

HAZARD. A sadistic creation of course designers to ruin a good round of golf. Usually an area containing sand or water, snakes and alligators.

HOLE. 1) The continuous area from tee to green over which strokes are played until the ball is holed out (hit into the hole). There are eighteen holes on a standard golf course each with it's own trials and tribulations. Each hole is scored individually.
2) A hole in the ground. The objective of the game. The source of joy, anguish and all humility.

HOLE IN ONE. Hitting the ball into the hole with the first stroke played on a hole. A rare and wondrous event that rewards the player accomplishing the feat by making he or she buy drinks for the entire clubhouse. A true indication of just how warped this game can be.

HONOR. Who has the honor of hitting the first ball on a hole. This is determined by scores from the previous holes, i.e. lowest score. The honor for the first tee is usually awarded the winner of a mutually agreed upon method such as flipping a coin or tee.

HOOK. A draw with an attitude. A ball flight that radically curves right to left. rph*

IN REGULATION. A hole is played in regulation when, a player makes par after two putts. I know, what's that mean? Stay with me here. A par four hole is played in regulation when the player hits his second shot onto the green, (this is called, on in regulation) then holes out his second putt for his par four. 2+2=4, basic math. On a par five hole, the third shot hits the green then two putts for a par five, 3+2=5. a par three hole, first shot hits the green, two putts for par. This is how the holes are designed to be played but in golf, design and reality clash violently.

IRON. A classification of clubs made from forged or cast metal. A typical set of irons consists of eight clubs usually 3 iron through pitching wedge. The numerical designation (displayed on the sole or back of the club head) is an indication of the clubs loft and shaft length which determines the distance a ball will travel when struck. A lower numbered club has less loft, a longer shaft and will travel farther than a higher numbered club, i.e. a six iron will go farther than an eight iron (in most cases). Individual differences in swing, strength etc. determines an individual's club selection for different shots. A flat bellied stud may hit a eight iron 170 yards while a pot bellied geezer may hit the same club a mere 110 yards.

LIE. 1) How the ball lies on the surface of the grass, sand, etc. A good lie (usually in the fairway) sits up and is easier to hit. A bad lie (usually in the rough or sand) the ball sits down or is embedded making it difficult to make good club contact.
2) An intentional error when recording your score. A good lie goes unnoticed. A bad lie doesn't.

LINE. Pre-shot. The intended or perceived direction the ball will travel when struck. Post shot. The actual direction the ball takes after being struck. Rarely do the two lines coincide.

LOFT. The angle of the club face in relation to the ground at address. The more loft a club has the higher the balls trajectory, that's assuming the ball was struck properly. Please see Chunk and Blade for exceptions.

MULLIGAN. A free stroke. A stroke that is not recorded on the scorecard. Mulligans are not recognized by the USGA (United States Golf Association) but are frequently invoked by duffers and hackers during the course of play.
The Mulligan is named in honor of Sedrick Mulligan, a golfing accountant at Arthur Anderson.

NINETEENTH HOLE. A watering hole, a bar, a place where players can go after play to hob-nob and tell good and bad lies. Alcohol is available for medicinal purposes only such as anesthetizing bruised egos and wounded pride.

ONE TIE ALL TIE. When two or more players tie for low score on a hole, the hole is carried over to the next hole and all players will have an opportunity to win that hole which is now double in value. A player usually wins two friends and loses one when he ties low score and forces a carryover. He loses three friends when he wins a hole. Golfers are a very fickle lot. Also see Carryover.

OUT OF BOUNDS. Out of bounds or O.B., is the mother of all golf boo-boos. A ball is deemed to be out of bounds when it 1) leaves the confines of the golf course. Or 2) goes into an area which is considered taboo by the course management (restrooms, clubhouse, snack bars, parking lot, etc.). Out of bounds areas are marked with white stakes aptly called O.B. stakes. Players hitting a ball O.B., incur what is called, a stroke and distance penalty which, means the player must replay a ball from the same spot from which he hit the out of bounds shot. The player must score both shots plus add one more as a penalty for being naughty. Due to the grievous consequences and O.B. shot can wreak upon a player's score, many players have devised means to avoid being out of bounds. Please see, Foot Wedge for more information.

PAR. The number of strokes it should take a player to play a hole. Ex: A player should play a par 5 hole in 5 strokes.

PIN. See Flag Stick.

PITCHING WEDGE. A lofted club used to loft or pitch the ball onto the green.

PRO SHOP. Where players pay their green fees to play. Most pro shops also have golf merchandise for sale such as clubs, balls, shoes, clothing, etc.

PROVISIONAL. In it's simplest form, a provisional ball is played to avoid backtracking to the spot from which an out of bounds or lost ball shot was played. A player must announce his intention of playing a provisional. It's a whole rule thingie.

PULL. A ball flight that travels straight but off line to the left. rhp*

PUSH. The mirror image of a pull. The ball travels right. rhp*

PUTT. A stroke played from on the green (sometimes referred to as the putting surface) and hopefully played in the direction of the hole.

PUTTER. 1) A club specifically designed for putting.
2) A person who putts.

ROUGH. Grass on either side of the fairway that is not mown as short as that of the fairway. Playing a shot from the rough, requires more strength and precision ball striking. Shots played from the rough are also harder to control. The rough, in effect, is a penalty for not hitting the fairway.

SAND WEDGE. A very lofted club specifically designed for hitting out of sand traps. It can also be used to hit short high shots to the green.

SANDIE. A player who makes par or better on any hole after playing at least one shot, on that hole, from a sand trap, is said to have made a sandie. Playing for sandies is optional and at the discretion and consent of the players involved. A sandie's monetary value is mutually agreed upon prior to the beginning of play.

SKIN. When a player wins a hole (has the lowest score) he is said to have won a skin. Don't ask!

SLICE. A fade run amuck. A ball flight that curves radically from left to right. rhp*

SNOWMAN. A score of 8 on a hole. Don't be misled by the cool connotation the name implies. Players who record a snowman are usually pretty hot.

STROKE. Any attempt to strike the ball with a club during the course of play is considered a stroke, even if the attempt was unsuccessful (please see Wiff).

SWING. The actual physical act of swinging the golf club. There are as many different swings as there are golfers.

TEE. 1) The starting area of each hole from which the first shot is played. There are at least three different tee areas (designated by color) on each hole. Each a different distance from the hole. For example: The ladies play from the red tee, which is located x-number of yards from the hole. Senior men and high handicap players (ego permitting) should play from the white tee, which is located x+y yards from the hole. Long knockin' flat bellies and players with illusions of grandeur play from the blue tees, x+y+z yards from the hole. This is done to afford players of different abilities a chance of making par on the hole.
2) A small wooden or plastic peg, which supports the ball when playing the first shot from the tee area. A tee can only be used on the tee.........yeah you read it right.

TEE BOX. The portion of the teeing area laying between two markers and extending two club lengths behind. The first shot on each hole must be played from within the tee box.

TEE MARKER. Movable colored markers (usually stone, wood or plastic) which mark the exact starting point from which the hole is to be played. The tee markers are usually moved daily by the course management to alter the holes distance and equalize wear on the teeing area.

THIN. See Blade 2.

TRAP. See Bunker

TURN, AT THE TURN, or MAKE THE TURN. An imaginary turn between the ninth green and the tenth tee. When a player completes the first nine holes (the front nine) he is at 'the turn' and now makes 'the turn' to the back nine.

UGLY. Optional. A player who holes a shot from off the green is said to have made an ugly. Usually, the ugly has to equal a score of birdie or better to realize a monetary reward. Be sure, prior to play, that all players are in accord on the definition of, the awarding of and value of uglies, otherwise, things could really get ugly.

WIFF. While attempting to execute a stroke the player completely misses the golf ball. Many players feel a wiff does not constitute a stroke, WRONG! Many others simply neglect or forget to score the stroke believing the embarrassment is punishment enough.

WOOD. A classification of clubs which originally had wooden heads, but today are mainly made from various metals and metal alloys. They are sometimes referred to as metals or metal woods. The driver or 1-wood is the longest club and is generally used when hitting from the tee. Fairway woods, 3, 4, 5, etc., are used for longer shots from the fairway or rough. Woods, in general, travel farther than irons due to longer shafts and lower lofts.

*rhp: for a right hand play. For left hand players the definitions would be mirrored, i.e. right would be left, left would be right.